## NIGH

Bobby stopped at the f
at his dog. King seemed to smile at the sight of him. He nodded his head as always, and as always Bobby thought that was his dog's way of saying good morning.

Bobby reached out to pet him, and pressed his face against King's strong, firm neck. . . .

The dog lunged forward, seizing Bobby just below the neck, digging his bottom teeth in and under the small deltoid muscles on the boy's shoulder.

Bobby's first reaction was such surprise and shock that he couldn't utter a sound. The stinging pain from where the dog's teeth had pierced his skin shot up and into his neck and head.

Then he screamed the loudest scream of his life. . . .

Also in Arrow by Andrew Neiderman

*Imp*
*Pin*
*Tender Loving Care*

# NIGHT HOWL

Andrew Neiderman

ARROW BOOKS

This novel is a work of fiction. Names, characters, places and incidents are either the product of the author's imagination or are used fictitiously. Any resemblance to actual events or locales or persons, living or dead, is entirely coincidental.

Arrow Books Limited
62–65 Chandos Place, London WC2N 4NW

An imprint of Century Hutchinson Limited

London Melbourne Sydney Auckland
Johannesburg and agencies throughout
the world

First published in Great Britain 1987



Printed and bound in Great Britain by
Anchor Brendon Limited, Tiptree, Essex

ISBN 0 09 949680 1

*for Nana*
*who tied us to all that was good and true*
*in the old world.*

# NIGHT HOWL

# *Preface*

HE PAUSED AT the base of the ridge that overlooked the south side of the lake. From this perspective he could see some of the houses situated to the east of the lake. There was something about the way they were built in relation to one another that attracted his interest. Geometric configurations fascinated him. He would stop and pause to study the way lines crossed one another and ran parallel to one another. He was intrigued with the rectangular and square shapes that resulted. He was hypnotized by the patterns in nature as well as in man-made structures. Trees and branches took on new meaning for him.

He looked behind him into the corridors of the forest and listened keenly. There was no one there; no one had been there for some time now. He had left them far behind, chasing shadows, hunting their own echoes. He had heard their curses and their cries of frustration and that had pleased him. He did not laugh in the same way they laughed, but his eyes grew brighter and his jaw loosened. He turned his laughter into a source of energy to propel him farther and farther away from them, and when he was sure that he had escaped for what he hoped was forever, he paused to howl his defiance and glee at the emerging stars. Then he hurried away from the spot, crossed over the mountain, and came down to this ridge where he slept. In the morning he fed on a fawn that stepped unwaringly into his field of vision. Anything within that field belonged to him. The fresh meat filled him with an animal strength that made him drunk on his own ego. He had the definite impression he could fly if he needed to fly.

For now he simply stood staring down at the houses. He was so still; he was a statue of himself. The birds of the forest that had been following him cautiously remained back within the sanctuary of the height of the trees. They fluttered about nervously, watching, waiting. A brave crow circled overhead, but when he turned in its direction, it shot off and disappeared over the rim of pine trees behind him and to the right.

He could see movement around the houses. From this distance the people looked small and insignificant to him. Their diminished size seemed to fit nicely into the way he related to people now. His confidence had grown and it wasn't only because of what he had accomplished recently. He had begun to sense something about people, to sense their deeper fears. They feared the darkness that he had come to cherish and they ran from the sounds he could make. He envisioned them clutching each other like the monkeys who had been a few cages down from him—their eyes bright with terror whenever he approached them or whenever they were brought near him.

He looked away from the houses, but all the other directions were far less enticing. There was something more here than merely the shapes of the structures. It was the territory itself. He didn't understand the force that was driving him toward it, but he didn't oppose it; it didn't make him uncomfortable. On the contrary, it filled him with a new sense of purpose.

All he knew was that he wanted to be down at those houses; he wanted to be able to move freely about them, even in and out of them. He wanted that space to be his space.

He growled instinctively before he took a step forward. It occurred to him that these houses and the land around them would not be taken easily. The inhabitants would put up a struggle. It was to be a contest, only now he didn't shy away from combat with people. Actually, he had a thirst for it.

He had a thirst for many new things. It was like being born again and again, each time growing into a different sort of creature, but each time becoming one with a wider scope, a greater list of needs and wants. He was far from being fully aware of just how far his capabilities had expanded. Every moment he seemed to learn something new about himself or about the world around him.

All of it stimulated him and made him feel taller and larger than he really was. The more distance he put between himself and his pursuers, the more confident he became. They had been the ones in control, doling out the food and the water and the small moments of freedom; he had defeated them, outsmarted them. The most important thing of all was that it had been easy, almost without challenge. All the while he had expected them to recapture him, but they didn't have his speed or his vision or his strength.

He sensed that those down by the houses wouldn't be any different. Despite his new confidence, he still relied on his instincts, especially when it came to things to fear. There were no warnings going off within him; there was nothing telling him to turn back or to turn away. All was quiet. The flight was over. He had nothing else to do now but feed his new hungers.

Before this, all his hungers had been simple. The new hungers were more demanding. They were all-encompassing. He should have been afraid of them, for they seemed to take complete control of him; but he was not afraid. He wasn't even sure what he had to do to satisfy them, but that didn't discourage him.

He knew it had something to do with the houses and the people around and in them. And so he stepped forward and began to descend the ridge, his eyes fixed on the lake and the homes beyond. Soon they would be his, not in the sense they were to the people who lived within, but his, nevertheless. He could go and come at will and he could feed off their fear.

In his mind's eye, he envisioned them all on leashes, tied to the walls of their houses. They strained and clawed at the air, screaming as he went past them, his head high, his chest up, his eyes gleaming. This was truly the greatest hunger he had ever known, and he longed to be satisfied.

# 1

EIGHT-YEAR-OLD Bobby Kaufman threw his blanket from his body as though he was breaking out of sleep instead of merely waking up. For the last two years, he had been the first to rise in the morning and, for the last two years, he had taken it upon himself to feed King his breakfast. Even during the cold Catskill winter months, he didn't mind bundling himself up, struggling with his heavy socks and boots, just so he could get King his food.

The Kaufmans had gotten their German shepherd when it was only six months old. Now, five years later, it was a husky, well-fed, well-exercised and cared for animal with firm musculature and keen eyes. Ever since the Levins were burglarized, Clara Kaufman had been after Sid to get them a good watchdog. King was everything they could have hoped for; he barked madly at a passing shadow. No one could approach the Kaufmans' four-bedroom ranch-style house on Lake Street without first being announced by King.

They had taken the dog to obedience school and given it the best possible training. Since the town of Fallsburg had a leash law in effect, they kept King on a one hundred-foot run just to the left of the garage. Sid had built him a nice size external plywood doghouse and he and Lisa, who was now ten, had painted it white, with the word *KING*, in black, on the front. The kids got more paint on themselves than they did on the house, but it was a fun day that they all remembered. Ken Strasser, a dairy farmer who lived a half mile down the road on an aging yet beautiful estate, told Sid to put hay inside the doghouse to serve as an insulator. It worked; the dog never seemed to be unhappy or cold, no matter how brutal the winter weather was.

After King was housebroken, they permitted him in the house for large portions of the day. Most of the time he could be found in Bobby's room, spread out beside the boy's pinewood bunk bed, watching him play. If anyone drove into their driveway or came to their front door, the dog would perk up, raise his head, listen hard, and then raise himself from the light blue shag carpet. Then he'd make his way down the hall to the living room and the entrance of the house, while a low, mechanical growl began in the base of his stomach and traveled up his body. Usually Sid or Clara would say "Stay," and King would sit and inspect the visitor or visitors suspiciously.

This morning, as usual, King's biological clock awakened him at almost the same time Bobby Kaufman threw his blanket from his body. King came out of his house and sat patiently, looking up and down the back country road. It was a sparsely populated street with each of the houses, up to this point, surrounded by sizable acreage. The unusually wet spring weather had filled the trees with rich green leaves, making the forest between and around the houses thick and dark, even on mornings as bright as this one.

The dog stared fixedly at the front door of the house, waiting for Bobby to emerge. Bobby slipped on his pants and pulled his Kermit the Frog sweatshirt over his head and down. Then he put on his thin white socks and his sneakers. Without taking time to tie the laces, he shot out of his room and went directly to the kitchen.

Clara Kaufman heard her son open the cabinet below the sink to take out the bag of dry dog food. She turned on her back and smiled to herself when she heard him shake the pellets into the dog's dish and wet them down. She envisioned him moving carefully and studiously, as he balanced what she was sure was a too-full dish, making his way across the kitchen, through the living room, and to the front door where he performed a minor juggling act to turn the lock on the door handle and zip off the chain latch. She heard him do it all successfully and then she looked over at Sid, who had slept through the whole event.

She pulled the blanket around her neck and pressed herself against him. The nudge elicited a groan from him, but he pretended not to realize what she was suggesting. She knew he was pretending, so she nudged him again and he began a slow turn, exaggerating the difficulty. Her laugh brought a smile to his face.

Outside, Bobby stopped at the front stoop and looked eagerly at his dog. King seemed to smile at the sight of him. The dog's tongue moved from the left side of his mouth to the right and then settled at the front expectantly. He nodded his head, as always, and Bobby, as always, thought this was his dog's way of saying good morning. Still moving carefully so as not to spill any of the precious breakfast, Bobby continued over the flagstone walkway toward the doghouse.

Before Bobby reached him, the dog snapped its head to the left and peered into the shadows of the forest across the street. There were no unusual sounds and nothing moved. It was just that in one spot, near an old, soft maple tree, the darkness seemed to grow deeper and darker. Perhaps it was caused by the movement of some leaves in the breeze or by a cloud that interfered with the sun for a few moments. Whatever it was, it wasn't enough to hold the dog's attention long, and it was certainly not enough to attract Bobby's attention. He was still very intent on performing his chore successfully.

There was no growl in the dog's voice. There was no tightening of its muscles as Bobby drew closer. It was as though King knew how important it was to remain calm and to remain in character. Only an experienced animal trainer might have noticed some nervousness in its eyes, and even he could have missed it.

Bobby set the bowl before King in almost the exact spot he had placed it time and time again. Then, as was his wont, he reached out to pet his dog and pressed his face against King's strong, firm neck. The dog waited with an apparently calculated patience and then lunged forward, seizing Bobby just below the neck, digging his bottom teeth in and under the small deltoid muscle on the boy's shoulder and clamping down with a ferocity the likes of which the boy had never seen.

His first reaction was surprise and shock, so much that he couldn't utter a sound. The powerful animal shook him from side to side in what seemed to be an almost playful grip, but the stinging pain from where the dog's teeth had pierced the skin shot up and into his neck and head. Unable to raise his left arm against the dog's body, Bobby tried pushing him off with his right arm and fell to the ground. At this point he screamed the loudest scream of his life. The dog began to drag him back toward the house, like a predator eager to secure its catch.

Clara and Sid heard the scream just after Sid had turned to embrace her. The ungodliness of the sound threw them both into a panic. Sid turned and spun off the bed. Just in his briefs, he rushed from the bedroom. Clara grabbed her robe and followed quickly behind. They both stepped outside in time to see King pulling Bobby's body back against the doghouse.

Shocked almost to the point of numbness, Sid Kaufman hesitated and then ran forward. The dog appeared to anticipate it.

He released his grip on Bobby, but he stepped over the wailing child, straddling the boy and growling. Sid stopped a few feet away from him. Lisa had come out behind Clara and was screaming almost as loudly as Bobby and Clara. Blood stained the little boy's sweatshirt and he pulled his legs up into a protective fetal position as he lay helplessly under the dog.

"Don't move, Bobby, don't move," Sid said. "Easy, easy. Hey, King, hey! What's wrong, boy? Why'd you do this?" he asked the dog as if he expected the pet of five years to respond and justify his action. Sid backed up to the garage and turned to Clara.

"Go around and open the garage door," he commanded. *"Hurry!"* She did so, Lisa following behind her. For a long moment, the seconds it actually took for Clara to go into the house and around to the garage-to-house entrance, Sid and King faced each other. He found the dog's look bone-chilling. It was as though the animal were gloating over its achievement and the man's helplessness. Confused and frightened himself, Sid realized that the dog could reach down and seize his son again at will.

The garage door went up.

"Get me Bobby's baseball bat," he said. Clara got it to him quickly. Grasping it firmly in his hands, Sid started toward the dog. "When I tell you to run out, Bobby, run." The little boy's whimper had become a dry, guttural sound. He was moving into total shock. "I'll move him off you, son. Then go," Sid said. When he got within striking distance of the animal, King braced himself for the conflict. Sid was surprised at the dog's look of calm challenge.

Sid feinted once and then swung as hard as he could

at the dog's head. King anticipated the move and brought his head back with perfect timing. Sid's swing carried him forward with the follow-through and the dog lunged out and clamped its jaws around Sid's naked right calf. The blood streamed out around the dog's teeth. Sid screamed for Bobby to move off and the eight-year-old had enough awareness left to do so. As soon as he did, Clara grabbed him and pulled him toward the house.

King's hold on Sid seemed unbreakable. He brought the bat down against the dog's side as hard as he could, but the animal was impervious to the blows. When Sid lost his balance, the dog released his leg in order to go for Sid's throat. His snap was so close that Sid actually caught the scent of the animal's breath. He moved just in time to avoid being seized at the throat. Then, turning over on his stomach, he spun away and got to his feet. The dog came at him, but Sid ran fast enough to get back to the garage.

There he fell against the back of his car and watched the animal lunge into the air. Its chain snapped and held him back. Sid moved farther into the garage and pushed the button to close the door. Then he stumbled into the house where his wife and his daughter and his eight-year-old son were all crying hysterically. Dazed, he looked down at his blood-covered lower right leg and went for some towels. After he wrapped his leg and got some towels to Clara, who was simply holding Bobby to her in the living room, he went to the telephone and called the Fallsburg police department. The dispatcher said he would call for an ambulance.

By the time the first patrol car arrived, the dog was sitting casually in front of the doghouse and eating his food. He didn't bark at the police; he simply stared at them with what was now a puppy's curiosity. The patrolmen were quite confused. They saw the bad gash on Bobby Kaufman's shoulder and the bad bite in Sid Kaufman's leg.

"Shoot him," Sid demanded. *"Shoot him!"* he shouted at the hesitant young cop, who looked to his older partner.

"What do you think?" he asked.

*"Shoot him,"* Sid repeated. The older officer looked at Sid and then shrugged.

"Shoot the bastard," he said.

The younger patrolman took out his thirty-eight, walked a few steps toward King, and fired directly into the animal's head. All the while the dog sat there peacefully. To the young policeman, it felt like a murder.

Afterward, it was clearly determined that the dog did not have rabies.

From the time he was a boy, Sid Kaufman demanded logic in everything. Contradictions, paradoxes, mysteries annoyed him to no end. He was downright intolerant when it came to confusion. When he analyzed it, he concluded that his attitude had found it's genesis on the day his mother gave birth to a stillborn baby girl. When his father brought his mother home and they all sat together in the gloomy living room after the comforting relatives had gone, Sid demonstrated a four-year-old's inquisitiveness, as precocious as it was.

"Why did God make a baby if the baby was going to be dead?" he asked. His parents looked at him, their faces filled with sympathy because they didn't have the answer and they knew he needed a satisfactory one very badly.

"It happens," his father offered.

"Why?"

"It just does. It's part of life, part of this world."

"That's silly," he said. He looked to his mother, but she offered nothing else.

But the frustration didn't defeat him. Questions continued to be a major part of his dialogue. He challenged everything and anything he could. In school his teachers saw him as a genuine pain in the ass, always wanting to know why things were due on a certain date or why they had to be done a certain way.

Perhaps it was only logical that he eventually became an efficiency expert. As a systems analyst, he traveled all over the state and country, going into factories, plants, corporations, and department stores to review practices and regulations and find ways of streamlining methods. He was good at it; he usually left a list of recommendations that resulted in increased production, if not more pleasant and agreeable working conditions.

Although his firm was situated in New York City, it didn't really matter where he lived. He was rarely at the office. Usually he received his assignments on the telephone, traveled to the location, did his job, and returned to file a report. So when Clara wanted them to buy the house in the Catskills in a town not far from her parents, he didn't resist. It was only an hour and forty minutes to the George Washington Bridge and the quiet country setting was very appealing. It was certainly a beautiful place for the kids to grow up. The school system was small and suffered from few of the problems that plagued more urban areas.

It was true that in the summertime, the resorts attracted thousands of tourists to the area, but their home was situated on a side country road, just east of a beautiful lake. In the fall the geese flew over on their journey south, and in the spring they returned, always in their remarkable *V* formation.

The air was clear, the people were friendly, the woods were beautiful, and the mountains were often awe-inspiring. A man could feel alive here and a father and husband could feel that his family was secure and safe. There was little crime, even though people were made paranoid by an occasional burglary and by television news crime stories.

All in all, settling in the town of Fallsburg seemed a smart and logical thing to do. He had been happy with his decision and proud of what he had done for his family. He had placed them in a simpler, happier world and they had loved it—until now.

Chief Michaels handed him a copy of the lab report and he read it three times before reacting.

"There's got to be some mistake. Can we have them redo it?"

"Believe me, they did."

"It doesn't make any sense. It wasn't a dog we just got."

"It happens," the chief said.

"You mean it's part of life, part of this world?"

The chief shrugged. "What can I tell you? It wasn't rabies. The dog just got a stick up its ass. Thank God it wasn't worse than it was."

"It was bad enough."

"It's dead. What else can we do?"

Sid simply stood there, staring at him.

"Go see a vet or talk to an animal psychiatrist," the chief added facetiously.

Sid nodded. "I might just do that," he said.

The chief followed him to the doorway of the station, which was part of the town hall and justice court. The hamlet of South Fallsburg, which was one of seven in the township, was the busiest and most populated. The Kaufmans lived a little more than two miles out of the business area, which was located on one main street that consisted of a variety of stores, luncheonettes, two bar-and-grills, two drugstores, two banks, a large grocery, and some professional offices. The town was so quiet during the off-season months, especially during the heart of winter, that a dog could go to sleep on the main street and feel confident of his security.

It was precisely this simplicity that made the area so attractive to Sid. Now, as he looked out at the intermittent traffic, he felt deceived. Terrible things could happen here, too. There were no guarantees.

Harry Michaels's weathered face softened as he stood beside Sid Kaufman. He was sorry now that he hadn't appeared more sympathetic. The father of two grown sons, he could understand Sid's outrage at what had occurred. It was easy to lose track of how fragile life was and how vulnerable to injury, illness, and disaster children were. How many vehicular traffic accidents involving teenagers had he investigated over the past twenty-nine years, and what about those two teenage suicides last year? Even a semi-rural police chief supervising a force of only twelve full-time men could grow hardened and insensitive, he thought.

"How's your boy doin'?"

"Thirty stitches," Sid said, looking out the window. It was as though he were talking to himself. "But the worst part of it is the psychological part. He doesn't sleep—nightmares. He's afraid to go out of the house. He'll probably be afraid of dogs for the rest of his life . . . maybe all animals. And my daughter . . . she's just as bad. Clara's just coming down from a peak of hysteria."

"It's eerie. I wish I had some logical explanation for you, but like I said . . ."

"I know." Sid looked at him. He was a couple of inches taller than the fifty-six-year-old police chief, but his slim build and fair skin made him appear slight beside the stocky, one-hundred-eighty-pound law officer, who often appeared more like a senior truck driver. He had big hands and large facial features. His hair had grayed and thinned, but he kept it brushed down and over so it didn't seem so.

"However," Sid said, "I'll find the logical explanation. That's for sure," he added. His blue eyes darkened with intensity and determination.

The chief nodded. "Wish you luck. Call me if you need anything else."

"Thanks."

The chief watched Sid walk out to his car. He limped because of the bite in his leg. After he drove off, Michaels went back to his desk and put the file on the Kaufman dog incident in his closed-case folder. As far as he was concerned, there was really nothing else to do.

Sid felt differently. As he drove back toward home, he considered the chief's half-facetious statement. Why not talk to a vet and get some insights into animal psychiatry? Could something mental have happened to King? Was it possible for an animal to become schizophrenic? The dog was so peaceful when the police arrived. Sid knew that if he and Bobby didn't have the wounds as evidence, the police would have doubted the story. The animal didn't growl or bark at them. It was as if . . . as if he had put on an act just for the cops.

This is getting insane, Sid thought. My mind is running wild. I have to talk to someone with expert knowledge and see if I can understand. And yet, in the back of his mind, he had a feeling, an idea that what had happened would be something even specialists would not fully comprehend.

When he arrived at the house, he found Bobby and Clara in the living room. Clara was playing video games with Bobby, even though she hated them. She gave him a knowing glance when he entered, signaling that Bobby was still on fragile ground.

"Where's Lisa?"

"Still at school. Tomorrow, Bobby's going to go to school. Right, Bobby?"

The little boy looked up at his father. Sid smiled expectantly.

"I guess so."

"Good," Sid said.

"My shoulder still hurts," Bobby said. "A lot."

"It'll get better fast."

"It's going to hurt to take the stitches out."

"Oh no. By then you won't feel a thing. I had stitches too, you know."

"Didn't yours hurt?"

"Sure, but it's getting better already. I just don't think about it. You shouldn't either."

"How about a little relief?" Clara said. "You know, substitution time," she sang.

"Oh, sure. Bobby's getting better at Breakout, huh?"

"I'm terrible at these things," Clara said. She got up and Sid went to take her place. "Anything new?" she asked softly.

"I just got a copy of the official results. The police don't know anything more."

"No other incidents like this?"

"Not that I know of or they spoke of. I think he would have told me if there were. He's a salty fellow, but not hard to read. He's as puzzled as we are, only his response is to shrug and file it away. Of course, it wasn't his family who suffered."

"Maybe he's right. Maybe it was just a freak thing."

"I don't think so. There's no such thing as a freak thing. There has to be an explanation."

"I just find it so hard to believe it happened. That dog was so . . ." She stopped talking when Bobby looked up.

"I know. Forget it for now. So, champ, what are we playing here?" he asked, squatting beside his son.

"I'm changing the cartridge to Asteroids, okay?"

"Sure. I don't know one from the other, but sure."

"Is King dead for good?" Bobby asked.

"You can only be dead for good, Bobby. There's no other way to be dead. He won't be coming back, if that's what you're worrying about."

"Yes he can," Bobby said. He pushed the button and started the video game.

"Yes he can? No, it's not possible, son. Don't think about that."

"But I saw him," Bobby said, looking away from the small television screen.

"Saw him? You mean King?"

"Uh huh."

"That's silly, Bobby. You probably mean you had a bad dream again, right?"

"Nope. It wasn't a dream. I heard him outside and I looked out my window."

"When was this?" Sid asked.

"Last night. I woke up and looked out the window and he was on the lawn. He was looking up at my window."

"Bobby, that was a dream. To you it seemed as though it really was happening, but it wasn't. You had a bad experience, a terrible experience, and when things like that happen, they stay with you for a while. It's like having a bad taste in your mouth after you eat something rotten," he added, searching for a simple analogy.

His son shook his head. "It wasn't a dream," he said. "I know it wasn't because I had to go to the bathroom and I went and I stopped by your door, but you and Mommy didn't hear me, so I went back to bed. I looked out again, but he was gone. He'll be back tonight, won't he?"

"Clara!"

"What is it?" Clara said, looking back through the doorway. She had gone to the kitchen to prepare dinner.

"Now he's saying the dog was here last night."

"I know. He told me the same story."

"Didn't you explain that it was a dream?"

"He doesn't believe me. You explain," she said and disappeared again.

"All right, I'll tell you what, Bobby. If King comes back, you come into my room no matter what and wake me up so I can see him too, okay?"

"All right."

"And I want to tell you something else, son. German shepherds are common. You'll see dogs that look like King from time to time. That doesn't mean it's King."

"Nobody else has a German shepherd on Lake Street," he said.

"That's true. As far as I know, that is." He thought about it for a moment. "I've been home for three straight days now and I haven't seen any," he added, more for himself than for his son.

"So then it must have been King," Bobby insisted.

Sid looked at his son. The kid has my serious expression, he thought. He has Clara's eyes and Clara's nose, but when he thinks, he looks like me. Bobby was always precocious. It wasn't surprising that he held on to his ideas.

"Listen, Bobby. Do you know what had to be done after King was shot? I didn't tell you all of it because it isn't pleasant. They had to cut off his head and send it to the laboratory in Albany for examination to see if he had rabies. Now how could he come around without a head?"

"I don't know."

"So it can't be King, right?" He could see that he had succeeded in placing some doubt in Bobby's mind.

"I don't know."

"You know. Don't say you don't know. He couldn't go get his head and put it back on again, could he?"

"No."

"Then it wasn't King or it was a dream, okay?"

Bobby didn't respond. Stubborn, just like I am, Sid thought.

"Why did he bite me?" Bobby asked softly.

"I don't know yet, son. But I will. You can be sure of that."

"He didn't want to bite me again. He sat down on the grass and looked up at me. He wanted me to come out and pet him and play with him, just like always."

"That was your dream."

"What if I'm having a dream and I go out?" Bobby asked.

"That's called sleepwalking. Don't worry, I won't let you go out."

"You didn't hear me go to the bathroom."

"I'll hear you open the front door. That's different. Besides, if you went out, there would be nothing there. You'd wake up and come back inside."

Bobby looked at the television set and began to work the video sticks, but Sid could see that the boy's mind wasn't totally on it. Suddenly, Bobby got up and ran to the front door.

"Hey, where are you going?"

"You'll see," Bobby said. He opened the door and rushed out. Sid got up reluctantly and followed his son out of the house. The gray afternoon seemed to have grown even darker. Sid thought he saw rain in the approaching overcast. He stood out on the patio and looked about, at first not seeing Bobby. Then he saw him crawling about on the lawn near the rosebush.

"What are you doing, Bobby?"

"Here," his son said. Sid walked to him. "He was here, looking up at me," Bobby said, pointing to his bedroom window.

"Bobby," Sid began, thinking he had to be as patient as possible. The kid had gone through a hell of an experience.

"Look," Bobby said, pointing to the soft earth around the rosebush. "See?"

Sid focused on the ground and then squatted slowly so he could inspect the area Bobby had indicated. There was a paw print there, a large dog's paw print.

"He was here," Bobby said. "It wasn't a dream."

Sid looked at the print and then looked at his son.

"It could have been one King made a while back, Bobby."

"It wasn't. He made it last night," Bobby said.

Sid studied it some more. "Okay," he said. "I'll look for him tonight—or whatever dog it was."

"Good," Bobby said. He wore a look of relief. He got up and ran back to the house. "Come on, Dad, let's play Asteroids."

"Right," Sid said. He stood up, but he couldn't take his eyes from the paw print.

When he looked up, he was sure it was going to rain. Answers. He had to have answers, and soon.

# 2

IT WAS OBVIOUS to him that the old barn was no longer in use, even though it was still structurally sound. He thought of it as an ideal location, warm and secure. He could easily move in and out unobserved. His own observations told him that only the old man inhabited the farmhouse, an old man so set in his ways that it was possible to tell the time of day by his actions. He watched the old man in the morning, working on his small garden, taking meticulous care of the newly planted crops. Everything was growing straight and proper. The smallest weeds were plucked and removed. The earth was pampered, watered, and fed the proper nutritional chemicals. And the fence around the garden kept out the deer and the rabbits. He saw them standing nearby, looking longingly and hungrily at the old man's plants, and he understood what the power of precaution, well-thought-out planning, could be. In a sense, the old man knew the future because he knew what would happen if he didn't take steps to prevent it. This was the power of foresight. How powerful it could be.

He had a healthy respect for these creatures. There was so much to learn from them, even though he had succeeded in outsmarting some of them. How simple his own kind appeared to be. When he had first come upon the dog chained by the house, he had sat there listening to it bark that same, monotonous, empty sound, a mixture of fear and warning. After he grew tired of hearing it, he growled with an authority that it had never heard from anything other than a human. It astounded and confused the dog and then frightened it. It crawled back into its doghouse, whimpering. He had all he could do to get it to come out again and to trust him. But it did.

It was dark. All the lights were out in the house. Nothing else moved. The dog came out to sniff in disbelief. It was easy to get to it, easy to make it understand and obey. All of its life, it had been a creature of commands. That was what it understood best. He got into its mind quickly, and because he understood the dog and its mind—and how that mind worked—better than any man could understand it, he could undo anything the men had taught it. The dog was to him what a child was to a grown man, and with the same ease that a grown man could exercise to influence a child, so he could influence this dog. It took him a while to train and retrain it to his satisfaction, but he was good at it. After all, he had been taught by the experts.

All the while he remained cautious. He sensed that those who pursued him were always out there. So he kept hidden during the daytime, venturing out carefully to observe and study the surroundings and the inhabitants. He moved through shadows, sometimes crawling on his stomach when he heard voices or saw movement.

After a short while, he got to know how many people lived in each of the half dozen houses on Lake Street. Plotting strategy, he recognized the need to center in on one at a time. All of this had the excitement and flavor of a hunt, only it was greater than any hunt he had ever undertaken. Chasing a rabbit was fool's play; he felt he could stalk a deer with his eyes closed. He was impatient with these traditional hunts and pursued them only when hunger demanded them. He wouldn't, as some stray dogs would, feed out of garbage cans.

He had come upon a stray dog here. The animal had come up the road from the east. It was a cross between a collie and a shepherd and even though it had been forced to live as a scavenger, it still had firm musculature and good size. As soon as he confronted it, he recognized its hunger and its antagonism. It had become a creature of violence, driven by fear and desperation, suspicious of everything.

It was angered by its own needs; it despised a body that called for food and water incessantly, a body that demanded warmth and comfort. There was no pride in its gait. It was always stalking, clinging to the side of the road, prepared at any moment to flee in any direction. Its eyes were filled with terror; they were wide, maddening. Its coat was mangy and dull and its ears were turned down, flopping loosely about to signal its sense of dejection.

The dog was instantly aggressive, expecting a challenge and an attack. It snarled and braced itself in readiness. He studied it carefully and silently and the dog sensed his extraordinary perception. This confused and frightened it. It was as though it had come upon a man with a club, a superior antagonist. It realized it was in some greater danger and moved aside. Then it began to whimper and plead. He could have killed it, cut it up in seconds, but instead he chased it off. He was quick to make it understand that this was his territory. The stray had no claim to it; it had no claim to anything but its own constant thirst and hunger; it had no stomach to fight for causes; the concept of loyalty to master and land was long gone from its consciousness. It ran as though it had seen some ghost of itself, and it didn't pause to hunt from any garbage cans along the street.

The day King had attacked Bobby, he was across the street in the shadows of the forest observing. He saw how helpless the boy was, and he saw how frustrated the man had become. He enjoyed every moment of it because he had designed it and it had happened just as he had foreseen it. The pleasure of accomplishment was extraordinary; it was greater than anything he had known before.

He hadn't even minded what resulted when the men with the guns arrived. He didn't care about the dog; he had used it, just as the men had tried to use him, just as they used other animals. Most often, from what he had seen, these animals would die too. The men weren't terribly saddened by that; they expected the death. This foresight was part of their intelligence. And so was all this part of his intelligence. He had winced when the shot was fired and the dog fell to the side. He had watched it jerk about spasmodically and then die, but he had watched with a scientific curiosity and not with a sense of compassion.

Afterward, when they had taken the dog away and night had fallen, he went down to the house and sat by that section where he knew the little boy to be. He called to him as the dog had called, and the boy appeared in the window. He wanted the boy to come out; he wanted to take them out of the house, one at a time, and the boy would be the easiest to get. He wanted to begin with him. The boy didn't come, but he sensed that he was close to coming. He decided he would go back and try again.

There was no moonlight, but the overcast couldn't prevent him from feeling the warmth of its glow, as it could prevent men. It was as though he could see through the clouds. It wasn't cool for him and it wasn't dreary. He wore the darkness like a second coat. For him the night was filled with excitement; his body tingled from his extrasensory perception. His ego made him defiant and he stepped out onto the road, unafraid.

He wasn't discovered.

He went back to the barn behind the old man's farmhouse and he crawled into a warm corner where he slept, dreaming of success. Before morning, the moon broke free of the clouds, just where he knew it to be.

At forty years of age, Sid Kaufman considered himself in the prime of his life. He told himself that he was in better physical shape than when he was eighteen. In high school and even in college, he had eschewed any sort of physical activity. At least now he jogged twice a week—three times a week when it was possible. He had even gone to health clubs from time to time and worked out on weight-training machines. They had a rowing machine, a stationary bike, and a trampoline in the basement, and Clara was into aerobics.

Sid had always been an enthusiastic student and an avid reader. In fact, he would read anything in sight, especially if he had to wait in airports or in waiting rooms. At the breakfast table he would read the backs of all the cereal boxes, if there wasn't anything else available. His studious demeanor, his air of seriousness, his intensity of thought made him appear quite introverted and withdrawn, when actually he was very curious and outgoing. It was never difficult for him to strike up conversations with new people.

He was just a shade under six feet tall and when he took his thick-rimmed reading glasses off, he had a Henry Fonda fatherly look, even when he was only in his early twenties. Perhaps his strong appearance of maturity was the best thing he had going for him.

Women and other men recognized it immediately. Sid Kaufman was not someone who would waste time or do meaningless things. He was purposeful, goal-oriented, ambitious, and confident.

For Clara Weintraub, he was the ideal man. Both of them were only children, but she had leaned strongly on her father and looked for that image in any man she dated. She wanted someone who was secure enough about himself to be able to devote a great deal of energy and time to taking care of her. She didn't like making decisions; she didn't like having major responsibilties. She wanted a world for herself in which everything was clearly delineated. There was no confusion about who would do what and when. She had thought about pursuing a career in child psychology, but she had put off getting her master's degree until after she had raised the children, and now she questioned whether or not she would ever do it. It didn't seem to matter as much as she thought it would.

Sid was working. They were doing well. She enjoyed taking care of the house and the children. She enjoyed her leisure time. She liked caring for her body, reading her books, spending time with her friends, and visiting with her parents. Life seemed enough as it was. She had no regrets and no anxieties about her self-image. In fact, she found other women, women who were constantly moaning and groaning about their failure to do more, curious. Some of them had so much and yet seemed so unhappy.

She regretted the fact that Sid's job took him away from the house and family for days at a time and occasionally for weeks, but she accepted it. She had complete faith in him. It wasn't as though she were married to some traveling salesman who had to seek out erotic adventures to compensate for an otherwise drab existence. Sid had his feet solidly planted in their life together. He knew what he wanted and he communicated that organization and strength so well that she was unafraid.

Her friends thought she was naive. She knew that in their eyes, every man was deceitful. These friends measured their lives against the fictional lives of prime-time soap opera characters. Some even behaved as though they were moving in front of cameras and audiences. But she could tolerate them because they amused her.

All in all, she felt that she and Sid had created a good life for themselves and she was about as happy and as satisfied with what they had as she possibly could be. She loved living in the Catskills, the place where she had grown up, and she thought they had bought a house in one of the most ideal locations in the area. They had privacy and yet they had neighbors within a reasonable distance. It was just a short ride to town to shop, yet they were out of the traffic and the hustle and bustle of the summer resort season when it came.

As she looked out at the woods and fields around her house, she couldn't imagine how it could turn sour. The incident with King was the most jarring and disturbing thing that had happened during ten years of her marriage to Sid. He was right about its being illogical and incomprehensible, but she didn't have his need for answers. She wanted to put the incident behind them as quickly as she could. She would work on the children and in time she would get them to accept and maybe even forget it enough so they could live around pets again.

But Sid's intense need to understand and explain what had happened was beginning to frighten her. He was making phone calls and looking for books with more ferocity than he would apply to one of his jobs. She could see that it was going to absorb him completely. It frightened her because she didn't think he would find satisfactory explanations, and she thought he was capable of monomania—devoting himself to a single purpose at the expense of some very important others.

They had their first fight about it one morning at breakfast when she tried to suggest that he ease off.

"What difference will it make to us now?" she asked.

"What difference? For one thing, the kid's got me looking out the window at night for a ghost dog."

"That's just part of the trauma he suffered. In time it will pass, but if he realizes you're still thinking about it and working on it, it won't pass. You're keeping it on his mind, on both the children's minds."

"Well I'm glad you can just accept what happened as though it was an ordinary, everyday event, but I can't."

"I'm not saying that, Sid."

"Look. It's not the kind of thing you just forget about."

"What else can you do? The laboratory checked him out. The police have no answers. . . ."

"I told you. I'll get the answers. Look, why don't you continue to live as though the whole thing was a fantasy and leave me alone about it, okay?"

"That's not fair. At night you're in the den reading those books about animals."

"It's only been two nights, for Christ's sake."

"I just thought it would be better for all concerned if we forgot about it. Besides, everyone I talk to has an animal story of one kind or another. Maybe it wasn't so unusual."

"I've got to go to Boston tomorrow and then you'll have a break from me."

"Oh, Sid!" She slammed her coffee cup down and got up from the table.

He didn't call her back, but after he considered what she had said, he went to look for her. She was making the bed almost viciously, snapping the sheets and blankets.

"Look," he said, "maybe you're right."

"You didn't have to say I'd be glad to have a break from you."

"I know. I'm sorry. This thing has gotten me crazy. I'll tone it down."

"Don't think the children don't sense it."

"I know. I'll be more subtle."

He kissed her on the forehead. She was satisfied, even though she wasn't convinced he would be any less intense. She knew him too well to believe that.

Later that day Sid went to see their veterinarian who had an office in Monticello, a nearby community. As usual the office was packed—people clutching sick-looking cats and unhappy dogs. There was even a German shepherd that looked remarkably like King. The dog had a mouth lined with porcupine quills.

The vet's name was Dr. Michael Fox. Sid had called him before coming, but now that he was here and saw all these people with real medical problems with their pets, he felt guilty about taking up any of the veterinarian's time. When Dr. Fox appeared at the reception desk, Sid told him that maybe he would come back at another time.

"Don't be silly. You had a very bad thing happen. I can give you a few minutes."

Sid followed him to the office adjacent to one of the examination rooms, where Fox closed the door and took his seat behind the desk.

"Sit down, relax. How's your boy doin'?"

"It's more psychological than physical now, even though he had a bad tear in his shoulder."

"And you're limpin' pretty well. That's why they call them "police dogs." They can be effective."

"Especially when you don't want them to be."

"Yeah. Well, my records show that King had all the

shots. With the old vaccine, there was a small percentage of animals who were actually infected with rabies, but the newer vaccines are foolproof. Anyway, it was too long a period after the shot for the shot to have anything to do with it," Fox said. He stood a stocky five feet ten inches, with a college wrestler's neck and shoulders. Sid hadn't thought about it before, but it suddenly struck him as ironic that a man with the name of Fox would become a veterinarian.

"I didn't think it could have. Anyway, as I told you on the phone, the laboratory reports were negative."

"Yes."

"What else could turn him that way?"

"Hard to say. It wasn't an uncomfortable day. The dog wasn't in any kind of pain?"

"No, he seemed perfect, healthy, and happy."

"You didn't notice any change in behavior coming on . . . irritability, loss of appetite, lethargy?"

"No, not that I can recall. I was away from home up until the day before it happened, but Clara didn't notice anything and my boy didn't say anything."

"They might not have noticed. Is it possible your son did something different to the dog, something he's afraid to tell you about?"

"No . . . at least I don't think so. Why?"

"Well maybe you remember the case of that St. Bernard that turned on this baby and killed it. It was a few years back. Same situation—unusual behavior that no one expected. Later, It was discovered that the baby had shoved a ballpoint pen deep into the dog's ear."

"Good God!"

"Exactly."

"Well, the dog wasn't only after Bobby. When I came out to help, he turned on me, too."

"Had to feel threatened at this point."

"I've been thinking about something else." Sid hesitated and then leaned forward in his chair. "Do you think it's possible for a dog to suffer some mental illness?" He was happy that Fox didn't smile.

"What did you have in mind?"

"Schizophrenia, paranoia . . ."

"You mean just like that? Get it like someone gets a common cold? No, I don't think that's possible. However, there are all sorts of new studies out on the psychology of animals. Dogs, especially, have personalities. It's what makes them so popular as pets, and I suppose it's within the realm of possibility that whatever has a personality can have personality problems. As you know, there are dogs that are far more aggressive than other dogs and dogs that are far more docile. You can have sharp differences within the same litter. A friend of mine who raises St. Bernards had to put one down recently. He had it for nearly three years and it was just becoming more and more vicious. It got to the point where he was afraid of it himself, afraid to feed it, afraid to go near it. What was more interesting, from your viewpoint, however," Fox added leaning over his desk, "is that this dog was beginning to influence the others."

"Like what we might call peer pressure?"

"Exactly. But, as I was saying before, you, your wife, or your children would have had to notice something unusual in King, some deviant behavior. It can't just happen."

"Why not? It often happens that way with people, doesn't it? How many times have we heard about someone nobody expected to become violent doing violent and crazy things? There was that boy who shot people from a tower in Dallas and . . ."

"Yes, but afterward, we learn that they had brain tumors or they had been doing little things people ignored . . . they checked King for a tumor?"

"Yes, the head was X-rayed."

"I don't know. Right now, I don't have any suggestions for you, and you saw what my office looks like."

"Yeah." Sid stood up. "I appreciate your giving me these few minutes, though."

"That's okay. I'm sorry I can't give you anything more. I know how you must feel."

"Perhaps, if something else comes to mind . . ."

"I'll give you a call. That's a promise." Dr. Fox extended his hand and Sid shook it. Outside in the lobby, he paused by the German shepherd. The owner was an elderly woman dressed in a long black overcoat. She looked fragile and afraid, with eyes sadder than the eyes of the dog that had quills in its mouth.

"Went where he shouldn't have, huh?" Sid asked.

"It's not like him," she said. "He's always right by me. Stays close to home. He's a good dog. But it's those dogs down the street that come up all the time," she added, her voice filled with vehemence, her pale, slim face becoming animated. "I tell those people they should keep their dogs leashed, but it's too much trouble to put up with the barking."

"You should report them."

"Oh, I have. The police come up; they warn them, and then they're at it again." She looked at her dog. The animal sat patiently and stared up at Sid. The dog's eyes were watery. Sid thought he looked remorseful, like a child who had been caught doing wrong and hoped to escape serious punishment by playing up his regret. "He's a good dog," the old lady said, stroking the animal's head and neck. "It's those others."

"He'll be all right," Sid said. He started to pet the dog and then stopped. "Good luck," he said and left the office.

She talks about him as though he were a child, he thought as he started for home. Then he thought, but so many people do. And the pet food industry and all the related pet industries cater to that, encourage that. He thought about the television commercials in which animals were shown having opinions about brands of food. People clothed their animals, bought health insurance for them, and even buried them in special pet cemeteries. No, the old lady isn't hard to understand, he thought. But how much of this stuff is true and how much of it is superimposed? Are animals really capable of the deep feelings and emotions we ascribe to them?

What was his relationship to King? He had liked the dog, had been impressed with him, especially after he had gone through obedience training. Sometimes when he sat there in the living room looking at Sid or at the kids, Sid thought he looked as though he were thinking. There were times when he seemed sad and times when he seemed happy. Yet was it possible to ascribe what had happened simply to a case of a bad mood?

People, who are far more intelligent than dogs, have been known to do impulsive and foolish things . . . things that hurt others and things that hurt themselves. Why was it so hard for him to accept that the dog might have done that, too?

Because it's precisely his lower level of mentality that makes him predictable, Sid thought. Someone once said, some philosopher, "To think is to be sad." The deeper one thinks, the more one philosophizes, the more unhappy one can become about this life.

Intelligent people are unpredictable because they see more choices and take more original routes. The dog, a lower form of life and intelligence, can't be as moody. He wasn't happy being chained, but it would be a stretch of the imagination to expect that to make him suicidal or conniving.

None of this satisfied Sid. All that he had learned

and thought about only deepened the mystery. Maybe Clara was right; maybe he should simply let it be: admit defeat and forget. It wasn't in his character to do so, but it wasn't in his character to be self-destructive, either.

He sat in the car for a moment after he pulled into the driveway; he stared at the empy doghouse. It would be best to get that out of here now, he thought. It was a shame to destroy it; it was a well-built doghouse. Maybe he could put an ad in the paper and try to sell it. It was worth a few bucks. There were people on the lookout for things like this. He should have put an ad on Dr. Fox's bulletin board in the office lobby. He'd just give the doctor's office a call and ask them to do it. He was sure they would.

There was certainly no chance, no chance in the immediate future, that he would get another dog, even though the doctor at the emergency room in the hospital had made that suggestion.

"Best way to overcome what could be a lifetime paranoia," he said. "Get him a puppy and let him start anew."

"Not a chance," Sid said. Maybe he'd been too quick to make up his mind.

Then he thought about the old lady and the dog with the quills in its mouth. Too much trouble, he thought. They're not worth it. I'd rather take my chance with the burglars.

He got out of the car, but before he reached the house, Clara was at the door. She looked white with fear.

"Oh Sid," she said, her voice thin and raspy, like someone talking in her sleep. "Thank God you're home."

"What is it? What's wrong? Bobby went to school, didn't he?"

"Yes."

"So? What is it?"

"It's King," she said.

"King?"

"I heard him."

"He's dead, Clara," Sid said.

But Clara went on as though he weren't even there. "So I came to the door and looked out and he was there." She turned slowly. "In the doghouse, just like always."

# 3

"I'VE TRACKED ALL sorts of animals in my life," Qwen said, "but I never seen nothin' like this."

Kevin Longfellow looked at the trapper. He didn't like the idea of going into town to find one of the locals to help in this search, but Dr. Bronstein was right when he said, "We're not trappers and hunters. We're scientists. We're not going to know the first thing about what to do out there. It's been nearly three days and those woods are deep." Kevin was a little wary of Mike Qwen, but everyone they talked to said he was the best. They said he knew the land so well he could read it better than one of those air traffic controllers could read radar. He knew just where every property line began and ended; he knew where the forest had thinned and thickened. He was a remnant of a bygone age, someone who lived off the land, a professional trapper and hunter.

As such, he was suspicious of technology; he distrusted a modern age that substituted so many devices and machines for human effort. He wasn't eager to work for them, but, if he succeeded, they offered half again as much money as he could make in a year. It didn't seem like much to do, so he relented and agreed to lead a search party.

"What the hell are you people doin' up there anyway?" he asked when Kevin drove him up to the institute to start the search.

"It's medical research. We're trying to find better ways to treat people who are sick."

"Why so secretive?"

"Everyone's out to steal everyone else's research. It's part of the game. There's more industrial and research espionage going on than espionage between countries."

"There was a big demonstration in New York City against experiments with animals," Qwen said. "I seen it on the television at Old Mill Tavern."

"Yeah, I know," Kevin said, "but if we didn't use animals, a lot of sick people would be a lot sicker today."

"I don't care one way or the other about it," Qwen said. "As long as you don't disturb what's goin' on out there," he added, indicating the forest. Kevin grunted. He was thirty and he didn't think Qwen was all that much older, even though he had a seasoned look about him. They were about the same height—five eleven or so—and Kevin imagined they were about the same weight, too, although Qwen's weight was firmer and better arranged. His skin was almond-colored and his sandpaper beard made him look as hard as a tree.

Kevin wore an army fatigue jacket and a pair of khaki pants with laced boots. Qwen wore only a flannel shirt, a pair of jeans, and a pair of moccasins. He said he liked to travel light. He had a long hunting knife in his belt, a pack of chewing tobacco in his shirt pocket, and a whistle dangling from his belt buckle. The whistle was "so you guys will know where I am when I want you to know. I've been on search parties before and lots of times the searchers get lost before we find what we're lookin' for."

"There's not going to be that many of us," Kevin said. "I've got two assistants who'll take the flanks."

"That's it? I thought this was damn important."

"It is, but that's all I have to bring. From what they tell me, you should be able to do it all by yourself," he said. Qwen laughed. He recognized that Kevin wasn't all that happy about this or about him.

"You ever go into deep woods before?"

"Not like this," Kevin said.

"What about him?"

"He was domestic from birth. Nothing wild about him."

"It comes more natural to him. He don't need no lessons, but if he's as domesticated as you say, he ain't going to be hard to find," Qwen said.

That was before they actually began. Now, he stood by the wild blueberry bush and shook his head.

"What bothers you?" Kevin asked him. As far as he could see, there was nothing, no hint, no tracks, nothing. Qwen squatted and Kevin squatted behind him.

"Most any animal would go right between the bushes. They don't consider that if they go right between these bushes, they'll probably break a branch or two and leave a sign, especially an animal bein' chased or an animal runnin' away from somethin'."

"So? He didn't break a branch."

"More 'n that. He didn't want to. Lookee here," Qwen said, pointing to the earth. "He crawled through the opening. He took care about it. This is an animal on its stomach pullin' itself along." Kevin nodded, but Qwen didn't look away. He had the eyes of a hunter and his prey was not only somewhere out in the wilderness; it was in the mind of the man beside him. "What is he?"

"I told you. Just a German shepherd, but one in whom we've invested a great deal of work and research. It would be very costly for us to lose him now."

Qwen stood up and took a chunk of chewing tobacco out of his pouch. "This isn't all," he said. "He started northwest and then went due north. He went northeast and back to due north. Then he turned back there and went southwest. Now he's come back to due south."

"He's confused."

"Yeah, maybe. Or he's zigzaggin' to throw off pursuit. Could he be doin' that?" Qwen asked. There was some laughter in his eyes.

Kevin bit his lower lip. "You'd better blow that whistle. Those guys are going too far ahead."

Qwen just looked at him. Then he took the whistle out and blew it. "He's movin' pretty fast," Qwen said. "He's not the lost animal you described searchin' for food and shelter. I'd say he's got a sense of direction and purpose."

"So?"

"So if we go on much farther, we're goin' to have to consider livin' off the land—huntin' for our own food and water. I think we're talkin' about days. We've been goin' three and a half hours; it's goin' to take us nearly that much to go back and it'll be close to dark by then."

"What do you suggest? You're the leader as far as this is concerned."

"Damned if I ever seen anything like you guys—bunch o' doctors and technicians rushin' out here to look for an escaped dog. What I suggest is we go back. You and I get some supplies together and we come back out in the mornin'. This ain't what you said it would be. I'm goin' to have to earn that money."

"Just the two of us?"

"You said he wears a collar and you got a leash and he'll come to you when we finally find him?"

"Maybe," Kevin confessed.

"I'll need to think about some trappin' gear, too. I

know you want to keep this quiet, Doc, and for now I'll go along with this worry about spies and all, but we're goin' to have to do it right. This is a real challenge. This animal knows we're comin'. Maybe you'll tell me a little more as we go along, huh?"

"Maybe," Kevin said. He smiled. Despite his initial feelings, he felt he could come to like this man. There was a refreshing forthrightness about him. Perhaps the simplicity of the natural world gave him more insight, even about people. He felt he could trust him and he knew that before it was all over, he would probably end up telling him everything, as wild and incredible as the story might sound. "We'll do what you say," Kevin said. "Take us back."

Ken Strasser paused at the kitchen sink and looked out the window at the barn. Maybe his old eyes were playing tricks on him, but he thought he saw something slip in through the partially opened door. He expected there would be all sorts of small wildlife in there by now: snakes, field mice, rabbits, and skunks. Maybe a raccoon and a possum would go in and out, but he didn't expect to see anything that big make its way inside. This looked big—as big as a large dog. A damn stray, he thought. A damn stray.

He debated whether or not to let the animal stay the night and then thought, if I give him an inch, the animal won't go. He'd seen it too many times before. When Ethel was alive, it was different. She took pity on anything. Every time he reached for the rifle to shoot a pesky skunk or drive off a coon, she pleaded for mercy. He always gave in, and even if he did shoot, he made sure to shoot too high or too low. It was because of Ethel that he hadn't gone deer hunting since he was eighteen. He stopped when they started courting, and after they were married, there was no chance. Of course, he could have resumed it after she died, but somehow that wouldn't have seemed right. He couldn't do anything she wouldn't have wanted him to do.

He even kept the house cleaner than she had kept it. The moment he finished a meal, he was up and about clearing off the table, scraping off the dishes, wiping and washing everywhere. God forbid there was a crumb on the floor. Charley would come and laugh at him, but he knew that his son was quietly pleased.

"Mom always said you could eat off her floor."

"You could. What can I do . . . she left me with bad habits."

"Bad habits." They both laughed about it. His son was fifty-one years old, and in some ways he looked older than his father. Didn't have the same good life, Ken thought. You can't compare the women. I was blessed with Ethel, he was cursed with Paula. Why his son had married such a woman, he'd never know. A home-cooked meal was always an ordeal, and to think, they lived in a six-room apartment and she needed a maid twice a week. No wonder Charley came here twice a week to eat and spend time.

Well, in a way Ken was happy about that. At least he had his son's company regularly. How many people his age could say the same thing? Oh, they had their share of arguments, most of them about whether or not he should keep the farm. It was a big house for one man, but it didn't seem right to even think about selling it. It was the only home he had ever known; it had been in the family back to his great-great grandfather. He hoped Charley would take it when he was gone; he had even hoped Charley and Paula and the girls would move in with him, but Paula hadn't gone for that. She wouldn't go for it after he died, either; she thought the place was too old and unattractive. The condo was more like it. Condo, he thought. Sounded like some kind of Latin music, not a home;

and how could you say that you owned an apartment? It didn't make sense. Right through the wall was another family who supposedly owned their apartment. There wasn't any land to speak of, and privacy was nonexistent as far as he was concerned. Bees in a hive, he thought. Bees in a hive.

Charley tried to make it sound like something. "We got a pool and a tennis court and a health club, all on the grounds."

"Hell, you coulda had your own right here. We got nearly eighty acres. A pool woulda fit in right nice over near the stone wall, and with the slate ground behind the house . . . you could probably lay out a helluva tennis court."

"Paula thinks this is the boondocks, Pop. She likes people around her."

"Citified."

"It's the way most people are nowadays. They feel more secure."

"Never felt insecure out here. You don't have people running about muggin' one another. A rapist would freeze to death waitin' for a woman."

"Yeah, maybe you're right about that."

"Look, I ain't one to interfere. Your mother wasn't that way and I sure as hell ain't. Do what makes you happy. Seems a shame though, all this bein' unused."

"It's too much for you, Pop."

"Well . . . I ain't doin' anything with the land . . . just the small garden is all. I think about gettin' a cow or two, just for the helluva it."

"Pop!"

"But I don't give it a second thought," he said. Charley smiled and nodded. "I'm eigthy-one years old, boy."

"I know, Pop."

"Ten years without your mother."

"I know."

"Been the saddest ten years of my life. Worse trick she ever played on me—dyin' before me."

"Just like her to upstage you, Pop."

The old man nodded. Deep in the back of his mind, rooted forever in his thoughts, was the permanent image of Ethel Marie Houseman, the anchor of his existence, her light brown hair brushed down softly over her bare shoulders, her eighteen-year-old body turned toward him, her arms out. It was right here in this house, with the moonlight tearing through the curtains and the peepers serenading them into the wee hours.

How many times during the past ten years while he moved through this house did he stop to think about her? How many times did he stop to talk to her? He wasn't alone as long as he was here. Give up this house and living in it? He might as well give it all up.

His attention came back to the barn. Night was falling quickly. Whatever it was, it had come to settle in for the evening. He was sure of it. If he was going to do anything, he would have to do it quickly. Best to drive it off, he thought; best to send it packin'. Sorry, Ethel, but I don't need no wild thing on the grounds. Got enough to worry about with the garden and all.

He went for his rifle.

He paused in the hallway by the telephone table before leaving and turned Ethel's picture to the wall. You don't have to see me doin' this, he thought. He laughed at himself. Funny, the things an old man livin' alone all these years would do. But he couldn't help it. So much in the house and on the land had spiritual qualities for him. Charley had wanted him to give away all her clothes, but he couldn't do it. What was the rush, he thought, even though he knew very well she would have wanted it that way; she would have wanted her clothes to go toward helping some poor soul. Forgive me for that one too, Ethel, he thought, and he went out the back door.

The sun had fallen faster than he had expected. It surprised him; he hadn't thought it was this dim out when he'd peered through the window. Must be my eyesight, he thought. Or maybe the world always looks brighter to me from the inside of the house. The idea made him laugh. He paused on the back porch, checked to be sure the rifle was loaded, and started down the short wooden steps.

If it was a dog, he didn't think he would have to shoot it. What he expected and hoped to do was scare the animal off so that it would never come back. It would run off and follow the road into town where maybe the police would pick it up or someone would take it in, some store owner who'd feed it scraps and keep it in the back of a store.

If it was a dog, he could call the dogcatcher, but as usual the stray wouldn't be around when he arrived and then he would take his time returning. Naw, there was no better way than handling your own problems yourself. That was the difference between men like him and men like . . . men like his son Charley. It made him sad to think it. He walked on toward the barn.

Somewhere from one of the shadowy corridors of his mind, he could hear Ethel saying, "You be careful, Ken Strasser. You're no young bull anymore. Don't go around acting like you are. You're foolin' nobody, least of all me."

"Right, right," he muttered. He shook his head. Didn't the shadow cast by the silhouette of the barn look long and dark, though. He almost wished he'd brought his flashlight along. Goin' to need it inside there, he realized. Probably will have to go back to fetch it anyway. Oh well, he thought, might just shake him out of there without much trouble.

He crossed into the shadow and moved like a shadow himself.

He heard the man coming even before the man emerged from the house. He was keen about any sounds in the rear of the building. Whenever he was in the barn, he was well aware of where the old man was at all times. Either he saw him move about the grounds, or he saw his shadow in the windows, or he heard him in the house. He wasn't afraid of him as such; he was simply alert and conscious of everything around him, more so than he had ever been. His senses were extraordinarily sharp, his perception far beyond anything he had ever known.

He had created a place for himself near the partially opened barn door. When he first discovered the hide-away, he brought large mouthfuls of hay to this location and created a warm and comfortable bed for himself. From this position, he could look out at the house and the yard and he could see and hear any potentially threatening movement.

As soon as the old man emerged from the house, he got to his feet. He knew that what the old man was carrying could inflict great pain and even death. He wasn't sure how he knew this. The realization came to him from a pocket of awareness fed by information gathered during some earlier time of his life. The intellectual process was quick and his resultant anger immediate. A low, threatening growl began in the base of his throat; he held it there in check, recognizing the need for silence.

He backed a few steps away when the man drew closer. In these few moments he was carved of stone. He remained outside the small ray of light that entered the barn, so that even his eyes were unseen. The old man paused a few feet from the door. He swung the rifle from the side of him so that the barrel faced the door.

*"Hey,"* the old man yelled, *"Get the hell outta there!"*

He didn't move. He heard the old man curse and then saw him come forward. He backed farther away, rubbing his body against the door, keeping himself close to it. When the old man slid it further open, he moved along with it as though he were attached to it. That made him invisible. He hoped that was all he would have to do. Attacking the old man wasn't part of his plan . . . not yet. But the old man entered the barn, rifle up and ready.

"Where are ya?" he shouted. "I know you're in here somewhere," he muttered to himself. He started to turn.

Before this, anything he attacked had been forewarned. His growl served as an announcement. The prey or the antagonist had an opportunity to bring up its guard and feign off his first thrust, or at least to block it. But this time he came out of the darkness, a fist of darkness, himself. He was an extension of the black, the air turned into a solid mass of muscle and bone.

He struck the old man in the chest and drove him back out of the barn, where he fell backward, the rifle flying over his head and bouncing somewhere in the yard. Still, he didn't growl. Once again, he lunged in silence.

Ken Strasser was confused by the blow. He wasn't sure what had come at him. The force of it was overwhelming, but the silence was shocking. It couldn't have been a dog, could it? Yet, when he looked up from the ground, that was just what it was . . . a large German shepherd, leaping in the air.

It never touched Ken with its mouth. He didn't even have to push its head away. This was like some kind of nightmare gone wild. He almost thought he had been attacked by a man dressed as a dog. The animal, or whatever it was, landed over his torso and dropped the center of its weight right over his face.

He pushed up with all his might, but Ethel was right—he was not a young bull anymore. The strength in these arms could serve to dig holes for tomato plants and maybe run the Rototiller over the ground, but even that was getting hard to do; he had to stop so often to rest. Pressing into this animal was like pressing against a solid wall. He couldn't budge it an inch.

He stopped his effort because the animal wasn't doing anything else to harm him. He expected it would get off him at any moment and run away, but it didn't. It rolled its body slightly, just so it could lean more of its weight against his face. Its coat was soft, but the scent of it was definitely dog, and not domesticated dog but dog that had been out in the wilds, dog that had been rained upon, dog that had dried in the sun, that had traveled through the forest, that had slept on the hay in his barn. All these odors were familiar to him. They greeted him like a montage of the natural world he had known and loved so long, only now they presented him with a most extraordinary kind of life-threatening problem. Why was this dog so contented with simply staying this way?

He pushed against it again and he turned his body from side to side to throw if off, but he might as well have tried to move a car. It was as though a decent-sized man had decided to sit on his face. The indignity of it all occurred to him, but that indignation was short because he quickly realized that his breathing was being cut off. As difficult as it was for him to accept, he was being smothered to death by a large German shepherd; what was most frightening about it for him was the realization that the animal seemed to know exactly what it was doing.

He gasped, closed his eyes, and gave a final push. The results were the same . . . failure. His lungs began to ache; his mind reeled. The last thing he thought of was Ethel's picture on the telephone table in the hallway. Thank God he had turned it to the wall.

"I have a very surprising, maybe even very stupid thing to tell you," Sid Kaufman began. The chief of police sat back in his chair. When Sid asked to see him privately with the door of his office closed, Harry Michaels's interest was piqued.

"Don't be afraid to say somethin' stupid, Mr. Kaufman. I hear a lot of that nowadays." He smiled at his own sense of humor, but Sid only nodded. "Sit down, sit down. You look awful. That leg acting up?"

"It thumps away, but I wish that was all of it." Sid took the seat and folded his hands on his lap. "I don't even know how to start this."

"Just start it. That's usually the best way," Michaels said.

"My son . . . my son, of course, has been having nightmares."

"Sure."

"Yesterday, he insisted that King had come to the house at night and sat by his window, whining for him to come out to play. The dog would do that sometimes."

"King was your dog? The one that . . ."

"Yes. Like I said, Bobby had been having nightmares, so I just assumed it was that."

"Uh huh."

"The kid's kinda bright. Top of his class, reads two grade levels beyond his age."

"I gotcha, but bright kids can have nightmares too, Mr. Kaufman."

"Oh sure. What I mean is, he stuck to his story and then took me out to where he claimed the dog had been."

"A young Charlie Chan," Michaels said. He took a cigar out of his shirt pocket, unwrapped it, and stuck it in his mouth without lighting it. "Doctor forbids me to smoke, but I like to pretend."

Sid smiled. "Anyway, I saw a paw print where the earth was soft."

"Paw print? You mean, a dog's paw print?"

"Uh huh. Just about King's size, too."

"I see."

"I thought the dog could have made that anytime."

"Sure. That makes sense."

"Even though it looked very fresh."

"Maybe it was another dog."

"I'm getting to that. This afternoon, when I came home, my wife . . . my wife was quite upset. She told me she heard King barking . . ."

"Mr. Kaufman," Michaels said, leaning forward, "you keep saying King, but that was the name of the dog that was destroyed, right?"

"Yes sir."

"Good. You're getting me a little confused."

"Well, that's because I am. She also said she came out of the house and looked at the doghouse and saw King in it."

Michaels stared at him. Then he moved the cigar from the corner of his mouth to the center and back to the corner again before taking it out.

"Saw?"

"My dog."

"Your dead dog?"

"Of course, I thought it was just another German shepherd."

"Of course."

"Even though one dog won't usually go into another dog's doghouse. I learned that afterward. I called my vet."

"You did? So what does that mean?"

"I began to call all the people who live on our street. There are a few with dogs, but no one has gotten a German shepherd recently. I reached everyone but Ken Strasser, so I went down to his place, but he wasn't around."

"Old Ken. He's probably with his son, Charley. You know Charley?"

"Just a nodding acquaintance. I didn't see any signs of a German shepherd at his place, though."

"So what's your point, Mr. Kaufman? I don't mean to sound rude, but . . ."

"Well, it's kind of a weird coincidence, don't you think?"

"What is?"

"Another German shepherd haunting our house."

"Haunting? Might be a stray. We'll have the dog-catcher make a few passes on your street."

"I was thinking maybe it was more than that . . . maybe someone's playing a sick joke on us."

"Oh God, Mr. Kaufman. That's stretchin' it. I don't know."

"My wife's pretty upset."

"I can see why. Tell you what: I'll send a patrol car up there two, three times a day and once or twice at night. He'll have a spotlight on the vehicle so he'll be able to keep a good lookout. And I'll call the dog-catcher for you, just as I said."

"Thank you."

"I know you people have been through a mess, but you can't let it get the best of you."

"You're right."

"And I'll speak to Charley or Ken later tonight, just to be sure Ken didn't take on a dog."

"This one would have to be along in years, at least four or five," Sid said.

"Okay," Michaels said. He put the cigar back in the corner of his mouth. "Seems a shame that smokin' has to be so bad for ya, don't it?"

"Yes." Sid smiled. "Thanks for being understanding."

"No problem. Just take care of yourself and tell your wife we'll be cruisin' along your street."

"I will. Oh, one other thing," Sid said after he reached the door. "No one else on the street has seen such a dog about. You'd think that if it was a stray, someone might have seen it, too."

"That's a thought, Mr. Kaufman," Harry Michaels said. He took the cigar out and used it as a pointer. "I'll keep that in mind."

"Thanks again."

After Sid Kaufman left, Harry Michaels sat back in his chair again. People sure can get wacked out of joint, he thought. This was one for the books.

"I'll meet you back at the institute at the crack of dawn," Qwen said. "Just the two of us is all we need. That is, unless this here dog of yours returns tonight," he added. That twinkle was in his eyes.

Keven knew the trapper was playing with him. "About six then?"

"That sounds right," Qwen said as he got out of the car. He lived alone in a small two-story house just outside of Margaretville. Kevin thought the seclusion fit a man like Qwen. A hound dog, tied near a doghouse on the side, began to bark a greeting.

"You going to bring your dog along?"

"I am now. Somethin' tells me we're gonna need all the help we can get. Bring something of the animal's—a collar, piece of bedding, somethin' Maggie can sniff and get a hold of."

"Okay."

"See ya," Qwen said and closed the car door. Kevin watched him walk toward his home and then he backed up, turned around, and headed for the institute.

There were no signs announcing what it was; there were only signs warning intruders away. The building, which had once served as a home for the elderly, was bleak and unattractive. Nothing had been done to the landscape except for the construction of a twelve-foot-tall chain-link fence all around the grounds. The agency had chosen the place because it was ideally adapted to what they required. Rooms had been redesigned to fit their needs, and equipment had been brought in. By the time Kevin had arrived, it was ready for the research and the experiments. When he saw how isolated the structure was and how deliberately obscure it had been kept, he was impressed. It gave him a renewed sense of the importance of their work, of how much their value had increased because of the success with the mice. If what they did could become transferable to people, human progress could take a giant leap forward. Everyone knew that a major ramification of that leap was power. Their discoveries, his discoveries, would be as important as the discovery of nuclear fission.

The security guard at the gate came out of his booth. As soon as he recognized Kevin, the guard opened the gate and Kevin drove up to the parking lot by the front entrance. He could see the lights were still on in his laboratory, and he imagined Ann was feeding the animals. His twenty-four-year-old assistant had taken the security breach rather personally. She was a perfectionist, a brilliant mathematician and logician who usually became emotional only over her work. The others had nicknamed her "Mrs. Spock," after the fictional character in *Star Trek*. Kevin couldn't blame them for it. He didn't really like Ann; there was nothing feminine about her. Her hair was cut shorter than his; her skin was sickly white. She never wore makeup, and the only time he had ever seen her out of that antiseptic lab robe was when she had first arrived. He thought it was possible she slept in it. But she had come highly recommended, and now she was an enormous asset.

After he got out of his car and entered the institute, Kevin walked through the lobby and went directly to Dr. Bronstein's office. The director had said he'd be waiting in his office. Kevin knocked and then entered. The fifty-five-year-old scientist looked up expectantly from a folder on his desk. His thin, graying hair looked disturbed again and Kevin smiled to himself, thinking how the director often ran his fingers through his hair nervously whenever he became engrossed in a new thought. It was as though he would stroke his brain into becoming more efficient. And wasn't that what it was all about?

"We're going to start again in the morning," Kevin said. "Just Qwen and me."

"Why just the two of you?"

"He wants it that way."

"Do you trust him?"

"I think we were told right. He looks damn authentic. He's pretty smart, too. He's figured out that we're not after just any lost dog."

"How much did you tell him?"

"Practically nothing, but I don't know how long I can keep him in the dark. Besides, once we find him . . ."

"You have to be careful, Kevin. Can't expect a layman to comprehend what we're about."

"I know."

Bronstein thought for a moment and then sat back.

"Maybe you'd better take Gerson with you," he said.

"Qwen wants only two of us."

"We're paying him. Besides, with the kind of combat training Gerson's had, he might be of some aid out there in the wilds. I'll tell him to be ready. What time?"

"About six. This Qwen is a kind of peculiar fellow. It wouldn't surprise me if he refused to take him along."

"Gerson's peculiar, too. That's why they assigned him to head up our security. Maybe they'll get along. Be careful out there. I've been going over Ann's report," he added, indicating the folder on his desk. "Apparently opening a door was quite basic for him and someone must have left that hall window open just enough for him to get his snoot into it so he could push it up."

"No, he's not going to have any problem getting out of a building."

"Which means the opposite is also true."

"Sir?"

"He won't have any problem getting into one either," the director said.

# 4

Harry Michaels got the phone call just as he sat down to have his dinner. Jenny shook the wooden spoonful of mashed potatoes over his plate with a vengeance. He was a half hour late as it was, and everything was overcooked. Even after thirty-one years of marriage, his wife had not gotten used to the unpredictability of their lives. They rarely had a serious fight about it. Her anger was usually directed at other targets: at herself for trying to lead a normal existence; at the community, which had no respect for its public servants; careless automobile drivers who never thought about other people; criminals who were growing in number; and fate, which had something against her serving a meal when it was hot and ready. Harry usually let her go on and on about it until her fuel ran down and she settled into a quiet tolerance. He never put up an argument. After all, she was right.

Jenny slapped the pot of potatoes back on the stove when Harry went to answer the phone. He could hear her mumbling behind him, sounding like a small outboard motor just starting.

"Michaels," he said. The forkful of potato was still on his tongue.

"It's Julie, Chief. Charley Strasser just found his father dead in the backyard. Clark went up."

"Aw, too bad. I'm on my way. Did you call the coroner?"

"Dr. Hamilton's on the way. The ambulance squad too."

"All right," he said and hung up. Jenny saw the expression on his face.

"What?"

"Ken Strasser was just found dead behind his house. His son found him."

"Oh my God." She bit her lower lip gently and they stared at each other. "He was the kind you think's goin' to live forever. Couldn't have been a nicer person."

"Yep."

"I'll hold the dinner," she said.

"Might be a while."

"Nothin' new about that. Must've been a terrible shock for Charley. I feel so bad for him."

He said nothing. She watched him strap on his pistol, slip into his jacket, and slap on his hat. Even though she complained regularly, she couldn't help being proud of him when he donned his police uniform. She knew there were those who sneered at a small town police force for being unsophisticated and simple, but Harry had never let that get to him. Although his men and their operation of law enforcement didn't seem as spit-polished as some big city forces, there was a quiet efficiency evident. She knew that Harry was respected by the sheriff and the state police. There were all sorts of letters of commendation and thanks in the den. To many, because of his longevity in office and his commanding personality, Harry had become Mr. Fallsburg.

"I'll be back as soon as I can," he said.

"Be careful. Tell Charley how sorry I am."

"Right."

He headed out to the car. After he started it and

pulled away from the house, he remembered Sid Kaufman's saying that he had been unable to contact Ken Strasser. Perhaps it was an irrelevant detail, but all his years of police training on the job had taught him never to neglect any piece of information, no matter how small or insignificant it might seem at the time.

Leon Clark, his night patrolman, and Charley Strasser were waiting for him at the front of the house. Dr. Hamilton's car was parked on the road and the ambulance was right behind it. The three volunteers, Marge Baxter, Tom Singleman, and Corky Wilson were standing beside it and talking softly. With the volunteers dressed in their white uniforms, the ambulance lights blinking, and Clark's radio amplifying static, the scene took on an eerie, dreamlike quality. It reminded Harry of the nightmares he had been having lately, nightmares that drove him out of his sleep and woke him with a start, leaving him sweating and breathing hard. Fortunately, Jenny hadn't noticed, or if she had, she hadn't let on about it. He ascribed it to mental fatigue and thought more seriously about his pension and his retirement.

He offered Charley his hand and condolences.

"It don't look right," Charley said.

"It never does, Charley. It never does."

"But this is different, Harry. I know he was along in his years, but I was here just yesterday. He was as spry as ever."

The chief nodded and turned to his patrolman.

"Coroner's back there?"

"Right behind me. Julie raised him on his car phone."

"Let me talk to him, Charley," Harry said. He and Clark moved through the darkness. Clark had taken the portable spotlight off the patrol car and left it with the coroner. Intermittent moonlight, breaking through what was now a partly cloudy sky, helped too. When they turned the corner of the house, they saw Dr. Hamilton kneeling beside the body.

"Any ideas yet, Doc?"

Hamilton looked up. He was a short man in his early fifties with wavy, reddish-blond hair and freckles, but his Van Johnson face was incongruous with his Peter Lorre voice. He always spoke slowly, methodically. Depending on accuracy, he looked at the world with microscopic eyes. Sometimes he gave Harry the creeps because he was so intense, even when he carried on an ordinary conversation. It was as if a simple "good morning" might turn out to be a clue.

"Well," he said, standing slowly. "Off-the-record first impression?"

Harry looked behind him to be sure the others had remained far enough behind to be out of earshot.

"I'm all ears, Doc."

"Well, we have peticial hemorrhage in the eyes. See the little round blood spots?"

"I'll take your word for it."

"There's swelling in the lips, tongue, and eyelids. You'll also notice the lips and earlobes are purple—cyanosis. Simply put, Chief, this man died from asphyxiation. He was smothered to death."

"A definite homicide?"

"No question about that. Whoever did it put some furry, hairy object over his face and blocked his respiration.

"Hairy?"

Hamilton took a sealed plastic sack from his pocket and handed it to Harry.

"I got those hairs off his face and hands. He struggled against whoever it was."

Harry looked down and saw that the coroner had placed plastic bags over Ken Strasser's hands to protect them for the autopsy and for the forensics team.

"How long has he been dead?"

"An hour, hour and a half tops. I have my pictures."

"Clark, go get the camera and diagram the scene. What about that rifle?"

"It's back there, Chief. From the grass stains on the stock and the indentures in the earth, it looks like it flew out of his hands."

"Bag it carefully after you photograph. Was there much of a struggle, Doc?"

"Not from what I can see now. He received a blow on the abdomen, a blow that sent him backward, I imagine. That was probably when the rifle left his grip." He turned toward the barn. "Probably heading toward the door. There are contusions on his back from the fall and from being pressed down. Held down, I should say. It wouldn't take much to hold down a man of his age and frame."

"Not now, maybe, but twenty years ago, it would have taken two fully grown men. I once saw him lift the back of a car to get the wheel off some ice."

"I'll tell the ambulance squad to take him to the hospital morgue as soon as you're done."

"Okay, I'll go up with them. I'd better call the district attorney," Harry said. But he looked toward the barn door again. He picked up the spotlight and went to it. Shining the light about, he looked in until he spotted the bed of hay by the door. He went to it and knelt down to inspect it. Running his hands over it, he found strands of hair similar to the ones the coroner had taken from Ken Strasser's body. He held one of them in his fingers and twirled it about. Then he put some in his shirt pocket. He went back outside and watched Clark take photographs and complete the diagram. After he called the district attorney, he joined Charley at the front of the house.

"Coroner won't say anything to me," Charley said.

"He's not supposed to."

"What happened to him, Harry?"

"We're going to have to wait for the autopsy before we make any definite conclusions, Charley. It's standard procedure."

"I know a little about police work, Harry. I watch television. You're treating this like a homicide, right?"

"Yes, Charley, we are. Now I got a crazy question for you. Did your father have a dog, even a stray he kept around?"

"A dog? No. A homicide. Who would want to hurt my father?"

"Let's wait until we gather all the facts together, Charley. I'm following the ambulance to the hospital."

"I'll go with you."

"It's going to be hours, Charley. I'll call you. That's a promise."

Charley nodded. They watched the ambulance squad lift his father's body into the ambulance. They handled it carefully, as if it mattered. As soon as the doors were closed, Charley shook his head.

"Kids are going to take this hard."

"Go home, Charley," Harry said and put his hand on Charley's shoulder. "Get your family together. I'll call you."

"Thanks. Thanks, Leon," he said, turning to Officer Clark.

After Charley left them, Harry turned to Clark. "I told Julie to tell you to be on the lookout for a stray dog when you made your sweep on Lake Street," he began. He didn't want to get into Sid Kaufman's story, so he added, "It was bothering some people."

"I ain't seen any sign of him, Chief. A German shepherd?"

"Right. Make another sweep down Lake Street tonight."

"Okay," Clark said. They watched the ambulance pull away.

"Did you put the rifle in my car?"

"Yeah."

Harry thought for a moment and then got into his car. When he came to Sid Kaufman's house, he slowed down and turned his spotlight on the doghouse. It was empty and there were no signs of anything about. Still, he felt uneasy. He took out one strand of hair he had placed in his shirt pocket and studied it in the car's interior light. It looked as if it very well could be dog hair—a German shepherd's hair.

What the hell was going on here? he wondered. He looked at the doghouse again, and the coldest chill ran up his spine. He looked into the darkness around him. If he were to believe in his instincts at all, he would be afraid, for they were telling him that something unusual, something very strange and very dangerous was here and might even be watching him at this very moment.

He chastised himself for permitting his imagination to run wild and sped up to catch the ambulance.

As soon as the scent of death came up to him, he released the pressure on the man's face and lifted himself from the man's body. It had been as easy as he thought it would be. How fragile they were when they didn't have clubs and fire and knives. He poked the body with his nose and sat back. It occurred to him that this was actually his first great kill. He couldn't help it; something stronger than logic came over him. He brought his head back and howled at the night sky. The sound entered the barn, reverberated, and came back out at him. Then it died away in the darkness. He understood that others would come and find the man dead, but he hadn't killed him the way he killed deer and rabbits. Perhaps they wouldn't know he'd done it and they wouldn't come looking for him in packs.

But he couldn't be sure, so he listened to his instincts and fled to the security of the forest darkness. He stayed close to the farmhouse, watching, waiting, and listening. He saw the other man drive up to the house and enter it. He saw him come out and he heard the man shouting. He watched the man find the body and he watched the pack arrive with their lights and noise. He thought it was wiser to go away from the farm and back toward the house where the dog had lived. There, in the woods across the road, he found a space between two large boulders and slipped himself securely within. Through the trees he could see the lights of the house and remain undetected. He rested his head on his outstretched front legs and waited.

When he closed his eyes, a hodgepodge of images and memories began to play on the inside of his eyelids. The earlier remembrances were disjointed and sensual; there were things that made his mouth water, tastes he had nearly forgotten; he recalled feelings of warmth, the tongue of a larger creature, like himself, stroking him. He remembered the sound of flowing water and he remembered running in a field, digging holes in soft earth, going in and out of structures that took him through darkness and into light; he remembered being lifted and stroked and then being kicked and slapped by the same kind of creature. Once again he felt himself being tugged; he remembered the collar being tightened on his throat until it made him gag and he had no alternative but to turn or stop or to lie down.

Then there was another kind of light, a brighter light, and the confinement of bars. He pressed his nose in-between them and took in the scents of things he didn't recognize. These images, which were more recent memories, were like nightmares now; they made him uneasy and he couldn't prevent a spontaneous growl from forming at the bottom of his throat. He pawed the earth and opened his eyes to escape the memories. Something burned at the base of his brain and he gagged on his own breath.

He started to stand but lowered his body immediately at the sight of the approaching ambulance. When he had heard it coming to the farmhouse before, it had made him think of some giant bird, some creature that had been in a cage not far from his. He recalled how it had lifted its claws through the bars and had thrust those claws repeatedly in his direction. Its eyes glowed like the tiny bulbs on the metal boxes around them and it screamed hideously at him until it fell over and lay still in the cage. He saw them take it out and he saw them put it on a table and cut it open.

He had gotten to the point where he was very content to simply sit there and watch them. They didn't seem to notice him as much as he noticed them. He watched what they did with their hands, with their tools, and with their bodies; he came to an understanding of the meanings in many of their gestures and sounds. After a while he was able to anticipate what they were going to do and he was cooperative or uncooperative according to his own curiosity. If he wanted to see the outcome of something they were going to do, he was as pliable and as easy as an obedient puppy, but if he was bored because he had done it so many times before, he put up some resistance.

When the police car appeared, his memories were interrupted again. He saw the car pause in front of the house and he saw the spotlight go on to wash away the darkness around the doghouse. He lowered himself into the full protection of the rocks and waited. To him the vehicle seemed like some giant creature, panting while it decided what it would do next. When it started away, he rose to watch it disappear down the street. Once it was completely gone, he felt safe enough to move to the edge of the woods. He lingered there for a few moments, studying the house. He could hear the sounds within and he could see the silhouettes of the people moving about.

He moved farther to his right through the woods and then crossed the street to circle the house widely. He moved swiftly and determinedly through the fields until he came out behind the house. Now, moving more like a fox, he crossed the yard in slow, methodical steps until he reached the basement door. There he paused and listened for a long time. Convinced that there was no one behind it, he sat back on his haunches and rose up like a performing dog about to receive its biscuit of reward for some trick learned through repetition and reward. He took the door handle in his teeth and clamped down until he could taste the metal on his tongue. He waited a moment, listened keenly, and then turned it slowly to the right. He wasn't disappointed; he heard the click.

He lowered himself as quietly as possible and waited again, sniffing and listening. Satisfied, he poked the door gently and it swung inward just enough for him to slip inside and enter the darkness. He paused again, this time to listen to all the sounds above him. There was nothing threatening, so he went on with his exploration.

The floor of the large basement playroom was carpeted and soft. It felt like trotting over a field of moss. He went between the two sets of oval tables and chairs, under the end of the pool table, to the entrance to the bar. He went around behind the bar and sniffed the bottles and dishes on the shelves. He picked up a slight leak in the piping under the sink and licked the droplets of water that escaped from the joint. Then he went back out to the center of the room and sat listening to the patter of small feet above him.

This was so much better than the barn; it was warmer and more comfortable. He felt a sense of possession, a sense of ownership, as if he had been the first to claim it. After all, it was within his territory; it was worth defending. He started to settle down on the rug to sleep when he was troubled by a pang of hunger. Some scent attracted him. He went back to the bar to search for it.

The box of bacon bits was slightly open. It was in behind a bowl and a glass. He reached for it, clamping it in his jaws and lifting it as carefully as he could, but he just grazed the glass and sent it toppling over the shelf. It smashed on the hard tiled floor behind the bar. To him the sound was like a commanding shout. He hesitated, the box still clamped in his jaw; he waited, but nothing changed in the sounds that came from upstairs.

He brought the box around to his spot on the carpet and there he proceeded to tear it open and spill out its contents. He consumed all of it in minutes, even licking the crumbs from the carpet. Now, more content than before, he settled his head on his front legs again, closed his eyes, and welcomed the relief of sleep.

This was good; this was the best he had felt since the escape. He had rewarded himself for doing the right things. And this was only the beginning.

Sid Kaufman rose from his chair quickly when he first heard the ambulance going down Lake Street. Clara was in the bedroom reading and Bobby and Lisa were sitting on the floor before him, watching television. He had been going over the prospectus for his new assignment. He went to the living room window and saw the ambulance rush by. A moment later Clara joined him to find out what was happening.

"What was that?" she asked.

"An ambulance went by. Maybe a car accident. How are you feeling?"

"All right. You didn't hear anything?"

"Not with the television going and all. Want some tea or something?"

"No thanks." She looked at the file of papers in his hands. "I wish you weren't going tomorrow."

"This one's supposed to take only two days. I'll call you at night and Chief Michaels said he'd have patrols up this street frequently. What's there to be afraid of, anyway? I'm sure there's a logical explanation for everything."

"Yeah, I'm going mad."

"Come on, Clara."

"You don't believe me though, do you?" She searched his face for a revelation of truth.

"Of course I do. I told you, it must have been a stray."

"But you said dogs don't do that—go into other dogs' houses so quickly after the first dog has died. You said the vet said . . ."

"I'm sorry I told you that. Look, they're animals. They can't be programmed like machines. They do unpredictable things, just like people."

"That's not what you thought before, Sid." She looked down at Bobby, who had his hand on his shoulder. "Are you having pain again, honey?" she asked. Without answering, he got up and embraced her around the legs. "Come into the kitchen," she said. "I'll give you an aspirin."

"Well I just can't cancel on this," Sid said, following them into the kitchen. "All the preparation has been done, schedules changed, people set up for meetings . . ."

"I didn't say you should cancel anything," Clara said.

"Not in so many words, but . . ."

"Look, I'm just being silly. Humor me. Ignore me." She reached into the cabinet for the aspirin. "Here, honey," she said, handing one to Bobby. He made a face. "It'll make you feel better."

"Take it, champ," Sid told him. The little boy plucked the pill reluctantly from his mother's opened hand and swallowed it quickly with the water chaser.

Clara looked at Sid. "I'm sorry," she said.

"Come back into the living room and watch some television," he said, putting his arm around her. "There's a good movie coming on. It'll get your mind off things."

"All right," she said. She was beside him on the couch when the ambulance went by again. "I wonder what it was." Then she added, "They didn't have their siren going."

"So?"

"Means it doesn't matter how soon they get to the hospital," she concluded.

Sid's eyes widened with the realization. When the police car stopped and the spotlight was turned on, the whole family went to the living room window.

"Just like the chief promised," Sid said. "He wasn't bulling me."

"What's he looking for, Daddy? King?" Bobby asked.

"No, not King. I told you, King's dead. They're looking for another dog that looks like King."

"Why do they have to look for him?"

"Because he's a stray dog, a dog nobody cares about, a dog somebody left or abandoned."

"I told him that, Daddy," Lisa said. "I told him all of that, but he doesn't want to believe me."

"He will after a while. Right, champ?" Sid said. He rubbed the top of Bobby's head and looked out as the police car started away. "Lisa, how about some popcorn?" he said.

"Yeah," Bobby said excitedly, "with butter and salt."

"Okay." She shot a quick look at Clara. "I'm going to do it all by myself, Mom."

"Okay with me. These two could keep you cooking and cleaning all day and night. Maybe something happened to Mr. Strasser," she whispered to Sid.

"I was thinking that."

"I wish there was a way to find out."

"I'm sure we will," he said.

She embraced herself.

"Come on," he said. "Let's smooch on the couch."

"What's smooch?" Bobby asked. Clara laughed for the first time all day.

After Lisa made the popcorn, they sat contentedly, the four of them huddled near each other, as magnetically attracted to the warmth and closeness of one another as they were to the glow and the movement on the television screen. The kids were absorbed by the movie, but both Clara and Sid were looking through the set, their eyes turned inward to their own thoughts. It still seemed like a bad dream. Only a short while ago, King was in here with them, his head down on his front legs as he slept beside Bobby. From time to time, Sid looked to the floor expectantly, almost as though he believed he would find the dog there.

But the place on the rug was empty and the doghouse was hollow and threatening, looming out there like some terrifying reminder—the tomb of a vampire, the deserted house of a ghost. He felt like getting up, taking his sledgehammer, and smashing it to bits. He regretted that he would leave tomorrow with it still there. Clara's story haunted him. Sure, she could have imagined it, just as Bobby could have imagined what he said he had seen. Clara could have been influenced by Bobby's tale. Adults could be influenced by children. Kids were always planting things in their parents' minds, things about school and teachers and about other kids.

And yet, he couldn't help believing her. Clara wasn't easily impressed. She was an intelligent and perceptive person who was usually very stable and strong. He remembered the time Lisa had stuck her hand through the storm door window, cutting her wrist dangerously near the artery. Clara had wrapped it quickly, calmed the girl down, and taken her to the emergency room at the hospital, all within half an hour. Afterward, she was mentally exhausted, but he was proud of her. He wondered if he would have been as cool and as organized if it had happened in front of him.

"You kids should start out for bed," Clara announced when the commercial came on. Both groaned, but neither put up any real resistance. They were tired. "Come on, I'll set out your pajamas, Bobby," Clara said, getting up. Sid watched the three of them go off toward the bathroom and bedrooms. Then he got up and went to the window again. The moon had gone behind some clouds and without it, it was too dark to see anything. Even the silhouettes of trees seemed swallowed by the inky night.

He thought about the ambulance and the police patrol car and went to the telephone. The dispatcher at the police station was a female. She seemed to know all about him, which was something that impressed Sid.

"Officer Clark is making the rounds on your street tonight, Mr. Kaufman. He'll be on his second sweep shortly."

"He's seen nothing?"

"No sir."

"Er, there was an ambulance by here tonight," Sid began.

"Yes sir, for Mr. Strasser."

"Oh, I thought so. How is he?"

"I'm afraid he's dead, sir."

"Dead." It was as though he had been slapped sharply at the back of his head. A mixture of hot and cold traveled down his spine. "How . . ."

"We don't know any details yet, Mr. Kaufman, and the chief is still up at the hospital."

"I see. Thank you," he said, hanging up the receiver slowly. For a split second he considered calling his boss and getting out of tomorrow's job, but he really didn't have any substantial reason for it and he knew how difficult it was to postpone an observation after everyone concerned had been prepared.

He went back to the living room and then to the kids' bedrooms when Clara called to tell him they were ready to be kissed good night. He was thankful that Bobby didn't talk about the dog; his son's mind was on the surprise Sid had promised to bring him when he returned. Lisa nearly brought him to tears with her remarks.

"Don't worry, Daddy," she said. "I'll take care of Bobby and keep him from thinking about King."

"Good girl."

"And Mommy too," she said. He laughed, but thought how perceptive children really were.

"I love you, baby," he said. Clara was waiting in the living room.

"I heard you on the phone," she said before he took his seat beside her.

"You little spy." He smiled, knowing she sensed trouble.

"Who were you talking to?"

"I just checked things out with the police. They're going to make another sweep down this street soon."

"Did you ask about the ambulance?" He hesitated. "You did, didn't you?"

"Uh huh."

"And?"

"It was Ken Strasser." He turned to her. "He's dead."

"Oh no. What happened? Heart?"

"She didn't know any details."

"My God! It's like something terrible has descended onto this street."

"Now Clara, you can't let your imagination run wild. Mr. Strasser was into his eighties and . . ."

"It's not imagination."

"I know," he said quickly.

"I'm tired too," she said abruptly. "I want to go to bed."

"All right." He turned off the television, checked the lock on the front door, and turned off the living room lights. He followed her to the bedroom, darkness falling behind them in the house. Now the only light was the small lamp by the side of their bed. When they were beside each other, she snuggled up to him and embraced him. He put his arm around her shoulders and she pressed the side of her face against his chest. They lay like that for a long moment, both silent.

"He was just down here the other day," she said. "He stopped during his walk and talked to King. King never barked at him. Did you ever notice that?"

"No, but I guess he sensed the old man was no danger. That dog—" He stopped himself. He had started to say that dog was pretty smart. He *was* smart, dammit, and well-trained and well-fed and loved. . . . "Maybe, maybe when I'm in Boston, I'll have a chance to talk to someone who knows more about these things." He expected Clara to chastise him at any moment, to bawl him out for still lingering on it. But she surprised him.

"Good," she said. "I want to know now," she said. "I want to understand."

He kissed her, held her tightly, and then put out the

small night light. Darkness dropped over them like a black shroud.

Downstairs, he awoke from his sleep abruptly. It was as though the same darkness that had fallen around Sid and Clara had come crashing down around him. He raised his head slowly and listened to the silence. Moving his gaze from one end of the ceiling to the next, he slowly inspected the floor above the signs of life. It was as though he could see through walls, but it was only his superior sense of hearing that guided him. He concluded that the people were gone from this side of the house, and he rose up from the carpet. He had been so still that when he finally did lift his body, he looked like some stuffed animal magically come to life. He paused and then moved cautiously to the foot of the stairs.

On the street outside, Leon Clark paused in his patrol car and snapped on the spotlight. He ran the beam along the edges of the woods and down the shoulder of the road to the start of the Kaufmans' front lawn. Then he edged the car forward and directed a beam of light to the side of the house, keeping it low so as not to shine it into an upstairs window. Some light did spill through the basement window.

Inside, he was already on the first step by the time the policeman's light pierced the darkness. He growled instinctively. He did not continue up the stairs after the light was gone. He remembered the previous patrol car and the light that it had shone.

So he retreated from the steps and went back to his comfortable place on the carpet. He spread himself out, listened keenly, and then lowered his head. He was satisfied that for the time being there was no immediate danger. In a few moments he was asleep again.

Upstairs, Sid had difficulty falling asleep. Clara was already deep in slumber. He recognized that for her, sleep was an escape, a panacea. He was jealous of it; he wished he could get the same quick relief. But he couldn't. Instead, he lay there battling against an ominous feeling of danger. It made no sense to him. There was no one battering at their door. All was quiet; all was still. And yet, it was that same quiet and stillness that unnerved him. Was it his imagination or were all the sounds that he had grown used to gone tonight?

He decided it was his imagination and he turned over to press his face into the pillow. When he closed his eyes, he saw King standing defiantly and confidently over Bobby's folded body. He couldn't shake the image from his mind until he suddenly realized what it was he saw in the dog's eyes. There wasn't any fear; there wasn't any hate. There wasn't even any recognition. It was as though the dog were in a trance, as though the dog had been hypnotized.

That's why King was so gentle when the police arrived; he wasn't aware of what he had done!

# 5

HARRY MICHAELS COULDN'T remember a time when he had gone up to the Community General Hospital and not seen the emergency room packed with people. It frightened him. The year-round population in Sullivan County wasn't that big. Someone once told him more people worked within the World Trade Center in New York City than lived in the entire county, yet there was all this sickness, all these accidents, all this confusion and pain. He imagined that working in the emergency room could distort a person's view of the world. It seemed more like a battleground.

He went out to the waiting area, got himself a cup of coffee from the machine, and then went to a pay phone and called Jenny. As he expected, she was quite sarcastic, but he enjoyed it. In fact, he'd made the phone call because he needed to hear her caustic wit.

"Well, maybe I'll wrap everything up and bring it to you. I'm sure we can eat our dinner off a small table in the waiting room. They won't mind."

"You'd just better go on without me, Jenny."

"I suppose you're right. If I didn't like eating alone, I'd be half the size. Johnny called. I told him he should call person-to-person whenever he wants to speak to his father. In the long run, he'd save money."

"What'd he say?"

"Dottie's pregnant."

"Again?"

"You should sound prouder, Harry. It means another grandchild."

"But on his salary . . . four children?"

"That's what happens when the husband is home more than he's away, Harry. We're lucky we had two. I guess I shoulda thanked old Chief Stark for giving you an hour off here and there."

"All right, Jenny. I'll be home as soon as I finish up here."

" 'Night, Harry," she sang. "Everything will be in the fridge as usual."

He had to laugh after he hung up. They broke the mold when she was born, he thought, but he was grateful he had found her. She was really his source of strength. Despite what she threatened, she'd be waiting for him when he arrived at home, and his dinner would be warm. Afterward, she would have him relate all the details and she would reminisce some more about Ken Strasser and his wife. Tomorrow there would be a cake for him to bring up to Charley Strasser's house.

He took another sip of his coffee and looked at his watch. When he turned around, he saw Steve Blocker, the district attorney, and Lieutenant Carlson of the state's I.D. bureau coming down the corridor toward him.

"Evenin', Harry. You know Tom Carlson from I.D., don't you?"

"Yes I do," Harry said. He had met Carlson on at least three other occasions during the last few years, and each time he had come away with the same bad impression. Most of the state people he knew were intelligent and skillful but unassuming. He wasn't left with the feeling that the pro's had come in to take over where the country bumpkins left off. They made him feel important and essential to any investigation. But Tom Carlson was different. He was smug and egotistical. His handshake was quick and perfunctory, as though Harry were the doorman.

Carlson was a slim six-footer who obviously took great pleasure and pride in his physical fitness. He stood erect, shoulders back in a military posture. His sport jacket looked custom-made; the firmness in his shoulders and arms was evident. Harry always liked to relate people to movie stars. Carlson, unfortunately, was good-looking and reminded him of Roger Moore. He imagined that Carlson thought himself to be the state's James Bond.

"You mentioned some hair?"

"Right," Harry said and handed him the packet Doc Hamilton had collected. Carlson turned it over in his hands and nodded as though he had just solved the entire case. "I have a suspicion about that," Harry said, nodding toward the plastic sack.

"Oh?" Carlson's expression was more of a smirk than a smile.

"I think it's the hair of a German shepherd."

"German shepherd?" Steve Blocker said. "You mean as in dog?"

"Right."

Carlson's smirk widened into a full smile.

"You think someone used a German shepherd dog to smother the old man?"

"I don't know the details. I just . . ."

"Harry, what the hell does a German shepherd have to do with a case of asphyxiation?" Blocker said. At thirty-four, Steve Blocker was one of the county's youngest district attorneys. He was six feet four and in Harry's mind, a Burt Reynolds type—handsome, quick-witted, capable but often impish in his dialogue and smile. He had creamed his opponent with one of the biggest majority victories in any district attorney election, more than six thousand votes. There was already a great deal of talk about running him for Congress in two years.

"I don't really know. Maybe after the autopsy . . ."

"Why did you move the body before I could get down there?" Carlson asked him abruptly.

Harry's face reddened. "We have good pictures, a diagram's been—"

"It's not the same thing. It never is."

"I was satisfied," Harry said. He wasn't one to back down from such a confrontation. "I didn't call you guys in. Blocker did."

"I'm sure Harry did everything on the money," Steve said. He had a way with compromise. "How's that coffee, Harry?"

"Liquid shit," he said, his eyes directly on Carlson.

"So what else is new? Come on," he said, nudging Carlson, "I'll buy you a cup." They walked past Harry and into the waiting room. He took another sip of his coffee and threw the rest into the water fountain behind him. After that, he deliberately involved himself in conversations with hospital staff so he could avoid talking to Carlson. Finally, Dr. Hamilton called them into one of the hospital conference rooms to discuss his findings. He also knew Carlson, but if he had any of the same impressions Harry had, he didn't show them. He seemed oblivious to his audience, anyway. Harry thought Doc might as well be talking to a classroom of criminology students.

"My initial diagnosis was correct. The subject died from asphyxiation. Aside from a fair-size hematoma on the diaphragm and contusions on the back, there were no other signs of struggle. I believe the subject was taken by surprise, had the breath knocked out of him, and put up only a small resistance. I found hairs in the fingernails and on the face and some strands on the clothing. The dirt, pebbles, embedded in the anterior of the head indicate strong pressure kept him down and under."

"Under what?" Harry asked quickly.

Hamilton looked at him as though he had just realized Harry was there; he seemed to snap out of a hypnotic state. "That's something Lieutenant Carlson will have to tell us."

"A pillow, a coat?" Blocker suggested.

"Or a dog," Carlson said. He didn't crack a smile, but there was laughter in his eyes.

Harry ignored his sarcasm for the sake of the investigation. "There's something else we'll have to check out," he said. He took out the strands of hair he had found on the hay in the barn and put them on the table in front of them. "I found these in the barn on a bed of hay right by the door. I'm pretty sure they'll match the ones you took off Ken Strasser," he added.

"Why weren't they placed in a proper container?" Carlson demanded.

"There's plenty more in the hay."

"So the killer was lying on the hay with a coat or pillow," Blocker said.

"Maybe," Harry said.

"I'd better head up to Strasser's farm," Carlson said, "before some other evidence gets misplaced."

"Nothing was misplaced," Harry said. His face reddened.

"There's no point in you two not getting along," Blocker said. "The only one to benefit from that is the killer."

Carlson smirked, but he nodded. "Well I gotta get up there," he said.

"I'll show you the way," Harry said.

Blocker caught up with him in the hospital parking lot. "Why do you keep harpin' on this dog thing?"

"There was a bad incident with a German shepherd

recently on that street. It attacked its master and his son. They'd had it for years."

"Rabies?"

"No."

"What happened to the dog?"

"We shot it and had it examined."

"So what the hell are you talking about, Harry, a ghost dog?"

"That's not as funny as it sounds. The guy's kid claims he saw the dog that night and the wife claimed she heard it and saw it in the doghouse today."

"Harry, for Christ's sake—"

"I'm just tellin' you what's been happenin' on that street."

"Do me a favor, willya? Let Carlson run this one."

"You know what, Steve, normally, I'd resent bein' cut out completely, but after tonight, he can have it." Carlson pulled up behind them. "Don't worry, I'll cooperate with him and I won't say anything about any ghost dog."

"I'll speak to you in the morning, Chief. Regards to Jenny."

"Thanks." He looked behind at the impatient I.D. man and then drove off. When he paused at the light by the hospital entrance, he reached into his shirt pocket and took out the few strands of hair he hadn't turned over. He looked at them again, shook his head, and continued on to Ken Strasser's.

Kevin Longfellow and Gerson Fishman stood talking to the security guard at the front gate of the institute when Qwen drove up in his '64 black Ford pickup truck. They heard him coming long before he made the turn toward the entrance. Although the engine sounded fine, the body of the truck was so battered and rusted that it was hard to believe it was still a viable means of transportation. He had somewhat worn snow tires on all four wheels, and a piece of rabbit's tail dangled from the inside rearview mirror. Maggie, his hound, sat beside him in the cab of the truck; she looked as nonchalant and as unperturbed about the bouncy, rough ride as Qwen did.

"This is your Daniel Boone," Gerson said. He laughed and shook his head.

Kevin told the guard to open the gate and let Qwen drive his truck into the parking lot. The brakes squeaked and the truck bed rattled as he did so.

" 'Morning," Kevin called out as he and Gerson walked toward the truck. Qwen stepped out, smiling.

"Glad you could make it," Gerson said and laughed again.

"Don't let her fool ya," Qwen said. He patted the roof of the truck cab. "Solid as a rock." He snapped his fingers and Maggie hopped out to stand beside him. She remained obediently nearby but sniffed the air suspiciously. Qwen noted his dog's natural paranoia. "Maggie doesn't like it here," he said, looking up from the hound and then at the building. "She must know something I don't know."

The security guard laughed quite loudly, but he stopped abruptly when Gerson Fishman turned his way. Kevin smiled and shook his head at Qwen. Fishman, who stood just behind him, folded his arms across his chest and straightened his posture. He scowled like a suspicious Indian. Qwen caught the look but chose to ignore it. Instead, he gazed out at the wooded area to the south of the institute. It was a clear morning, although a little cooler than usual. Some fog had yet to lift from the tops of trees in the distance, and the mountains that loomed ahead looked silvery and wet. For Qwen it was a good morning. The air invigorated him. He felt his heart pumping joyfully, his blood moving richly through his body. Today he wore a flannel shirt over an undershirt, a pair of very worn-looking jeans, white wool socks, and his moccasins. He had his hunting knife and his tobacco, but he had some sticks of beef jerky and a pocketful of dried apricots, too. He enjoyed them as dessert. Before anyone spoke, he reached into the truck cab and took out his twenty-two automatic rifle and a box of shells. He put the shells securely into his back pants pocket and clipped on his canteen.

"What the hell's the gun for?" Gerson asked.

"Dinner, breakfast, maybe another dinner," Qwen said. He looked at Kevin. "You ready?"

"As ready as I'll ever be," he said, smiling. "Oh, this is Gerson Fishman. He's the head of security here and my director thought that he should go along with us."

Qwen looked at him more closely. Gerson had lowered his right hand to his side, catching his thumb in his wide belt. He wore army fatigues and high laced boots. Qwen could see that the bulge in the side of his jacket was made by a pistol. It looked like a forty-five.

There was something in the security man's demeanor that caused Qwen to reject him immediately. He was a big man, probably six feet three and at least two hundred and thirty pounds, but it wasn't only his size that was intimidating. There was a cold, calculated look in his eyes that Qwen usually saw in mad animals.

There was no softness in this man's face; it was as though compassion and pity had been extracted from him as a dentist might extract a tooth. The gaping holes in his personality had been quickly filled with harder, insensitive material, giving him the look of someone driven by cold efficiency, concerned only with achieving a single goal. He looked as though he had been wound up and pointed in one direction and God help anyone who stood in his way.

His uncovered dark brown hair was closely cropped in marine boot camp style. While he looked at Qwen, he narrowed his eyes to make a quick evaluation. Qwen imagined some kind of computer printout forming on the surface of the man's brain. Gerson tightened his lips and nodded.

"What's the pistol for?" Qwen asked.

"I might not like what you make for supper," Gerson said. He laughed only with his eyes.

Qwen shook his head and turned to Kevin. "You bring something for Maggie to smell?"

"I've got a piece of his blanket in here," Kevin said and reached into the backpack he had at his feet. He took out the material and Qwen inspected it.

"Okay," he said. "Put the bag on and let's get started." He knelt down to let Maggie get a whiff of the blanket. At first she backed away from it as though she smelled something very unpleasant. Qwen sniffed too to see if there was something, but he didn't detect anything unusual. Still, the dog didn't like putting her nose right up to it. "Where the hell's this from?"

"The dog's cage."

"Where was the cage?"

"In the institute laboratory."

"What's the problem?" Gerson asked.

"Some other odor from something in there got onto it. I don't know if it's going to do us any good." He took hold of Maggie's collar and forced her to get closer. She whined and struggled to get away, so Qwen released his grip on her and threw the cloth back to Kevin. Just as he turned to start away to begin the search again, their attention was drawn to Ann Bergman, who had come out of the side entrance of the institute and called to them. Kevin was surprised because she was dressed in a jacket, jeans, and sneakers. She, too, wore a backpack.

"What the hell—" Gerson began.

Qwen was amused by his anger. "Looks like this is becoming a regular garden party," he said.

"Ann, what are you doing?"

"I'm coming along," she said.

"You can't do that," Gerson said. He stepped forward as if to block her from joining their group.

"Who says so?" She widened her hazel eyes and tightened her lips. Qwen stepped back, a half-smile on his face. This woman was a little over five feet two and probably weighed just about a hundred pounds, but she showed a genuine sense of authority and firmness about her. Obviously the giant security man didn't intimidate her one bit. Qwen thought the brightness in her eyes was the only thing that suggested anything feminine about her. She had the build of a small teenaged boy. He hated women who cut their hair that short. When she relaxed her lips, the paleness didn't leave them. Her face was bland. She looked like a flower shut away from sunlight.

"Dr. Bronstein didn't assign you to this," Gerson said. His voice quivered a bit with uncertainty.

"So what?" She turned to Kevin. "I have to go along, Kevin. You know that."

"This isn't going to be a little walk in the woods, Ann. We might have to be out for a couple of days."

"I've camped out before. I have what I need," she said. She turned to Qwen.

"I don't care if you go along or not, lady, but like the man here says, it's not a picnic."

"I'm very well aware of that," she said.

"But what about your work?" Kevin asked. He stepped forward so that he could be between Ann and Qwen. Qwen understood that Kevin wanted some privacy, so he went to the truck and leaned against the bashed-in fender.

"You know as well as I do that I need him back in the laboratory before I can go much further."

"Dr. Bronstein said we have to think about working around that."

"Listen to me, Kevin," she said. She drew him farther from Gerson, who glared hatefully at her defiance. She took a deep breath. "I haven't told you everything. I haven't told anyone."

"What are you talking about?"

"There was something I saw happening. I didn't say anything because I didn't want to see any delays or participate in any stupid roundtable discussions about morality."

"Ann, what the hell are you talking about? I've got this guy ready to go. We're already wasting precious daylight . . ."

"I knew that eventually he would escape," she said.

"What?"

"He was making judgments about us, about what we were doing."

"I don't understand."

"Dammit, Kevin. He didn't want us to know how intelligent he had become. He deliberately failed tests. He deliberately made mistakes. Don't you see, that's more than intelligence growth. That's . . . that's foresight. We didn't just expand an animal's perception and ability to make conclusions on a higher level. We've developed something beyond that. We've created a creature with ego. You know he has self-awareness. You know what that means."

Kevin stared at her.

"We should have talked more about this. You were in there doing all those tests, all those other things . . ."

"I know, but I thought it was interesting," she said, looking down, "and I didn't want to fill the others in on everything just yet. You know how it gets to be, everything becomes a committee decision."

"It's supposed to be a group effort, Ann. For Christ's sake—"

"I don't mean to interrupt," Qwen said, "but we could have been a half a mile or so by now."

"Right. One more moment."

"I've got to go along," Ann said when Kevin turned back to her. "Don't you see? I know things about him that you don't, and when you confront him, it might come in handy."

"Okay," he said. "But when we get back, we're going to have one helluva meeting with Dr. Bronstein. And no holding back on anything."

"It's a promise," she said.

"Ann's coming along," he said, turning to Gerson and Qwen.

"Bullshit," Gerson said.

"What the hell's the difference to you?" Kevin asked. Gerson shot a look at Qwen and then at him.

"Dr. Bronstein said—"

"I'll take full responsibility for her going. Don't worry," Kevin said.

"Why don't we ask the dog how he feels about it?" Qwen said and then laughed, but he stopped when all three of them turned toward him and looked at him as though he had just solved some great mystery.

"Let's go," Kevin said, and the four of them started toward the gate. Qwen took a chaw of his tobacco, chewed it vigorously, and then spit a glob high in the air to his left. It wasn't until after the institute disappeared behind the forest that he began to feel this little trip could somehow become life-threatening. He made a mental note not to trust anyone or anything but himself and Maggie's instincts.

Sid was up at dawn. He wanted to be on the road by six-thirty because he had a good five hours of driving ahead of him. Clara heard him in the bathroom and rose to make the coffee and get him some breakfast, even though it would be a quick one. He had done almost all of his packing the day before, so he expected his departure to be smooth and fast.

"I don't think I fell asleep," Clara told him. "I think I passed out."

"You're right. I thought I'd wake you with my tossing and turning."

"Didn't hear a thing," she said.

They spoke to each other softly, almost as softly as they had when he'd courted her on a summer night, the two of them sitting on the porch of her house, her parents just inside, watching television, the sounds of the neighbors subdued, their own conversation broken occasionally by her parents' laughter within. There were strong feelings just under the surface of things, passions and emotions lying dormant, just below the thin membrane of courtesy and restraint. He wanted her in his arms just as much as she wanted to be in them. The truth of their desires was written between sentences, in the lingering glances, and in the closeness of their bodies.

Now, in the early morning hours, there was a similar thin membrane of courtesy and restraint between them, only this time it covered disturbing tensions, aroused by the events of the past few days and Sid's impending business trip. They both searched for small talk to avoid any references to the pain and fear.

"What's this place like?" she asked him. She usually inquired about his projects.

"They make paper containers for things like dairy products, ice cream. That kind of thing. They're growing, but not at the rate they should. They've had some labor problems, but I think they're top-heavy in management. There's a lot of duplication."

"I guess you won't be too popular with the executives."

"Doesn't matter. I'm in and out. If they want to listen, good, it's their nickel. If not . . ." he shrugged and she forced a smile.

"You have everything?"

"Just about. I was looking for that new calculator Morris gave me last time I was in New York."

"Oh, Bobby had that." She thought for a moment. "He was down in the basement with it, last I remember. It's probably right on the bar or the table. I'll look for it."

"No, that's all right. I'll go." He got up quickly. "You've got to get the kids up for school soon." He was hoping they'd be awake before he left.

He went to the basement door, flipped on the lights, and descended the steps.

In the darkness below, he had awakened with the first sounds of Sid's rising. He had listened intelligently to the movements upstairs, recognizing the heaviness that identified the adults. He was naturally more afraid of the man; he was keenly aware of Sid's location above him every moment. It wasn't his intention to go right into battle now. He wanted to wait and look for opportunity. Although he liked where he was and was comfortable here, he wasn't satisfactorily familiar enough with all the surroundings yet.

The early dawn light that flowed through the basement windows gave him a better view of the room and its contents. He explored with a sharp curiosity, looking for familiar things. There was another part to the basement, a room that housed the water pump and hot water heater, as well as the box of circuit breakers. There was no oil burner or gas heater, since the house had electrical heat. The room had no carpeting, nor did it have paneling on the walls. There was a cold cement floor and rough, poured cement foundation walls. Pipes and wires were freely exposed. Because they weren't heating the basement playroom at this time, the door to this utility area was left open. The morning light penetrated a single basement window here, too.

One corner of the room contained the family's older possessions. There were some cartons of clothing, some pieces of furniture, boxes of pictures and books, and a variety of knickknacks, including small lamps and a small desk. He moved around the items slowly, inspecting, sniffing, searching for anything that would have value to him. There was nothing of any particular interest as far as he was concerned, and he would have gone out of the utility room and gone directly for the stairway if he hadn't heard Sid descending.

He went to the doorway and looked out into the playroom, debating whether or not he should attack the man now. He heard the footsteps of the woman above and he wondered whether there would be any more men coming. He had a healthy respect for packs. It was one thing to take down a single man; that was relatively easy, but groups of them presented other dangers. For one thing, he didn't like the possibility of battling them in a confined area. It was still their environment. They knew it best. Successful predators chose the time and place best suited for them.

These conclusions didn't come to him quickly. The alternatives presented themselves in a logical fashion, and he made his choice just the way a well-programmed computer might—moving ahead only when the correct set of variables existed. His decision was to wait.

When Sid made the turn at the bottom of the stairway, he saw the shredded bacon bits box immediately and went right to it. It was curious that the box had been so torn up and left in the middle of the floor. He knelt down and inspected it, noting how cleanly it had been emptied. He smirked and shook his head. He was about to stand up again when he saw the dog hairs just below the box. There were only a few, but he thought they were King's.

"Dammit," he muttered. He stood up and looked about, remembering that he had to find that calculator and get a move on. He went to the table and moved some books and papers around, but the calculator wasn't there. He thought about the bar and the shelves behind it. When he went there, he saw the smashed glass on the floor. "Shit. What the hell went on here?"

His first thought was to yell for Clara. Then he realized that the mood wasn't right for him to raise his voice. It would just frighten her unnecessarily. But he didn't have time to stay down here and clean up the mess. He'd have to tell her about it and leave it for her. He found his calculator at the corner of the bar and turned to go back upstairs. That was when he saw it.

The basement door to the outside was slightly opened.

"For Christ's sake," he muttered and went to it. "Jesus," he said, closing the door. "Talk about making it easy for burglars. You might as well put up an invitation." He slid the latch-lock to the right, securing the door, and then he turned around and considered the rest of the basement playroom. Nothing else looked disturbed and it was already six-thirty. He couldn't tolerate any further delays, so he ascended the stairway and turned off the lights.

Clara was just rousing Bobby and Lisa when he came to her.

"You found it?"

"Yeah, but I found something else too," he said.

"What?" She held Bobby's shirt to her bosom.

"Seems Junior there was down in the basement with King. There's a torn-up box of bacon bits and a glass smashed behind the bar."

"Oh, Bobby." She looked at the little boy, who was just stirring. He sat up and rubbed his eyes in confusion.

"Why didn't you tell me you broke a glass downstairs, honey?"

"I didn't break a glass," he said.

"The dog probably did it," Sid said. "And he covered for him."

"I'll go down and clean it up later, after they're off."

"That's not all," he said. "He left the basement door open. Anyone could have just walked into the house."

"Oh no! You know, I always mean to check that at night before I go to sleep. Bobby, you're getting to be impossible, do you know that?"

The little boy stared up with growing confusion. He was no longer sure himself when he had last been down there. He had gone down there with King, at times, but he couldn't remember doing it recently. At the moment, he had a poor perspective of time, anyway. And his father was talking as if King were still alive. For a moment he wondered if everything hadn't really been a dream.

"I gotta get going," Sid said. He went into the bedroom, put the calculator into his suitcase, shut it, and started out. He paused at Lisa's doorway and gave her another kiss good-bye, kissed Bobby and shook his head gently, and then went to the garage door. Clara followed him to the car and watched him throw the suitcase into the trunk.

"Have a good trip," she said.

"Thanks. I'll call you tonight. You've got the name of the motel and the numbers where I can be reached if you need me for anything."

"Right." She smiled. "Don't worry. I'm going to be all right."

"Sure." He kissed her and got into the car. She

watched him back the car out of the garage and then waved one more time as he turned and headed down Lake Street.

As soon as he was gone, her sense of dread became terribly heavy. She closed the garage door and busied herself with the children to keep herself from crying. But when the school bus came and they got on it, she couldn't hold back the tears. It was irrational; it was weak, but she couldn't help it. She stopped when she remembered the mess in the basement. She was almost grateful for it. She was grateful for anything that would keep her mind off her seemingly inexplicable sense of doom.

# 6

For the first few hours of the morning, they traveled in relative silence. To Qwen there was something monastic about the forest in the early morning hours, anyway. The crack of a branch, the heavy shuffle of feet, a cough, a grunt, even the sound of his own breathing were all amplified tenfold. In the weaker, early morning sun, the shadows of the taller, wider trees loomed around them like cold stone walls. He had a religious respect for the stillness. Ever since he was a little boy, since his grandfather began teaching him lessons of nature and making it seem like a living, intelligent being in and of itself, Qwen imagined the forest housed some great, wild, night creature, a beast unseen by men, feeding off the darkness and retreating into the trees and dark earth with the coming of the morning light. It was an irrational thought, a ghost of childhood past, the product of a young boy's imagination, but a product that lingered in the closets of the adult's mind, peering out whenever an unusual sound was heard or a shadow moved quickly and mysteriously across the surface of his peripheral vision. Like a descendant of some indigenous Indian tribe, he clung to a belief in the spiritual life of the forest.

Qwen kept Maggie close to him until they reached the spot from which he had turned back the day before. She was eager to be turned loose, to follow the commands of instinct and do what she was genetically programmed to do—search and discover. He could see the anxiousness in her walk, the way the muscles in her legs and flank tightened, and the manner in which she kept her head high so she could sift through the breeze and hone in on the scents. But Qwen didn't see any point in having her confirm the zigzag pattern the dog had taken. It was a particularly arduous path, designed, it still seemed to him, to make things more difficult for pursuers.

Qwen was surprised about the direction in which they had to travel. This part of the Catskills was vast and undeveloped. He was puzzled as to why a so-called domesticated dog would head into the wildest areas. In his experience strays and lost animals usually sought out familiar ground: houses where they might beg food, populated areas where they might find scraps. Unless, of course, they became attached to a pack that had been running for some time.

He had heard about packs of strays, lost and discarded dogs, that would make long journeys through the forest, taking down deer and, although he never really came upon it himself, a bear here and there. Some of the old-timers talked about strays attacking men. The strays had been wild so long, they had lost all their domesticity. But this animal was alone and not that long away from civilized conditions.

As they walked on, the rising sun began to warm the air considerably, but they felt the warmth only when they traveled through opened or cleared areas. The forest was so thick, the trees growing so closely to one another, that at times it seemed as though they were traveling through a long green tunnel. In this part of the woods, there was a great deal of white and yellow birch, knotty and twisted softwood trees that were distorted and weakened by their proximity to one another. How clearly was illustrated the law of survival of the fittest. The roots of the thicker, healthier trees invaded the territory of the thinner, smaller ones. There were many trees broken and split by the force of the wind and the weight of the ice and snow in winter. There was so much of it in some sections it looked as if a battle between opposing spirits had been fought, the only casualties evident in the fallen birch.

Occasionally, they moved through long and wide sections of pine, the fallen needles making a natural carpet of green and brown. Qwen loved the pungent scent of fresh pine. He always thought them to be regal and aloof. They remained green in the winter and seemed undaunted by the change in seasons. Sometimes a birch started its growth very close to a pine, but the pine continued its development as though it had turned its back on the audacious intruder. If the pine could speak, Qwen imagined they would tell him that the birch were ignorant, the peasants of the forest.

For a man like Qwen, the forest never ceased to be a wonder and an entertainment. He was never bored with it because to him it was different everywhere. The others walking behind him didn't catch the quick, nervous movement of squirrels, the gazing, curious but cautious rabbits, and the variety of birds that flittered from branch to branch, peering down at them, whistling and singing warnings and announcements to unseen brothers and sisters somewhere in their general direction. He was amused by the animals and he wondered what they thought of this strange entourage moving somewhat boldly through their woods.

As soon as Maggie was released, she shot out about fifty feet or so in front of them and began barking and whining, serving them like a sonar device. To the others her sounds were monotonous, even idiotic. This was especially true for Gerson Fishman. Finally he stepped forward and reached out to seize Qwen's upper right arm.

"How the hell are we gonna find him if that dog keeps barkin' all the while?" he asked when Qwen stopped and turned. "He'll only keep runnin' from us. Shit, he could hear that a mile away." Qwen didn't respond. He continued walking, moving as though nothing had been said. "Hey, I asked you somethin'!"

Qwen stopped again and turned slowly. "Well, I'll tell you, Mr. . . . Fisher, is it?"

"Fishman. Gerson Fishman."

"Fishman. First off, any dog worth his Ken L Ration would hear us comin' a mile off. You've been smackin' the branches and kickin' your feet like you want to be announced. Second, when Maggie there gets within a mile of your pup, she'll let us know and we'll decide our strategy then. Feelin' better about it?"

"Pup? Did you say pup?"

Qwen looked at Kevin and shook his head. Then he started on again, but this time Ann moved up beside him quickly. He looked at her, but neither of them spoke for a while. He decided that she was a great deal tougher than she had first appeared. Most women unused to this kind of difficult travel would have shown some signs of discomfort by now, but she looked as cool as she had when she came out of the institute. In fact, she had a look of determination in her eyes that frightened him a bit. Her pale complexion had reddened and blotched on her cheeks and over her forehead, but her lips were moist and her breathing was still quite regular.

"Where do you suppose he could be heading?" she asked. She didn't stop or look directly at him; she spoke as though she were talking to herself. He actually turned to her first to be sure she was speaking to him.

"Well miss, pretty soon we're gonna know if he's headed for population, although it's a mystery to me why he'd go so far into the undeveloped woods first. I'm expecting him to head southeast eventually."

"And if he doesn't?"

"I'd say he has it in his mind to be a wild thing. Could he have that in his mind, miss?" Qwen asked. He had that gleeful glint in his eyes again, but Ann didn't notice it. She was thinking too deeply about his question.

"He might," she finally replied. "He might not like what he's seen of civilization."

"And just what might that be, miss? What has he seen?"

"The world of science, Mr. Qwen. In all its majestic promise."

"But would he know what he's seen, miss? He's just a dog."

"What's all the gab about?" Gerson said, coming up behind them. "Your dog seems to be gettin' farther and farther away."

"Oh," Qwen said, pretending some surprise. "I hope she's not after jackrabbits."

"What? You mean . . ."

"Relax, Mr. Fishman." Qwen paused and knelt to show them a very clear paw print.

"How do you know that's not a fox?"

"Fox? Look at the size of the print and the distance between each. You can measure the dog's size from this. He's big, about as big as a German shepherd gets," Qwen said, looking up at Kevin. "Maybe even a little bigger than a German shepherd gets. Is that possible, Kevin?"

"He's been given some growth hormones that have had a positive effect on his maturation."

"I'd say about a hundred, a hundred and five would be a good-size dog." Qwen looked at the depth of the impression in the earth. "How much, Kevin?"

"About a hundred and . . ." Gerson spun around, but Kevin shrugged, as if to ask what difference does it make. "A hundred and a half."

"More like a St. Bernard." Qwen stood up. "There's a creek a little ways ahead. Maggie'll be waitin' there. We'll take a breather when we get to it," he said and started on.

Gerson seized Kevin's arm before he could continue. Ann kept moving.

"A bit mouthy about him, arent' ya?"

"What's the difference? If we're successful, he'll see him anyway, won't he?"

"He doesn't have to know about growth hormones and the other things."

"He's been around animals, Gerson. He's gonna know things. He already senses it. Let's quit kidding ourselves about it and just do the job we're out here to do."

"Amen to that," Gerson said and released his grip. Kevin started, but Gerson remained behind a few steps. He looked back as though he expected company, lit a cigarette, and walked after them, glaring from side to side with the suspicious and aggressive eyes of a man in combat. He had been in woods like this before and he was never comfortable about it. He didn't like the shadows and the silence. Birds fell through the trees like heavy stones. He resented their confidence. Mostly, he resented the confidence of the trapper. The man radiated an inner strength that came from an inner peace. It was almost oriental—inscrutible, controlled, and deadly to a man like Gerson. He felt himself shudder like a drug addict who, for one split second, had imagined himself without supply. He shook the uneasiness from his mind and plodded on with heavy steps, moving as though dragged by some unseen chain.

Qwen was constantly aware of the three people beside and behind him. Each of them gave off different vibes. The woman was intense and alert. She moved with definite, strong steps, full of purpose, but even though she was the closest to him now, he sensed her aloofness. It was as if she were transmitting her thoughts on a frequency far above him. She was an alien creature; he imagined that if he were in a room with her, he'd feel alone.

Kevin was the warmest and, it seemed to him, the most reluctant. His steps were uncertain, cautious. When Qwen looked back at him from time to time, Kevin seemed distracted by his own troubled thoughts. He walked with his head down, like a truant schoolboy being escorted back to the classroom. Much of this Qwen attributed to his uneasiness in the forest. Kevin was a city boy who rarely, if ever, went deeply enough into the woods to lose sight of all civilization.

The big man who haunted the rear was also uneasy, but his irritability came from other sources. His steps were ponderous, angry. He was impatient with the pace of the search and the prospects of difficulty. When Qwen gazed back at him, he thought he caught a hateful gaze. Why this man should resent him so, he did not know; but he understood that the so-called security chief felt threatened by him.

Qwen wasn't very comfortable with any of them. Because he had been self-reliant all of his mature life and because he lived in a world in which all the important laws were natural and obvious, he disliked police and military types. He respected the conservation laws and appreciated their need and purpose, but he adhered to a higher code—the law of survival. He spent so much of his time in the forest and among wild creatures that he considered himself a citizen of a different country. If he was out in the forest for days, he wouldn't hesitate to shoot a deer or a rabbit to eat, even though the season for such hunting might not be in effect. And yet he thought himself more moral because he saw those who hunted during the correct season to be invaders. Their kills were wanton; they did it for the sport or the fun of it; his life in nature had taught him that animals take the lives of other animals only for a necessary end, usually, only for food. Only man killed for the trophy.

Fishman, the police type, struck him to be a man who could kill for any reason, or maybe even for no reason. He had seen that, too—hunters who shot animals they didn't want. They were the servants of a callous and impish Death, the Death of no purpose.

Kevin and the woman were academic types. They made him uneasy because he felt as though they spoke another language. No one felt safe in the company of people who could speak in a tongue he did not understand. It brought out the paranoid in him. They were talking about him, laughing about him, manipulating him somehow.

Maggie was waiting at the creek, just as he had expected. She barked and came running to greet them. Qwen laughed and knelt down to pet her as the others gathered about. Then he studied the ground and nodded to himself. Kevin had taken a seat on a big boulder. Ann stood beside him, waiting and watching Qwen search for signs, while Gerson stood right behind him.

It was relatively quiet except for the sound of the water rushing over the stones. In the distance, just over two tall hickory trees, two crows taunted one another. Their caws seemed to be seized by the forest below and tossed back and forth by the large maple and oak, the sounds dying somewhere below the ridge to the left. No one spoke. They were all watching Qwen closely and waiting for his conclusions.

Suddenly he took off his moccasins, stepped into the water, and began to make his way across the creek. Maggie began barking madly and then went in behind him. The water wasn't deep; it came to just below Qwen's knees. The dog swam and used large stones to keep up. Since the creek was only about twelve feet wide, Qwen was across it in seconds. On the other side, he rolled down his pants and put on his moccasins. Then, without saying anything to anyone, he began to move down the bank of the creek. He went about twenty feet, paused and came back to the spot on which he had landed. He went upstream about twenty feet, stopped, scratched his head, and laughed.

"What's so damn funny?" Gerson asked. He came to Kevin's boulder and lit another cigarette.

"You guys are gonna hafta tell me a little more about this dog," Qwen said. He sat himself down on the ground, laid his rifle beside him, and folded his legs under one another in Indian fashion. Maggie sprawled out beside him.

"What the hell . . ." Gerson looked at Kevin. He slipped off the rock and stood up beside Ann. Now the three of them stared across the creek at their trapper guide.

"What is it?" Kevin asked. "Why do you ask such a thing?"

Qwen shook his head. He took out a chunk of tobacco and bit off a piece. The crows flying over the hickory trees spotted them and flew overhead to inspect and report. Qwen watched them bank through the two large maples on the left and disappear.

"Well," Qwen said, "I've tracked a few animals in

my time, animals that lived all their lives in the forest and knew something about flight from other animals. They all do something different to protect themselves. I've known hunters to walk right past a deer because it planted itself so successfully and so quietly in the bush, but anyone who could track worth a shit could come up right behind them and blow them to kingdom come because wild animals, as nature smart as they are, don't know what we're looking for. They don't know what to hide, cover up, understand."

"So?" Gerson said.

"Kevin, yesterday when I showed you what your dog did at that bush, you didn't seem that surprised."

"Well, he's smart," Kevin said.

"Smart?" Qwen laughed. He pointed to the area about ten feet below them. "Look carefully over there. You'll make out the dog's tracks. You'll see where he came to the creek. What I was thinking was he'd go either east or west along the bank of the water, follow it somewhere. Okay, he didn't do that. He went into the water."

"So? What's so smart about that?" Gerson asked.

"What's so smart about it, Mr. Fishman, is he didn't cross the creek."

"He remained within it," Ann said quickly. "So we'd lose his tracks."

"Exactly," Qwen said, "and I ain't never seen . . . no animal . . . think that far ahead."

The three stared at him for a long moment. Qwen stroked Maggie slowly and watched them. They were strange, all right. This whole thing was strange, but he'd be damned if he'd go any farther until he found out why.

"All right," Ann said. "Tell him."

"Are you crazy?" Gerson said. "What if we never find the dog?"

"No one's going to believe him anyway," Kevin

said. The three turned to one another for their conference.

"Bronstein's not going to like this. I'm warning you."

"Don't be illogical," Ann said. "Dr. Bronstein wants the dog back more than anything else. This man can't do the job if he doesn't know the full extent of what he's up against."

"She's right," Kevin said. Gerson's eyes narrowed as he turned and contemplated the trapper across the creek.

"Okay," Gerson said. "Do what has to be done."

"Mr. Qwen," Kevin said. "Why don't we break out some lunch and talk?"

"Well it's a little early for lunch," Qwen said, "but under the circumstances . . ." He got up, took off his mocassins again, rolled up his pants, and came back across the creek.

After leaving the hospital the night before, Harry Michaels had no desire to remain long with Lieutenant Carlson. There wasn't any gratitude or camaraderie in the I.D. man's voice when he spoke. He made Harry feel like an underling assigned to do some insignificant "gofer" work. After Harry pulled up in front of Ken Strasser's house, Carlson, parking behind him, took out his portable spotlight and washed the front of the home in its rays—as though the killer might be found plastered to one of the outside walls. Harry reached into his glove compartment, took out his flashlight, and stepped out of the car.

"He lived here alone?"

"For about ten years. That's when his wife passed away."

"And he was in his eighties?"

"Right."

"I assume you checked the house for burglary," Carlson said. Harry hadn't personally done so, but he knew Patrolman Clark had been inside and that Charley had started looking for his father there.

"His son ransacked the place looking for him first. He didn't mention any kind of robbery."

"But you didn't check it out yourself?" Carlson didn't put his light directly on Harry, but he pointed the beam so it would strike that portion of the road before Harry and the illumination would encompass him.

"I had a patrolman in and out of there."

"In a case like this, involving an elderly person, that is the most likely motive."

"No shit."

Carlson chose to ignore the sarcasm. "Show me where it supposedly happened first," he commanded.

"Supposedly? The coroner pulled pebbles out of his head. He was killed outside, unless of course, he has a sandbox inside." Harry turned on his light and started around the house. Carlson kept his light on and followed closely behind him, moving in silence. "That's the barn," Harry said, hitting it with his beam. "The coroner and I feel he was heading for it when something, someone, came out at him. I don't know what that would do to your most likely motive, but . . ."

"Doesn't do anything to it, Chief. The thief could have just escaped detection in the house and fled to the barn for cover, not knowing that the old man had seen him. The old man went for his rifle. He was probably the self-reliant type. And the rest is police history," Carlson concluded. He had a tendency to speak a little through his nose and hold his head back. Harry hated to admit it, but the I.D. man's theory sounded very logical. He regretted now that he hadn't gone through the house. All alone out here and a man of his age, Ken

Strasser would have been a prime target for some burglar.

"Has there been an upswing in burglaries in your jurisdiction, Chief?" Carlson asked. Harry didn't have to think long. Statistics showed they already had doubled last year's.

"Yes."

"Any on this road lately?"

"On this road? No, not for nearly five years," he added. He recalled the burglarization of the Levins' home because it had been an incredible job. The story had even made the New York City papers. The thieves, after having well scouted Phil Levin's family, pulled up in a moving van while the Levins were away for a weekend. They had practically emptied the house. Witnesses saw the truck, but no one called the police station. Who would suspect such a blatant theft performed in broad daylight? Some of the men even waved to passersby. They did nothing to hide the name on the truck—CARE FREE MOVERS. Harry suspected a little irony and humor deliberately placed there. Afterward, there was no sign of such a truck and the conclusion was that the wording had been painted over quickly or somehow quickly removed. Most people minded their own business and simply assumed the Levins had bought new furniture and sold the old.

Carlson studied the diagram and measured out the distance to the barn. Inside, he inspected the hay bed that Harry had described. He said nothing while he did all this and Harry debated whether or not to simply leave. What kept him was the thought that he hadn't personally inspected the inside of the house and he had better help do so.

"I see what you mean about a dog," Carlson said suddenly. "There are prints all over the place here."

"What do you make of it?" Harry asked quickly. He hadn't meant to; it went against his grain to show this man he respected his opinion or his intelligence, but his own driving curiosity was too strong.

"There was a case we had back in the early seventies," Carlson began. He set his spotlight down at his feet and took out a cigarette. "Fascinating, I thought. Most people, especially today, are buying and training guard dogs, German shepherds, police dogs, to help protect them. It's becoming a booming business. Anyway, this guy, a good trainer himself, used a dog to help rob people."

"Rob people?"

"Yeah," Carlson said. He blew his smoke into the darkness. "He'd confront people with his dog and the dog would growl and show its teeth and he would say, 'Empty your pockets,' whatever. Better than a gun. I mean, is that armed robbery?"

"Hard to make an escape though, wasn't it?"

"Not really. He drove around in a station wagon and the dog would stay down between the seats."

"But he got caught, didn't he?"

"Oh yeah, by a police dog too," Carlson said and laughed. "One night he chose to rob this little diner just outside of Jamestown, New York. He picked a time when the place was empty, just before closing. What he didn't know was the owner had his own dog and the two got into a real battle. The diner dog tore his dog up pretty badly and while that was going on, the owner had time to get to his pistol."

"If you had a story like that on the records, why did you laugh when I mentioned a dog?"

"Well, I didn't know about the paw prints and it's one thing to have a dog growl and threaten people and another to train one to smother a man to death, wouldn't you say? A dog would bite, if he's a killer, trained to go for the throat, but once the coroner confirmed asphyxiation as the cause of death . . ."

"Well, what do you make of it now?"

"I don't know. I don't see any evidence of a human being around that bed of hair . . . no cigarette butts or anything. Of course, it's dark and even with the light, it's hard to search. I'll come back first thing in the morning and scout this whole area. I'll bring in some of my people and we'll have forensics work out this animal hair. Can we get into the house?"

"Yeah," Harry said. Despite himself, he felt he was getting so he could tolerate Carlson enough to work with him. They walked up to the back door and entered the old farmhouse.

"Big place for one old man," Carlson said. "Did he have a housekeeper or something?"

"I don't know. I don't think so, but I'll check with his son. I've got to call him now. I promised I would."

"Do you have any reason to suspect him?" Carlson asked. Harry thought for a moment. Again, here was something he hadn't even considered. It wasn't good police work. Maybe this was a job only for men like Carlson.

"I don't, no."

"Inheritance. Is the son in any kind of serious debt?"

"I can't say for sure, but I haven't heard anything."

"We've got to consider it," Carlson said.

"Yeah," Harry said, the realization settling in. He watched Carlson inspect the kitchen. "It's all right for me to call him though, isn't it?" In a matter of moments, Carlson had made Harry feel insecure. Maybe we are the country bumpkins, he thought. After all, they are the experts. Their days aren't filled with the same kind of trivia. You don't have to like the specialist that the GP calls in, but you damn well need him when things get serious. It was a matter of the experiences. Harry could count on his fingers all the homicides that had occurred in the township since he had become a police chief, but for a man like Carlson, homicide was his daily work.

"What are you supposed to tell him?"

"The cause of death, that it was a definite homicide."

"All right. Ask him if there was some kind of housekeeper and ask him how thoroughly he went through this house first. See if there are any valuables we should look for to find out if they're still here. I assume you asked him about a dog."

"Yeah. The old man didn't have one, but there have been some problems with dogs on this street. I'll tell you about them."

"Good," Carlson said. "While you're calling him, I'll start looking through the house." He went on to the living room.

When Harry was finished with Charley, he joined Carlson in the hall at the foot of the stairway.

"No housekeeper. The old man was just very particular about how the place was kept. Charley hadn't really checked the place, but he says his mother's jewelry is still up in the bedroom and his father kept some savings bonds in a dresser drawer."

"All right. Let's check that," Carlson said. He stopped before taking the first step and went to the small table by the phone. Ethel's picture turned to the wall caught his attention. "Funny, isn't it? Why would someone do that?"

"Cleaning maybe, and forgot to turn it back."

"Maybe."

"Jesus, you are a stickler for details," Harry said, half admiringly.

"It's in the smallest, seemingly insignificant acts that people leave their signatures," Carlson said.

Harry nodded and then followed him up the stairs. Everything was there.

They didn't part on what he would call friendly terms, but the case itself had caused a natural truce to form between them. Carlson's gesture came when he said he would contact Harry in the morning and keep him abreast of events. He didn't laugh or smirk when Harry told him about the near tragic incident the Kaufmans had had with their dog and the strange things the family had seen and heard afterward. At the moment he couldn't see how it related, but he promised to speak to the Kaufmans. Harry said he would start investigating Charley Strasser's finances immediately. They shook hands and parted.

Harry checked in at the station first and was grateful that everything was quieter than usual. It wasn't until he was halfway home that he realized he hadn't eaten a thing since twelve o'clock. As he expected, Jenny was waiting for him in the kitchen, preparing his late supper. As soon as she saw his face, her expression softened.

"I earned my money tonight," he said. He sat down and as she served him, he told her about the autopsy, about Carlson, and about their investigation. He didn't mention Carlson's suspicion of Charley Strasser, but he told her about the dog hairs.

"Eerie," she said. She sat across from him, watching him eat.

"Well, Carlson has a theory based on a case that occurred before, but . . ."

"But you don't think it's the same thing?"

"No, and neither does he, as far as I can tell."

"You'd better call the boys," she told him after she served him his coffee. "Larry called an hour ago because Johnny called him. They're both worried about you."

"A conspiracy," he said. "I smell it."

"Conspiracy?"

"Don't tell me my retirement didn't come up in your conversations, Jenny Michaels."

"Why Harry, do you think I would stoop so low as to use our children as a way of influencing you?"

"Yes." They stared at each other a moment, neither changing expression.

"Well, it's only natural," she said, and he laughed. Later, he did talk to his sons. He told them something about the case, and during the conversation with both of them, he promised he was going to seriously consider his future. It was enough to quiet everyone down for the evening.

He was up at the start of dawn, actually a few minutes before the first rays of sunlight broke the wall of darkness. It had been a restless sleep, and although Jenny didn't say anything, she was just as disturbed. She watched him slip silently from the bed and begin to dress. For a few moments she debated whether or not to pretend to be asleep and then decided that it was no sense kidding anyone, least of all herself.

"What do you expect to find this early in the morning, Harry? Even thieves and killers sleep."

"No sense in me just lyin' here. My eyes won't close and my mind don't stop."

"Wonderful." She started to get up.

"You just sleep. I'll make some coffee. That's about all I'm havin' now anyway. I'll eat later at Willy's luncheonette."

"So everyone can say I don't get up to give you breakfast?"

"Now you know no one would say that."

"I'll make the coffee," she said. "You go shave. At least you could look like you live a normal life," she added. He shook his head and did as she suggested.

He was downtown early enough to see Sid Kaufman come out of Lake Street and head for the New York State Thruway. Kaufman must have been in deep thought, he figured, because although they clearly faced each other and Harry waved, the efficiency expert drove by looking like a man hypnotized by his own thoughts.

# 7

WHEN HE SAW the man bolt the basement door shut, his first reaction was to charge out to attack. He saw him discover the torn box and the broken glass and he assumed the man had come to the realization that he was here. It looked as though the man had decided to trap him. He hesitated and in that hesitation, he saw a second possible conclusion. Although his ego had been swelling like an infected area of skin, he was still governed by logic. From the early days, days when he had been drilled in the most elemental behavioral tasks, he relied on the distinct steps of observation, action, reaction, and conclusion. The Pavlovian games the man and the woman had made him play gave him an understanding of relationships and rewards; and when they changed the stimulus and stung him with electricity, it didn't take him a second or third try to change his awareness of what was pleasant and what was not. He respected logic; he relied on it. It was one of his chief weapons.

The man didn't come in his direction; he did nothing to threaten him. He simply shook his head and went back upstairs. After the man was gone and it was completely still in the basement playroom, he came out and boldly went to the door to inspect what had been done. The latch wasn't unlike some of the metal devices he had used during the tests. He felt confident that when the time came for him to leave, he could leave. He turned and studied the surroundings again. He was hungry and thirsty. He went back to where the pipes under the sink leaked, but he was impatient with the tiny amount of liquid available to him. He didn't know what was in the bottles on the shelves under the bar, but he knew from his experiences in the lab that bottles often contained liquids that were tasty, if not refreshing. He often watched the man and the woman pour some of these liquids together into a bowl and serve him the bowl.

Without concern for the voices and footsteps he now heard above him, he went forward and seized a bottle at its nape. He brought his head back and then forward hard and fast, releasing the bottle from his teeth at the same time. It hit the tiled floor and the glass broke. Its contents rushed about. Careful to avoid the pieces of glass, he lapped at it. At first the taste was bitter and unpleasant to him, but his thirst was great and he ignored that. When he swallowed the liquid, he lit a fire down his throat and dropped the fire into his stomach, but surprisingly, he didn't mind it. In a strange way, he enjoyed it. It made him curious and he licked at what remained. For a few moments he just stood there contemplating how it made him feel. Then he remembered his hunger.

Under the bottom shelf behind the bar was a small carton filled with bags of potato chips, pretzels, and a mixture of nuts and raisins. He had been fed from bags, so it was logical to him that what was in these bags could be eaten as well. He dipped into the carton and chumped through the cellophane packages, spilling the contents on the floor about him. He tasted everything. The salty potato chips and pretzels brought back his thirst even more fiercely than it had been before and he went for another bottle, smashing it the same way, licking up its contents carefully.

This feast was one of the most interesting dinners he had eaten. He didn't like all the flavors, but most of the foods seemed to satisfy him, although when he sat back, he couldn't help imagining the opened side of a rabbit or the deep red flesh of a deer. Freshly killed forest animals filled him with a strength and energy that brought all of his senses to an ecstatic height. He loved the feel of the blood on his jaws and the way the meat softened in his bite. There was no challenge in this food, but the liquid . . . the liquid was different. It was like drinking fire, and fire was something he had always feared.

They had taught him about fire early on. As a puppy he had once been curious enough about a flame to go up to it to sniff it. Suddenly it seemed to turn his way, reach out for him. It barely touched his nose, but it sent him howling into a corner. The pain was so great and lingered so long, he never forgot it. Just the sight of fire froze him in fear.

But this, this was different. He felt as though he had conquered it. It made him proud; it made him boastful. He was about to howl his exaltation when he reminded himself of where he was. By now the footsteps above had grown louder and the number of them had increased. He went around to the front of the bar, sprawled out on the carpet again, and pressed his snoot in and under his extended front legs as though he had to keep himself from making any sounds. Indeed, he did snort and hiccup. He gnawed at some of the carpet and then, for absolutely no reason he could think of, he rolled over. He liked the feeling, so he did it again, this time the opposite way. Once again it was good. He repeated it until he grew dizzy and tired.

He felt the acid building in his stomach. It rose up his throat so quickly he had no time to swallow it back.

Before he knew it, it was in his mouth and he opened quickly to release it in a small puddle on the rug. He stood up and backed away from the sour scent, but the acid built again and rose again and another puddle was created. He did it twice more at different spots on the carpet and then retreated to a corner under the stairway, where he spread out and lowered his head. He closed his eyes to keep the room from spinning and kept himself as still as he could. It felt better not to move, and his stomach started to settle.

He slept in short spurts, each one bringing with it a montage of terrible images. He felt and saw the prongs being pressed into him. He saw himself completely ensnared, tied down, his legs against his stomach. He could barely move his head. He saw the flashes of light and envisioned himself moving down the narrow corridors, some of which had led to painful experiences. The first time they put him down a maze shaped like a Y, he mastered the two distinct choices so quickly they had to create a maze shaped like a pitchfork to give him more of a challenge. The additional choices didn't confuse him, so they tried deliberately to deceive him by plugging the wire into the steak meat. He didn't understand the meaning. It filled him with anger. He heard them laugh at his barking and he retreated. The next time, however, he looked for the wire and they took him out of the maze.

Faces and sounds flashed before him. Each time an image woke him, he lifted his head and looked about fearfully, and each time it took him a few moments to remember where he was. His head felt heavy, so he lowered it and tried for sleep again. Finally, he had a peaceful ten minutes. That restored him and when he awoke after it, he didn't seek any more sleep. He stood up, shook his body and urinated, directing his stream against the electric heat panel. Relieved, he thought about the people upstairs.

The sounds had grown softer, fewer. He sensed an emptying. He heard the school bus when it stopped in front of the house and he listened keenly to the thin, excited voices of the children. After it was gone, he waited patiently. He was about to conclude that there were no more footsteps when he heard Clara Kaufman approaching the basement door. The click of the door-knob sent him into a very slow kneel. His eyes widened; his ears perked. He sniffed the air and caught her scent and then he heard her first footsteps on the stairway. It was too late to hide.

Clara paused when she had descended only a little more than a third of the stairway. The way the stairs had been built, anyone coming down them wouldn't become fully visible until he or she was nearly halfway down. Clara saw only a portion of the basement playroom, but it wasn't what she saw that made her hesitate. She knew her house as well as she knew her own body. As soon as she fully inhaled the air, she stopped. This wasn't the way her basement always smelled. It had the odor of one of those cheap bar and grills downtown. What the hell did that boy and his dog do down here? she wondered, continuing her descent.

She stopped again when she saw the bags of pretzels, potato chips, and mixed nuts and raisins strewn about, the putrid puddles on the carpet. Sid had only mentioned a torn box of bacon bits and a broken glass. Why would he neglect to mention all this? She nodded and smiled.

"Just like him to try to diminish the impact," she muttered. She had to love him for it. He wanted to get on the road before she started ranting and raving about the mess. He knew how she could be when it came to cleanliness and order in the house. "You coward, Sid Kaufman," she added. She turned, deciding she'd better go back up and get a pail of hot water and some sponges.

Then it occurred to her. Bobby and the dog couldn't have done this recently enough for the puddles to still be wet. The carpet would have absorbed it. Sid didn't tell her about this because it wasn't here when he came down! The realization sent a terrific chill up the back of her legs and into her spine. She felt her legs weaken. That odor . . . that odor was definitely the odor of spilled whiskey. Something had happened behind that bar.

She was caught in a dilemma: she wanted to rush back up the stairs and slam the door shut behind her. Some siren of instinct had begun to send warnings into her consciousness, even though she had yet to confront anything threatening. On the other hand, her curiosity as to what had caused this mess and this horrible stink pulled her toward the bar and deeper into the basement. Her possessiveness that characterized her feelings about the house filled her with indignation. Anger rose to confront fear. She looked back once at the still opened basement door, turned toward the basement again, and continued down the stairs. When she reached the bottom, she turned.

Once again he sprang out of silence. He had to learn the value of that only once for it to stay with him forever. That was part of the beauty of what he had become. He had been slinking against the wall, moving toward the stairway in tiny, quiet steps, muted further by the softness of the carpet. When he leaped through the air at her, he pushed himself up and out with such a well-coordinated movement it was as if he were made of a single, powerful muscle. His legs and thighs, his sides and back all joined with the power in his neck to make him into a new breed of giant bird.

He had his head lowered so that the center of his skull would strike her like a giant fist. The point of impact was well-plotted; he hit her on the left side at the center of the ribcage. The blow sent her flying backward. She hit the wall with her right shoulder, and her neck, still loose and relaxed as it was before the instant of attack, didn't tighten fast enough to prevent her head from snapping to the right and striking the wall as well.

She went unconscious immediately and slumped to the floor, falling first into a sitting position, her arms limply at her sides. Then she toppled over to her right. A small trickle of blood emerged from the right corner of her mouth where her teeth had come down hard into her lower lip. She hadn't even had time to release a cry. The whole affair, except for the clunk of her body and her head against the wall, was done as if it were a scene in a silent movie.

He waited a moment, watching her closely and looking for any signs of life. When she didn't stir after a few seconds, he stepped up to her body and sniffed around her face, putting his nose right up to hers. He licked the trickle of blood and then sat back, contemplating his achievement. This, too, had been so easy. She wasn't any smaller than the woman in the laboratory, but at times, he had had such fear of that woman. The memory of her stirred the anger in him and he transferred that rage to this woman before him. He snarled, hoping she would move, hoping she would do something to challenge him.

When she did nothing, his fury subsided. He went to the foot of the stairs and looked up at the opened basement door that led to the interior of the house. Then he looked back at the unconscious woman. He didn't feel safe with her behind him in the open. He wished there were a cage to put her in, like the cages that trapped the animals in the laboratory. He thought about the other room, the darker, colder room of cement floors and walls, and he made a quick, logical decision, just the way he had been taught to do it—lining up the possibilities, weighing the positive and negative of each, and concluding. Once the conclusion was made, there was to be no hesitation.

He went directly to her right arm. It had fallen with her palm facing upward. He took the small, limp wrist into his mouth and clamped down firmly on the bone. His sharp teeth pierced the skin and the taste of blood filled his mouth. Then he backed toward the doorway to the other room, dragging her along with relative ease. Her head bobbed on the carpet and her legs straightened out, one shoe coming off and then the other. In a few moments he was into the room of darkness. She seemed to move more easily over the cement floor. He paused, looked to both sides, her wrist still in his mouth, her arms moving along with his head and neck like the appendage of a puppet with broken strings.

He decided to put her in the corner behind the water heater. Once he got her there, he released her wrist and her arm fell to the floor, the wrist slapping the concrete. He studied her for a moment. There was no scent of death, but her stillness made him think that she wasn't far from it. He nudged her once with his snoot just to be certain and then stepped over her body and went to the doorway. There, he looked back into the darkness. Confident she was no longer any possible threat to him, he sat up, took the door handle into his mouth, and pulled the door closed.

He waited a moment and listened keenly for any sounds in the house. There were none. He approached the stairs and began his ascent toward the door. When he reached the top and stepped out into the house, he turned sharply and pressed himself against the basement door. It slammed shut. Then he looked about slowly. Although the human scent was strong, there was no movement, no sign of any other. He went forward into the house, confident that the entire domain was his to do with as he liked. There was food here and comfort and things to explore.

They hadn't come out as he had hoped they would, but he had done something better—he had come in. Of course, he understood that others would come in, too. They would return. But that thought didn't frighten him. Instead, it stimulated the pleasure of the predator. He had only to wait.

Sid Kaufman wasn't comforted by his car radio. He put thousands of miles beyond those of the average driver on the car during the course of a year and he had become quite dependent on the radio for company. There were times when he wanted to pick up hitchhikers, but he always hesitated to do it. Clara, worried about some of the things that could happen to him on the highways, had made him promise not to give strangers lifts. Sometimes he felt terribly about passing up what was obviously a college kid trying to get home or back to school, but he couldn't help it. So the radio was all important—the music, the talk shows, the news. Actually, he concluded, the radio could keep a citizen very informed if he used it well. There were times he wished he had a car phone so he could call in and give his opinions, too. Frustrated, he often carried on whole conversations with an imaginary passenger. As far as that part went, today was no different.

"I shouldn't have left them," he muttered. He turned to his imaginary passenger. "The horrible incident with King was still too fresh. I should have called Carl Pearson in New York and told him I couldn't go. Why didn't I do it?"

He didn't have any satisfactory answers for himself. The sky ahead of him was gray and overcast; he knew soon he would be riding into rain. The dreary propsect fit his mood. Usually, when he was on a highway like the New York State Thruway, he put on the cruise control, setting the speed at just over the speed limit; but this morning, in deep thought, he forgot about that and paid no attention to just how fast he was traveling. That is, until he went through the radar trap. He looked down at his speedometer and cursed. He was going seventy-five miles an hour. Sure enough, the state policeman parked ahead was in the road waving him to the side.

He had no defense and told him so.

"My mind wasn't on my driving. Sorry," he said. The policeman was silent. He looked at Sid's license and registration and then went back to his vehicle to write the ticket. When he returned, he had his comment.

"When people don't have their minds on their driving, they get into accidents and hurt themselves and others, Mr. Kaufman." He handed him the ticket.

"Yeah," Sid said, his face reddening, "but if you went through what I've been through these past couple of days, you wouldn't have your mind on your driving either."

The policeman ignored the comment. He politely explained that Sid could pay for his ticket or contest it. The state patrolman's even, matter-of-fact tone of voice annoyed him. It was as though he were giving Sid directions about finding some address.

"Well thank you," Sid said, "you've been very kind and considerate."

The patrolman's eyes narrowed, but he didn't respond. He waved Sid on and went back to his position. To catch another forgetful idiot, Sid thought. Actually, the incident had a good effect—it took his mind off his guilt for a while. He reminisced about other tickets he had gotten and about the ones he'd escaped. He recalled the time he and Clara and Lisa (Bobby wasn't born yet) had driven to Florida. They were pulled over early in the evening in North Carolina and Clara put on a beautiful performance, explaining that Lisa had to go to the bathroom and they were closing in on their motel for the night. The cop must have seen or heard something that struck home, for he let them go with only a warning.

Clara was really a very resourceful person, Sid thought; thinking this helped to relieve his guilt too, for he truly believed that she could take care of things while he was away. He looked at his dashboard clock and envisioned what she was doing. The kids were off to school; she would go down to the basement and clean up the mess and then . . . that mess; there was something about the whole thing that bothered him. It was like a tickle at the base of his spine. He couldn't quite reach it, but it wasn't all that annoying. It was just there. But what? What?

He was a great deal more careful about his driving on the Massachusetts Turnpike, and he was glad that he was. It seemed to him that there were many more highway patrolman out than usual. Must be quota day or something, he thought. In any case, he pulled into Boston on time and reached his destination according to schedule. Once he set his eyes on the project, he was able to put everything else aside. He had that ability to concentrate, to direct his attention solely on the problems at hand. It was what made him successful in his job—the ability to avoid any distractions.

The company was called Star Products. He went right to the president's office and introduced himself to the secretary. Almost immediately he sensed a familiar fear and distrust in her face. He expected that she, being secretary to the president and owner of the company, knew Sid's purpose and had warned some of the management staff. She also knew that he might very well make some recommendations concerning her own job. But Sid was used to this. In fact, to be honest about it, he had to admit he even enjoyed it to a certain extent. He enjoyed the feeling of power that came from being able to instill such fear in some people, especially those who made a great deal more money than he did.

George Friedman, the president and owner of the company, came out to greet him. He was a short, stocky man with a round face dominated by soft, rubbery lips. He had heavy cheeks and small, dull brown eyes. Sid placed him in his fifties, but imagined the man's balding, thin brown hair might have begun shedding as early as his late twenties. He was dressed in an opened white shirt with the sleeves rolled sloppily to the elbows. Sid noticed that his shoes were scuffed and his pants were somewhat wrinkled.

Sid always believed one could tell a great deal about a man's productivity and success in his work from his appearance. Disheveled-looking people were rarely organized and efficient. Their lackadaisical attitude about themselves often transferred itself to their work. Conversely, people who had pride in themselves, in their appearance, usually took pride in what they accomplished. What they did had their personal stamp on it.

Friedman shook Sid's hand and led him into his office. The inside confirmed Sid's initial impression. Friedman's desk was disorganized. There were even papers piled on chairs. The room looked dirty as well as messy, a stale coffee cup remained on the windowsill, and a paper bag stuffed with remnants of that morning's take-out breakfast remained on a small table in the right corner. Sid's first question, unvoiced, was, "Do you have your managerial meetings in this room?"

He didn't offer his criticism at that moment. His technique was to hold everything in abeyance until the report was completed. That way he held everyone's attention until he was finished with his work. He didn't know yet if George Friedman was a man who could take criticism. He seemed friendly enough, a man with a jovial personality. If anything, Sid thought, he was too easygoing.

"Right on time, right on time," George said. He slapped his hands together, indicated an empty chair, and went behind his desk.

"Time is money, Mr. Friedman."

"Oh, call me George. Everybody does. Yes, you're right, time is money. So, where do we begin?"

"Well, I've gone over your layout. What I'd like to do first is inspect your plant and then walk through the procedures. I suppose everyone knows I'm here."

"Oh, sure, sure. No secrets in this place."

"Well then, I'll get right to it," Sid said. He reached into his briefcase and took out a folder and a long yellow notebook with lined paper.

"Cup of coffee first? Some lunch?"

"Not just yet. Oh," he said, looking back at his notes, "this coffee break you give your employees in the morning . . . they all take it at the same time?"

"Pretty much. Started with ten minutes, but it crept into twenty. I've spoken to the union reps about that," he said, putting on his tough face.

"Any improvement?"

"Not to my satisfaction, not yet. Maybe after we receive your report . . ."

"Don't look upon my report as a panacea, George. Usually ideas have to be implemented. Attitudes have to be changed, some things done the same way for years might have to change. It's going to take time and leadership."

"I understand. You guys have a good reputation. You come highly recommended."

"That's nice to hear. Thank you. Well, then . . ." Sid stood up.

"I'll go along with you for a while," Friedman said. "Introduce you to some people."

"Fine."

"Staying over at the Holiday, are you?"

"Yes. It seemed convenient," Sid said and pasued near the doorway. Looking over at some of George Friedman's knickknacks on a wall shelf, he saw the pewter replica of a collie. Just the sight of another dog, even a fake one, triggered all sorts of quick associations. He saw King standing over Bobby and threatening him. He closed and opened his eyes, moving out the office door to flee from the memory.

George Friedman followed quickly behind him. He tugged on the handle of his office door to shut it, but his effort was halfhearted and the door did not close all the way. While George paused to say something to his secretary, Sid stared at the partly opened office door for a moment, and the image of his partly opened basement door returned.

What was it that bothered him about that? Whatever it was, that was the tickle at the base of his spine, that was what bothered him about the mess. He began to recall what he had done yesterday after Clara had told him about her seeing the German shepherd. He had gone around the house looking for signs of another dog, and he was sure, absolutely positive now that he thought hard about it, that the basement door had been closed.

Bobby and Lisa hadn't been down there with King yesterday; King was already gone. And Clara certainly hadn't been down there. Why was the door opened? Who had opened it?

"Mr. Kaufman? Mr. Kaufman?" George Friedman repeated. He and his secretary both had puzzled looks on their faces.

"What?"

"Hope this place didn't put you into a daze already," George said. "That's what happens to most of the people who work here." He laughed at his own joke.

"Oh, sorry," Sid said.

"It's all right," George said and started out. Sid nodded to the secretary and then made a mental note to call Clara the moment he had an opportunity.

"Well hello," Harry Michaels said. Lieutenant Carlson was on the other end and Harry was a little surprised, even a little flattered that the I.D. man had decided to call him so soon.

"I thought you'd like to know," Carlson began, "that I followed up on your hunch about that hair we found on the old man and in the barn."

"Oh?"

"You were right. It was German shepherd. Forensics confirmed it for me early this morning."

"What do you make of that?"

"Don't know yet. I went to see the Kaufmans, the ones you told me had trouble with a dog."

"Yes?"

"There was no one home. I'll go back later."

"Yeah, I saw Mr. Kaufman leaving town this morning. His job takes him away often. They have school-age kids. I guess his wife's out shopping or something. I know she doesn't work anywhere. Outside the home, that is," he added, remembering Jenny. She'd hang him by his short hairs if she ever caught him belittling what a woman did in the home. "Do you think this might be something similar to that case you described?"

"To tell you the truth, Harry," Carlson said, "right now I'm kinda puzzled. According to the old man's son, there's nothing of any value missing from that house. I don't have anything to indicate there was a man with the dog, although we're not finished combing the place, and according to what you, the son, and other people have told me about the old man, he didn't have any fierce enemies. All I've got, if you'll pardon the expression, is a 'hairy' cause of death."

The chief almost laughed. Difficulty made this guy Carlson almost human, he thought.

"Let me know if I can do anything more," Harry said gently.

"Thanks. I'll talk to you later."

After Carlson hung up, Harry put his unlit cigar in his mouth again and worked it around. He thought about his weird conversation with Sid Kaufman when the man had come down to tell him what his wife had seen. Maybe the conversation wasn't as weird as he had thought.

An idea came to him. He imagined Carlson would think of it sooner or later, but just in case, he thought it wouldn't be a bad idea to get a start on it. He buzzed the town clerk's office and asked Charley Cauthers to look up his dog license records and give him a list of anyone who owned a German shepherd.

"Not everyone who has a German shepherd got a license, you know," Charley remarked. He started in about the lousy job the dogcatcher was doing and why the police department should become more involved in the problem. Before he was finished, Harry questioned the wisdom of asking him for anything.

"Whatever you have might be of some help," Harry finally said and hung up. He thought for a moment and then got up and went out to the dispatcher. "Who's in South Fallsburg today?" he asked.

Benny Berstein looked up. He was a semiretired policeman who was actually two years older than Harry but who had become a policeman much later in life. Now he performed an eight-hour shift at the desk three times a week.

"Lenny Sidewater," he said.

"Raise him for me." After the contact was made, Harry took the microphone. "Park your carcass on Lake Street," he said, "close to the Kaufmans and stay there for a couple of hours.

"Chief? You said stay?"

"That's correct."

"What for?"

"I want you to." He looked down at Benny, who was looking up at him curiously. "I want you to keep your eyes open for a German shepherd dog," he said. "If you spot one, call in right away."

"Dog?"

"You heard me," he said and handed the microphone back to Benny.

"I guess the town clerk's got to you, huh Chief?"

"What's that?"

"About the dog problem."

"Yeah," he said and shook his head. "Dog problem. Dog problem," he repeated and went back into his office.

# 8

"TO BEGIN WITH," Kevin Longfellow said, "I wasn't truthful about our purpose here."

"I gathered that much myself," Qwen said. There was a twinkle in his eye. He, Kevin, and Ann sat in something of a circle on a clearing by the stream. Gerson remained apart from them, leaning against the big rock, looking at them sullenly. The water that rippled around the small rocks and against the banks of the stream maintained a soft murmur that created a dreamlike sound track. Qwen chewed on a piece of beef jerky, but neither Kevin nor Ann ate anything. Gerson took a gulp of water from his canteen and wiped his mouth with the back of his hand.

"In a way you're forcing us to be unfair to you," Kevin continued. Qwen saw that he was being very careful about his words, thinking it all out before speaking. He was impressed with that and for a moment he wondered if he should let the young scientist go on with it. "What we are about to tell you is top secret information. I'm not trying to be overly dramatic or anything," he added quickly, seeing the smile widen on Qwen's face. "You, yourself, will have to come under a security clearance when we get back and you will have to keep everything we say and everything we do to yourself. You could even be arrested for not doing so."

Gerson grunted and they all turned to him. He looked out over the stream.

"Do you insist that I continue?" Kevin asked.

Qwen thought a moment. "The thing is," he said, "do you insist *I* continue?"

"Stop playing games," Ann said. "Tell him and get it over with. You know we need him. Probably more than ever now," she added.

"All right," Kevin said. He straightened up. "I'm going to explain this in the simplest way I can. Not that I think you're stupid," he added quickly. "It's just that it's complicated."

"My father used to say that anything that's honest and good could be told to a nine-year-old," Qwen said. Ann smiled.

"Yes. You know that the major technological-industrial nations of the world are in a race, not just a race of weapons, but a race to win the world's markets, to do things most efficiently, to make the best use of fuels and energy, to make themselves as self-sufficient as possible." Kevin paused, but Qwen just took another bite on his beef jerky. "Everywhere, in all sorts of laboratories, scientists are working on projects, on research, trying to discover answers, methods, secrets, if you will."

"Don't tell me the dog is a scientist," Qwen said and laughed.

"Jesus," Gerson said. He spit and took out a cigarette.

"No, he's not a scientist, but he's a product of science."

"Product? You mean like a box of tissues?"

"In a way, yes. The process that was used to create him could mass produce hundreds like him, if we wanted to."

"Wait a minute," Qwen said, "let me understand you. You made this dog in the laboratory? From scratch?"

"No, not scratch." Kevin smiled and turned to Ann, but she was stone-faced. "We began with dog genes, genes from a natural dog, and we duplicated those genes and then began to experiment with them . . . what they call genetic engineering, today."

Qwen didn't say anything. He folded the paper over his remaining beef jerky and stuffed it into his shirt pocket. "I've heard about that," he said. "Science changing nature. Sounded very dangerous to me."

"Oh, there have been some very good things," Ann said. "The mass production of insulin, for one. It's a great deal cheaper. And there have been some very promising experiments with produce—larger vegetables, greater amounts of grain, not to mention bigger farm animals for meat. It's the way we'll stop starvation, for sure."

"What the hell's all that got to do with a dog?"

"Well, it wasn't just a dog. We've used the process on other animals as well. You've got to understand," Kevin went on with more energy and animation, "that what might look grotesque to you now is part of what is necessary for us to gain something very beautiful and very valuable later on. After all, remember Doctor Frankenstein had very good motives for what he began," Kevin added. Once again he looked to Ann and once again she was nonplussed.

"So you made a German shepherd in your laboratory and from what I gathered before, you made him larger than the ordinary German shepherd. What does that lead to—bigger and better pets?"

"No," Kevin said, smiling. "Not at all. As I started to say, everywhere in the world there are scientists working on problems, trying to discover secrets. Well, what's the most important ingredient in all that? What's the most necessary thing?"

"I give up," Qwen said.

"Intelligence. It's as simple as that. Whoever has the most intelligent people will have the most progress." Kevin held his hands out as if that explained everything.

Qwen looked from him to Ann and then back at him. "So?"

"So what we've been doing is working on increasing intelligence. What is intelligence? Why is one person smarter than another? Why is one animal smarter than another? You know, using dogs, that some dogs are smarter than others, even within the same species. Ann and I, and our superiors back at the institute, belong to that school of science that believes increased intelligence can be genetically engineered. Simply put, we believe we will be able to isolate genes that have to do with intelligence and create smarter people. Eventually," he added. "We're not there yet, but when we get there . . . try to imagine what it could mean. Intelligence is power, power greater than anything that now exists. We can outsmart the enemy, outthink him, outdevelop him, outcreate him. Think what it would mean if the average man, the average man, mind you, had the intelligence of an Einstein."

"And you think you'll do all this by pickin' and pokin' around with genes."

"Yes, sir."

"And you've been doing it with animals up to now?"

"Exactly. With very satisfactory results, I might add. Satisfactory enough to get the kind of financing and support from our government that we get."

"So," Qwen said, leaning in toward them, "you made a smarter dog."

"In a matter of speaking, yes."

"So smart that it would perform like a human at times?"

Kevin looked to Ann and both of them looked at Gerson, who had come up behind them.

"You'll have to tell him all of it," she said.

"Part of our theories, part of what we do required us to perform some unusual experiments," Kevin said. "In the course of doing one of them, we isolated a gene relating to human intelligence and we . . . we implanted it in the brain of the dog. Before birth, of course. We didn't expect it to take. There were so many reasons why it shouldn't, but we've made remarkable progress with the problems of rejection. You must remember the transplanting of a baboon's heart into a human baby."

"There was the orangutan's kidney in that man in Australia last year," Ann said.

"Yes, not to mention some of the experiments behind the Iron Curtain. As far as we know, though, no one's ever done what we've done. Thus, the importance of secrecy."

Qwen looked over at Maggie. The dog had been lying quietly a few feet from him, but she stirred and produced a low growl as she eyed Gerson. The big man's shadow fell over the group and reached the dog. Qwen looked up at him.

"What part of our government do you work for?"

"Oh, what's the difference?" Gerson said.

"That's all right," Kevin said. "It's a legitimate question. I've asked myself the same one from time to time. I suppose if you trace all the lines back, you'll reach the CIA."

"Had that feeling."

"We're concerned with the research," Ann said, "not the politics."

"Anyway," Kevin said, "you can understand now

why the dog is so important to us. He's one of a kind and we've spent the better part of two years developing him, learning from him and about him, actually."

"How did he get out?"

"He opened a door," Ann said, "went to a window that was partly opened, forced it up enough, and jumped out. You know how he got past the fence."

"Has he been out before? I mean, has he been with people before?"

"Yes. It was part of his testing program, but we had no idea how far he had developed. We were just learning new things about him when he escaped."

Qwen nodded, took a chunk of chewing tobacco out of his pouch, and stuck it between his gums and his cheek. Ann and Kevin watched him patiently, but Gerson turned away again and flipped his cigarette toward the stream. Maggie watched it fly, and then she rose and shook herself. Somewhere in the forest behind them, a crow complained. Its cawing sent a flock of sparrows skywide and to the west.

"So if I'm to understand you," Qwen finally said, "there's a dog with human intelligence out here."

"To some extent, yes," Kevin said.

"But you don't know exactly to what extent?" Qwen tilted his head after asking the question.

"Well . . ."

"No," Ann said quickly. "We thought we knew his limits, but there have been some new conclusions."

"Such as?"

"Ego. He has a well-defined ego. Ordinary animals have no mirror consciousness. Some monkeys have been found to have it, but by and large, it's not in the ken of lower animals. In other words, Mr. Qwen, if you put Maggie there before a mirror and she saw herself, she wouldn't know herself. She has no self-awareness. And you can't just say it's not in her experience. You can leave her in a room with mirrors from the day she can see, and she won't develop it, whereas a human baby will."

"By the way, does this dog have a name or did you give it a number?"

Ann looked at Kevin and he laughed.

"I gave it a name," he said, "but no one liked it."

"What?"

"Phantom."

"Any particular reason?"

"Well . . . a phantom is something that is not really what it seems to be or should be. I thought that fit. You understand, don't you?"

"I understand that you people are weird as hell. Does he come when you call out that name?"

"Yes."

"If he wants to," Ann added. "He can make decisions independently, think for himself. Maggie will respond automatically when you call her. It's the training, and it's inbred by now. She won't challenge it. She won't reject you or your command." Qwen just looked at her a moment.

"Well," he said, "if I didn't see some of the things he's done up to now, I might think you're all lunatics. Maybe I still do."

"Haven't we wasted enough time?" Gerson said. "If you're a trapper, you should be able to track the bastard no matter what he is. You can track a person too, can't ya?"

"That's true, Mr. Fisher . . ."

"Fishman."

"Fishman. Sorry. But an animal in the wild's got certain advantages over a man, and when you combine that with higher intelligence, you've got a challenge. What I mean," Qwen said turning his attention to Ann and Kevin, "is he's got instinct. He's got speed. His senses are keener."

"We know," Kevin said softly.

"In your experiments," Qwen began, "did you have him matched up against people? I mean as a way of measuring his intelligence?"

"Yes," Kevin said, "especially against children of comparative age. A dog's year is supposed to be equal to seven human years."

"Did he . . ."

"Win? Often."

"One more question," Qwen said, turning to Ann. "Did he like it?"

"Most definitely," she said. "More and more so during the last few months and weeks."

"All right," Qwen said, standing, "we'll go southeast."

"Why southeast?" Kevin asked. He and Ann stood, too. Gerson moved in their direction.

"Because that's where he'll find people the fastest," Qwen said. "And from what I gather from this mess, that's the direction that holds the most promise of any satisfaction for him. Phantom," he muttered and walked on.

Tom Carlson stood on Ken Strasser's back porch and looked out toward the barn where his men were wrapping up their materials. This part of his investigation was over and the clues and information were quite unsatisfactory. Usually there was something about a murder that placed it in one or another of the common categories of crimes. Once that was accomplished, he had a systematic way of proceeding. This was not the case. The substantiated involvement of a dog confused him. If the old man had gotten into a confrontation with a German shepherd, why did the animal smother him to death instead of biting him? He had heard of animals smothering babies, but a grown man?

It was difficult to believe in an imagined scenario. The old man came out with his rifle to chase off a big dog. The dog knocked him down and then . . . maybe the dog was knocked unconscious and fell over him and the old man, weakened by the first blow himself, was unable to move the dog off his face. Then the dog came to and left.

He couldn't blame anyone for laughing at his theory, but there wasn't even another man's footprint, and it would be stretching it awfully far to suspect that a man used dog fur to kill Strasser and then covered up his own tracks by marching a dog around the place. No, from what he had learned, he had to conclude that this was a man-animal confrontation.

One of the primary things to do after any crime had been committed was to look for the weapon. In this case, the weapon was an animal and since the animal wasn't here, since there were no signs of its having been wounded, it was logical to assume it had escaped to someplace else, perhaps someplace nearby.

After hearing the German shepherd story from Harry Michaels, Carlson concluded that his investigation should now center in on the Kaufmans. The coincidence of something terrible happening with a German shepherd there and something terrible happening with one here was too significant. Especially since, for the moment, it was all he had to go on. Even so, he didn't discuss these ideas with any of his men. He felt he had to do some personal footwork and gather something more concrete before he presented his theory to anyone else.

His ego required it. He hated the thought of being laughed at, and he remembered how he had reacted when Harry Michaels had first brought up the involvement of a German shepherd. He had always prided himself in being methodical and concise, bringing true scientific observation and scientific detachment to all of his cases. Police detective work wasn't as glamorous and romantic as it was depicted to be in television and movies and books. It was nitty-gritty, detailed, careful analysis carried out with a monotonous uniformity of procedure. Anyone following him around through the investigations of most of his cases would become bored quickly. That was all right; he wasn't in this business for the headlines.

Why was he in it? What had brought him to this farmhouse and this case? He couldn't claim to be on some moral crusade, eager to dedicate himself to the capture of evildoers. He had to admit that his first interest in police work had been whetted by movies and television, but he'd never really seen himself as the heroic type. Throughout his public school education, despite his good looks and athletic prowess, he was still quite standoffish.

Close to being a loner, he was never really popular with the rest of the student body. In fact, those who knew him well resented his egotism and the cold pleasure he evinced whenever he achieved anything academically or athletically. He knew that they called him Mr. Clean behind his back and even slipped it into the senior yearbook, but he didn't let that bother him.

After he joined the junior police auxillary in his hometown and began spending a great deal of time with policemen, even his closer school acquaintances became aloof. There was talk about his being a teenage "narc" and he was no longer trusted at parties. None of this dissuaded him, however. He had, by this time, developed a strong intellectual interest in the science of police work, and his ability to achieve in it reinforced his ego.

In fact, now that he thought about it, if he had to center in on one thing that had driven him to become what he was, he would have to admit to ego. He liked the feeling he got whenever he packaged a solution to a crime and brought a guilty person in to face justice. It made him feel superior to be able to defeat the criminal mind. He believed that it had to take a certain arrogance for someone to commit a crime anyway, the arrogant belief that he or she could get away with it, could confuse and puzzle the authorities, men and women like Carlson.

If his admittedly wild theory was correct now, he wasn't up against another human being; he was up against an animal. It wasn't the same kind of challenge, and he debated whether or not he'd be better off turning the whole thing over to some animal experts. Let them go track down this dog—if it was indeed only a dog.

And then he thought, if this case did involve a killer animal, albeit a unique killer animal, he would have achieved something remarkable in proving it so. Surely this was strong enough motivation to want to continue and to want to succeed. After all, if it had happened to this old man the way he suspected it might have, it could happen to someone else, maybe even a small child.

Talk about headlines, talk about glamour, talk about movies and books, this could be one for the records. The only other person who had any idea what he might be thinking about was this small-town police chief, hardly a man of his vision, training, and experience. Who would expect him to solve such a crime?

No, this was important, he thought. He would proceed with vigor.

Barry Foster, one of his assistants, came around the corner of the house to approach him. He had put Foster on the dog tracks because he knew Foster was a hunter. He always put in for a day off on the first day of deer season. "You got to get your deer the first day," he said when Carlson once questioned the man about it, "otherwise you'll be traipsin' forever through the woods. The mob of idiots drive the deer farther and farther in and you're better off not bein' out there when some of those so-called big-game hunters from the city come up."

"I picked up his tracks down the road aways. He went into the woods across the street and headed southwest."

"Lose 'em?"

"No, I don't think so, Tom. I think he's still pretty close by."

"How close by?"

"Well, he seemed to be around that ranch house down the street. 'Course, I saw a doghouse there, so I can't be sure it's not theirs."

"The Kaufmans," Carlson muttered to himself. "Yeah, I was down there," he said. "They did have a dog, but they had trouble with it recently and it was killed. How fresh were the tracks you found?"

"Not too much more than a day, Tom."

"Then that's our dog. These people haven't had their dog for a few days now. Okay, wrap it up with John and Stanley. I'm going to talk to some of the other people on this street and go to that ranch house later."

"Right. Oh, one thing about this dog though, Tom."

"What's that?"

"I can't be sure, but I think he's big."

"How big?"

"He's heavy and his prints are larger than usual. German shepherds can run a little over a hundred pounds, but this one could run forty or maybe even fifty over, as hard as that is to believe."

"What do you think?"

"Maybe it's not a German shepherd; maybe it's something else. Something *like* a German shepherd."

"Wolf?"

"No, a wolf would be smaller."

"What, then?"

"I don't know, Tom. You're going to have to bring

in someone with more experience with animals. I'm just a country boy."

"Thanks, Barry. I'll probably do that."

Carlson watched his men pack up and leave. Then he proceeded to visit the different houses along the street, leaving the Kaufmans until last, since the woman wasn't there when he had gone there earlier. None of the people on the street had seen a German shepherd other than the one the Kaufmans had owned. They all told Carlson about Sid Kaufman's contacting them earlier and asking the same question. This reinforced his theories.

Just as he pulled into the Kaufmans' driveway again, Lenny Sidewater drove up. Carlson waved him over and showed him his identification.

"The chief had me parked over there looking for signs of a German shepherd," he explained when Carlson asked him what he was doing.

"Oh he did, did he? See anything?"

"Naw. I almost fell asleep. Time for lunch, though, and the chief says I can come in."

"Do you know if Mrs. Kaufman's returned? I was here early this morning, but no one came to the door."

"I didn't see her pull in, no."

"Oh." Carlson turned and looked at the house and at the doghouse. "All right," he said, "thanks."

Sidewater drove off and Carlson stood in the driveway, debating whether or not to go somewhere for lunch or wait around for the woman to return.

Inside, Phantom rose up slowly from the living room couch. He had gone through the kitchen, leapt up on counters, and pulled open the cabinet doors until he found something appetizing. What he found was King's dog food. The Kaufmans hadn't gotten around to throwing out or giving away the large bag of dry dog food. Phantom tore it open quickly and spilled its contents all over the kitchen floor. Then he proceeded to eat ravenously.

He had seen refrigerators in the laboratory and knew what they were. This one was even simpler to open. It took only a small amount of pressure on the handle to have the door swing out. Once it did so, he perused the contents, sniffing around the shelves, pulling out packages of cold cuts and a plate of leftover chicken. Everything dropped to the floor and was wolfed down quickly. Afterward, with his appetite sated, he sought out some comfort and settled on the couch in the living room. His sleep was interrupted when he heard Carlson's car pull in and the car door open and close.

Now he peered out through the curtains over the bay window. He sat back on his haunches and studied the man and the police car that arrived soon after. When the police car began to pull away, he braced himself on a side table to get a better view of where it was going and what was happening outside. But he weighed too much for the small marble-topped side table and it tipped enough to send the ceramic vase lamp to the floor. It struck the electric heating unit against the wall and shattered.

Carlson had just turned toward his car, concluding that he would go into town for a quick bite and then return. He heard the sound of the lamp and stopped to listen. The silence that followed made him question whether or not he had really heard anything.

Phantom knew that the sound might have been heard. He placed his front paws on the top of the couch and leaned forward to press his snoot into the curtain and get a better view of the man. In doing so, he moved the curtain emphatically.

Carlson saw the movement in the window and stepped away from his car. Perhaps Mrs. Kaufman was there after all; perhaps the policeman had done what he said he almost had done: fallen asleep and missed her return. It was certainly possible and worth investigating.

The state I.D. man headed determindly for the front door of the Kaufman house. He rang the buzzer and waited, but no one came to the door. He knocked and waited. Puzzled, he went to the garage door and peered in. A car was there; the woman had to be home. He went back to the door and tried the handle. He was surprised the front door was unlocked. He would have thought, with all that had been happening on this street, that a woman alone in a house outside a populated area would keep her front door locked. This, plus her not coming to the door at all, triggered the policeman in him. He unbuttoned his jacket so he could get to his revolver easily, and then he entered the Kaufmans' house.

"Tell me more about him," Qwen said as he walked along. Ann was at his side. Among the three from the institute, she seemed to have the most physical endurance and kept right up with his pace. About half a mile upstream, they had found the dog's tracks on the south side of the water. Maggie, once again with a strong lead, forged ahead, yapping continually. Her bark was like the puttering of a small gasoline engine. Qwen could see that the noise aggravated the big security man. Qwen felt the man's tension and moved faster and farther ahead of him just to keep more distance between them. He could see that Kevin Longfellow had difficulty with the pace, but he felt he couldn't be concerned about that. After all, they had gotten themselves into this situation, not he.

"What do you want to know?" Ann asked.

"Why do you bother with animals if you want to do research and find ways to increase human intelligence?

There's a big difference between animals and people, isn't there?"

"Not really. You'd be surprised at the similarities. It would reinforce your belief in evolution."

"Who said I believe in it?"

"I meant anyone who did believe in it as an explanation for all this. Anyway, to get back to your first question. We use animals for two basic reasons. It's possible to control their entire learning history. We know exactly what they've been exposed to, how much and what kind of training they've had, and we can keep accurate records of their achievements."

"What's the other reason?"

"Animals are simpler to observe and understand. The reactions they have and the mechanisms they use are obvious. There's no deception, deliberate deception, that is."

"Except for him, is that it?"

"Yes, that's true, which is another reason why we can say he's so advanced."

"So lying and cheating make him more like us," Qwen said and spit. Ann laughed. It was a strange kind of laugh, a thin sound, punctuated by a kind of gasping. Qwen looked at her; it was as if she didn't know how to really laugh.

"Funny way to put it, Mr. Qwen, but you're right."

"There's got to be more to it than that, more of a difference between us."

"Well I am simplifying, but all higher mammals possess intricate nervous systems and can solve complex problems. There are some behaviorists who believe it is doubtful that man possesses any fundamental intellectual process, except true language, that is not also present in lower biological life."

"I can't believe that," Qwen said. He gestured forward. "Maggie's loyal. She's done some pretty smart things for a dog, but I wouldn't go around sayin' she thinks like a man. Or a woman," he added quickly.

"What do you think thinking is? It used to be that we thought Pavlovian conditioning and Skinner's imprinting were too crude to be considered thinking, but the theory today is that trial and error and insight are but different phases of the same long, continuous process."

"You lost me."

"Sorry. I have a tendency to assume that everyone knows from where we come. You taught your dog to do something by using carrots and sticks. If it did well, you gave it a carrot, a dog biscuit or something, but if it did it wrong or did something wrong, you punished it, wacked it with newspaper or something, right?"

"So?"

"So it learned by trial and error. Say it urinated in the living room when it was a puppy and you wacked it and stuck its snoot in it. It didn't have to urinate in the bedroom and have you wack it there to know it can't urinate there, either. It formed what we call a learning set, an organized set of habits that enables the animal to effectively meet each new problem of similar kind. This second stage is insight, what we call thinking. Humans go through the same process, only faster."

"So what the hell's the difference between us?" he asked. He couldn't help sounding the note of frustration. This asexual female who spoke with a little nasality and sounded like a talking computer was beginning to annoy him.

"Language, for one, and as I told you before, self-image."

"All right. This son-of-a-bitch can't talk, can he?"

"No, but he was making such progress with simple sign language."

"How did you find out he understood sign language?"

"All dogs do to a certain extent, don't they? If you

had Maggie's attention and gestured for her to come to you, she probably would, right?"

"That's nothin'."

"Not much, no. We went further with him. Take the simple trial and error selection test." Her voice rose in pitch. He detected an obvious note of pride and he realized that whatever happened here, they thought they were doing wonderful things. "I had three small containers, two shaped like a square, one like a triangle. In the triangle was a sweetmeat. If he chose that one, he got the meat. It didn't take more than twice for him to select the correct shape all the time."

"He formed a learning set."

"Right. Now you're getting it. I haven't even discussed this with Kevin," she added, looking back, "but I'm sure Phantom has gotten to the point where he could read us."

"Read you?"

"Maggie knows when you're happy with her and when you're angry—by the sound of your voice, by a gesture, whatever. She might even have reached the point where she reacts to your simple smile, no words, no sounds. I think he read our most subtle gestures and knew when some test result pleased us or got us intellectually excited."

"That doesn't sound as fantastic as some of the other stuff you described."

"No, not in and of itself, but he was taking it a step further. I think he reached the point where he was testing us."

"What?" He paused and then started up quickly.

"He would deliberately fail tests to frustrate us, to see what we would do next. I've been keeping accurate track of things and some of the inconsistencies point to nothing else."

"That's the deception you were talking about before, huh?"

"Some of it."

"What else is there?"

"Well . . ." Her free flow of answers suddenly stalled. Kevin and Gerson were drawing closer to them and he thought that might be the reason. It whetted Qwen's interest and curiosity.

"Why stop now? You've told me so much already."

"Because this is very unscientific of me. It's in the realm of pure conjecture. I don't have enough evidence, data, to even suggest such a conclusion."

"Hey, I'm not giving you a grade, miss. I haven't decided yet whether I'm going to buy any of this, even the stuff you claim you can demonstrate with graphs or notes or boxes, triangles, whatever you got."

She was quiet for a few more steps and he didn't try to pump her any further.

"I think," she finally said, "that he got to the point where he knew what we were about. He didn't want to let us know just how intelligent he was and he rationed what he'd let us know about him . . . rewarded us in a way not too different from the way we rewarded him. He was conditioning us," she added. Qwen didn't say anything, so she looked at him. "Do you understand what I'm implying?"

"Sure," he said. ""That's why I asked you back there if he was put into competition with humans."

"How did you come to such a quick conclusion?"

"Instinct," he said and smiled. "I've been among animals all my life. I don't have to read about survival of the fittest. I've lived it. Everything livin' wants to run herd over somethin' else. There's nothin' surprisin' about that."

"You're a remarkable man, Mr. Qwen. Now tell me honestly, since I've been honest with you, what do you think of our chances of recapturing him?"

"Well, miss, from what you've been telling me, you

might better ask what I think of his chances of capturing us."

She stopped in her tracks, but Qwen kept walking.

"What's the matter?" Kevin called. "What is it?"

"Nothing," she said quickly and jogged to catch up with Qwen again. "What do you mean by that?" she asked him.

"This hunt, this chase, maybe it'll turn out to be like one of your mazes and tests. Maybe you taught him too well, miss."

Maggie's barking suddenly grew shriller.

"Pick up the pace," Qwen called back as he surged forward.

# 9

"MRS. KAUFMAN?"

Lieutenant Carlson paused in the foyer and listened. All was quiet, but ominously so. He put his hand on the handle of his revolver. He didn't want to draw it out just yet. The sight of a stranger dressed in a jacket and tie entering a house with a gun in his hand could be quite a shock to anyone. Perhaps she was lying down; perhaps she was in the bathroom or taking a shower and simply didn't hear the doorbell or his calling.

"Hello!" She should hear that, he thought. *"Hello, Mrs. Kaufman! It's the police! Mrs. Kaufman?"*

Nothing returned but the echo of his own voice. He took a few steps further into the house. The living room was to his right. He could see that the dining room and kitchen were ahead to his left, and straight on down the hall led to the bedrooms and bathroom. The hallway veered to the left after the entrance to the dining room.

He surveyed the living room. At first, everything appeared normal, undisturbed; but when he looked to the right of the couch, he saw the overturned end table and the smashed ceramic lamp. This was different; this required more precaution. He drew his revolver from his belt holster and listened more intently for any sounds of stirring within the house. It was still deadly quiet. He went directly to the end table and lamp and knelt down to inspect them. There was a print on the window and it was distinctly the paw print of a dog. The realization sent a cold tingle down the back of his neck to the base of his spine. It felt as though someone had sprayed ice water on him. Still squatting, he turned slowly and looked behind the couch. Nothing was there.

He stood up and studied the rest of the furniture: the chairs, the larger center table, the reading lamp in the corner, and the bookcase. Nothing else looked touched and nothing was big enough for anything or anyone to hide behind. The bookcase was smack against the far wall.

It occurred to him that he should probably go outside and radio for assistance, that this was the most intelligent way to handle the situation. He might have done that, too, if he hadn't heard what sounded like heavy breathing coming from the area of the bedrooms. He thought it was possible that Mrs. Kaufman might be in trouble; she might be hurt. So he started down the hall, pausing only at the door to the basement. He listened for anything or anyone behind it and then opened it slowly to peer down.

The light that Clara Kaufman had put on when she first went downstairs was still on. Carlson was encouraged by this. He thought the woman was somewhere in her basement and that was probably why she hadn't heard him enter and call to her. He called again, this time from the top of the basement stairs.

He waited. There was no response, but even though all was quiet below, he decided he had better go down there first to check before going through any other portion of the house. He started down the stairs and had descended about halfway when he heard the sounds behind him.

Phantom had been waiting down the hall in the first

bedroom, Lisa's bedroom. He had wanted the man to come further into the house, away from the entranceway and away from the windows that looked out on the driveway. He heard the basement door being opened and he peered around the corner of the bedroom doorway in time to see Carlson begin his descent. Then he went down the hallway, hesitating, out of sight by the doorway. Phantom wanted Carlson to be halfway down before he turned the corner and made the leap.

Stalking and attacking humans seemed to come as easily to him as stalking and attacking a deer. He anticipated their moves, the way they looked about. He knew the man's attention would be fully on the basement below; he knew he'd be moving slowly, cautiously, looking from side to side. The sounds the man had made when he first entered the house weren't threatening, but Phantom had observed him long enough to sense a threat.

Anyone seeing Phantom move around the corner of the basement door would have thought he was something mechanical. It was as if levers had been pulled and circuits had been connected to permit the flow of violent energy through his body. He moved forward like a computerized weapon. There wasn't the slightest indecision. It had all been programmed a thousand years before. This time he permitted himself a short growl, but he was already in the air when he did so. He sprang off the top step and shot downward with spearlike accuracy.

Carlson's turn seemed timed to fit the dog's attack. In doing so, he exposed his throat. His left arm was at his side and his right arm, the hand holding the revolver, was about chest-high. He didn't even have time to think about pulling the trigger. The big dog clamped its jaws on his throat and then threw the rest of its body out and behind him, its force and the weight pulling and ripping Carlson's throat out. His eyes bulged at the sight of his own blood spurting upward and away.

The impact of the blow and the bite spun him around and he folded like a broken puppet, collapsing and tumbling the rest of the way down. Phantom had landed on all fours at the base of the stairs, a piece of Carlson's flesh still in his teeth. He stepped aside as the body rolled past him and came to a stop against the wall. Carlson was on his right side, his feet twisted, legs turned inward. Blood continued to flow freely into the carpet. Incredibly, the pistol was still in his hand, his trigger finger having gotten caught around the trigger. Carlson's voice box had been torn; there were no final sounds. His head simply slumped a little further down into the carpet.

Phantom nudged the body with his snoot and then sniffed around the head and face. Satisfied that death had claimed the man, he sat back on his haunches and contemplated what had transpired. The attack had excited him; his heart still beat quickly. He lowered his jaws and let his tongue hang freely to the side. He looked up the stairs and then back at the body of the man.

Once again he was filled with pride and satisfaction. His confidence bloated. No matter what size, shape, or sex they were, he could defeat them. He remembered how they had treated him back at the laboratory when he completed a test, especially when they had given him a difficult task and he had been successful. He felt the same way now; he needed some reward. It was part of what he had learned and what he had come to expect.

Before he could think about it any further, the telephone rang. It seemed to be ringing everywhere. There were four phones in the house: one in the kitchen, one in the living room, one in the master bedroom, and one down in the basement, so the ringing was duplicated and amplified.

He turned around and looked at Carlson again. Despite the fact that the man was dead, he almost expected him to get up in response to the sound. It rang and rang and rang. Even when it stopped, he felt the sound lingering in the air. There was a hum in his ears.

He shot up the stairs quickly and went back into the living room. He liked the view of the driveway and the road from there. As before, he hopped onto the couch and peered out. When a car went by, he put his paws on the sill and the pane to see where it went. It disappeared down the road and things became quiet once again.

A great thirst came over him, so he went to the kitchen, opened the refrigerator door, and pulled out a container of milk. The cool white liquid spurted freely from the top after he dropped it hard to the floor. He lapped it up greedily and then, impatient with the flow, tore open the container and finished what remained.

This was good; he felt good about everything in here. There was so much to please him, and he hadn't really gone through all of it. There was more to explore. He trotted down to Bobby's bedroom and nudged open the door. The scent of the other dog was still in the room; indeed it was still throughout much of the house, only humans wouldn't sense it as keenly as he could. He thought about that dog for a moment and remembered how defenseless it had been against the man with the gun. The man he had just killed had a gun, too, but it hadn't seemed to matter.

He hopped up on the little boy's bed and sprawled out against the quilt and the pillow. This was even more comfortable than the couch. He lowered his head between his two front legs and closed his eyes. For a few moments he saw nothing; all was dark. He could sleep. Then, as though a shock passed through his body, he jerked his head up and listened.

There was no sound. Nothing that anyone could hear, but there was something . . . his sixth sense, his instinct, had begun the first in a series of upcoming small warnings. They came in the form of a quickened heartbeat, a stirring in the blood. His eyes widened and, without willing himself to do it, he growled. The rumbling died slowly in the base of his stomach and then all was quiet with him once more.

But a thought was born in his brain. He could do more with his instinct: he could bring it to a fruition, envision things, realize things concretely enough to give them lasting power. He looked in the direction from where he had come and he understood that his pursuers had not given up. They were still out there, moving toward him. This instinctive knowledge provided him with the first real pangs of fear since he had escaped. He had almost forgotten what fear was like.

After a while his heart slowed again; the pace of his blood went back to normal. He returned his head to the comfortable spot he had found and closed his eyes. For now he was safe; it was good here and there was more he wanted to do yet. He would have time to flee.

Downstairs, in the rear room of the basement, Clara Kaufman stirred. Her first movements were a kind of spasmodic jerking in her hands and feet. The twitching served as a preface to her regaining consciousness. She opened her eyes and confronted the unfinished basement room. She was completely disoriented and confused. How had she gotten here? Why did she have all this pain—pain in her wrist, pain in her lip, pain in her side, and an aching in the back of her head?

She put her hand on the pipe of the water heater and tried to boost herself into a sitting position. When she turned her torso however, the sting from her broken ribs sucked the breath out of her. She gasped in disbelief and fell back to the cold, concrete floor. She remembered now that she had been struck by something. The image of it in her memory was blurred, but it was something large and hairy like a . . . like a dog.

The thought nearly brought a scream to her lips. She wanted to raise her voice, but the expectancy of agony that would result from the extra effort kept her from doing so. It was a dog, she thought. The colors, the shape . . . it was like King. It was the dog she had seen near King's house, the dog Sid had labeled the ghost dog of Bobby's nightmares. Oh God, she thought.

She felt around her right wrist. Blood on the punctured skin had clotted, but the pain was still there. The bone felt bruised. She raised her arm slowly to catch a view of it in the afternoon light that penetrated the one basement window and saw what looked like teeth marks in her skin. She was sure of it—they were teeth marks. The dog had bitten her.

She had a fantastic thought after she saw what had been done to her wrist. She was almost happy about it because now, she told herself, she could prove that this dog existed.

Her head was spinning, but she fought to keep consciousness. She had to put intelligent thoughts together; she had to realize all that had happened and deal with it. She was not one to back away from crisis, no matter how horrible it seemed.

Something terrible had gotten into the house, she thought. This dog, be it King's ghost or whatever, had done the damage in the basement, and Sid hadn't seen it—or it hadn't seen Sid when he was first down here this morning.

This morning, she thought. How long have I been down here? She lifted her left arm and turned it to the light too, trying to get a clear view of her watch. Damn the small face, she thought, hating it for being so elegant and so dainty. The numbers were blurry. She focused and refocused and finally came to the conclusion that she had been down here for hours.

She had to get out and get to a phone. The closest one was behind the bar in the playroom. She took hold of the water heater and used it to brace herself into a sitting position. Even that simple action brought excruciating pain, and she had to rest and catch her breath before attempting any further movement. One of her cracked ribs pressed dangerously against her lung. A puncture was more than possible. Any abrupt, hard move would guarantee it.

She thought about Sid, miles and miles away by now, working on his job in Boston, concentrating in his inimitable way, blocking out all the bad memories until the work was completed. Never in his deepest imagination could he envision her the way she was now—crumpled up in the basement, barely able to stir, strapped down by pain and probably still in great danger.

There was no one here to help her; she had to help herself. In a few hours her children would be arriving on the school bus. What if she didn't get out of here? What if that animal was still in the house? The thought of such a possibility gave her the grit to face the pain. She made an attempt at standing but found she could get herself only into a squatting position. Straightening her torso brought more pain than she could bear. She had to make her way across the basement floor in a kind of crawl, inching forward, step by step, careful not to place too much pressure on the side that sang the song of agony.

It seemed to take half an hour to reach the door. Every few moments along the way, she felt nauseated and battled to keep herself from blacking out. Slowly she reached forward with her right arm and took hold of the door to pull it open further. She emerged from the rear room on all fours and faced the body of Lt. Carlson. The sight of his opened throat and the blood was too much to behold.

She couldn't hold back the terror and the scream. The effort constricted her upper body and a rib slipped into her lung, the jagged bone tearing into it like a pin puncturing a balloon. Such a shot of pain was rejected by her brain. It shut down quickly and she fell forward on the basement playroom rug, once again losing consciousness.

Clara's scream brought Phantom to the basement door. He growled a warning and then came down the steps quickly to confront the woman's body. He studied it for a moment, sniffed about, and then concluded there was no danger. He thought about dragging it back into the room and maybe even dragging the man's body in, too, but the prospect of all that work was not appealing to him now. He had been awakened from a comfortable sleep and he felt like getting back to it. He trotted up the stairs again and looked back only once from the top of the step. The two crumpled human bodies side by side encouraged him. There was a kind of evil, aesthetic pleasure for him in the sight. He continued on back down the hallway, back to Bobby's room and the bed and the comfort he had so easily earned.

Qwen knelt over the carcass of the dead fawn. Maggie sat by, looking proud of her find.

"He's been through here, all right," Qwen said. "It's been days, though." He looked up at Kevin. "You should have started this search earlier."

"Oh, we searched."

"He means you should have come to him earlier, Kevin," Ann said. He didn't like her tone of voice.

"You know very well why we didn't. It wasn't our intention to involve any layman if we could help it,"

Kevin said to Qwen. Qwen nodded and stood up. Then he started to the right.

"Shouldn't we take a short rest?" Kevin asked. "We've been going steady for more than two hours."

Qwen paused and looked back.

"Think that would bother your man-dog?" he asked. "Think he'd hafta stop and rest after two, three hours of travelin'?"

"We ain't dogs," Gerson said, but there was a growl to his voice.

"Good predators think like their prey, move like their prey."

"Who was it told me this wasn't going to be a Sunday picnic?" Ann asked sarcastically. "Go on, Mr. Qwen, I'm right behind you." Qwen smiled and walked on, Maggie surging forward.

This part of the undeveloped land they traveled was more mountainous. The reason for Kevin and Gerson's complaining related to the fact that they had been walking uphill for the last hour and a half. Qwen wanted to stay as close to the dog's trail as he could. Often that meant taking a harder than necessary path. When he moved through the forest, he didn't think much about the people who were with him, anyway. He got lost in the flow of things—the rhythm of his own steps, the sound of Maggie's barking, the ever-present indication of wildlife.

His pace was vigorous. His legs were sinewy and strong and he had the wind endurance of an eighteen-year-old. Much of his time was spent traveling by foot. In high school he had been a cross-country runner, amazed at how hard some of his fellow teammates had to work to do what he could do naturally.

Before he had spoken to the scientists and learned the nature of their work and what the dog was about, he had seriously considered the possibility that the dog had created a home for itself somewhere in the forest.

He really didn't think they'd have to go as far as they had, and he half-suspected that they might end up circling back somewhat, anyway.

But now he was convinced that they were easily a few days behind the creature. It had a destination and had made its way there. It wasn't just wandering aimlessly through the woods. He couldn't point to any one thing, any sign, and say this or that proved it. If the others wanted an explanation for his theory, he couldn't even give a satisfactory reply, but he still felt as positive as could be about it.

The stories the scientists had told him should have caused him to think of some horrible, distorted terror-creature seen in movies and television, yet he didn't have those images. He was never one to let his imagination run wild. If anything, he had an image of a pitiful creature. He saw it as somehow wounded and suffering. These Frankensteins, no matter what they wanted to call themselves—research scientists, CIA operatives, whatever—had, in his opinion, tortured and tormented the animal. Whatever they had done to it with their so-called genetic engineering had put it in a painful state. Now it was a mad, unnatural part of nature, even though it still performed in a certain, predictable way.

His problem, as he saw it, was how much of the animal was still in it and how much of the human had taken control. The big man behind him was right—he could trap another human being as easily, if not more easily, than he could trap an animal. He was confident that in the end he would find the animal, no matter what genes they had put into it. What Qwen wasn't sure of was what he would be able to do when he found him. But, he thought, maybe that will be their problem. Maybe that was when they would have to use their "magical, scientific ways."

The woman was beside him again, going stride for stride. He paused to look at some tracks and then continued on, bearing to his left. The afternoon sun had dipped considerably to the west. Because the trees were so tall and full here, they had to move through long corridors of shadow. Qwen thought the cool air was invigorating; his pace kept him snug. But the two men behind him began to look more and more grumpy and uncomfortable. The woman was different, though—she seemed unaffected by anything.

Qwen had a funny idea about her. It brought a smile to his lips and eyes, but she didn't see it. He thought about *The Invasion of the Body Snatchers* and envisioned her to be nothing more than a large portion of brain matter housed in a human body. This was why she was so indifferent to her body, why she didn't care if it was attractive or if she abused it in any way. Whenever he did talk to her and look at her eyes, he had the eerie feeling he was talking to a mask. Someone else was inside that frame.

"Tell me more about this genetic material you implanted into this dog," he said without breaking stride.

"What else do you want to know?"

"How much do you know about it?"

"You mean what can it do for him? That's what we were learning about ourselves."

"From where did you get it?" He spit some tobacco juice to his left. "My mother usta have this saying, 'The apple don't fall far from the tree,' if you know what I mean."

"I know exactly what you mean. In her crude way she was expressing the theory of genetics."

"Crude?"

"Well, I mean unsubstantiated. In her time it was just a feeling people had."

"Sometimes it's better to trust your feelings."

"Maybe. But you see, I believe, we believe, I should say, that even your feelings are preconditioned by your genetic makeup. It's not something that happens spontaneously. You know people who have habitually sour, cynical personalities and people who are habitually optimistic, even annoyingly optimistic, maybe. Why, two people like that could be from the same family, could be brother and sister. What makes them different? They had the same home environment, the same basic conditioning. It's got to be in their given, in their genes."

"Hmm." He had to admit she made sense.

"Do you have any brothers or sisters?"

"Got a younger brother."

"Are you very alike?"

"Night and day," he said and laughed. "He teaches high school English in a little town in Pennsylvania. Went to college there, met a girl, and settled down there."

"See what I mean? Would you mind if I tried to guess more about the two of you?"

"Go ahead."

"My guess is your brother never liked to hunt and be outdoors as much as you do. When you said he was an English teacher, you indicated he was a good reader. How many years difference between you?"

"Three."

"Was your father disappointed in him?"

"Hell, no. My father never stopped braggin' about him."

"Really?"

Qwen paused.

"Maybe you ain't as perfect about this stuff as you think. Sure, I spent my life outdoors and I love the land, but that don't mean I'm stupid or that I think people who spend most of their time indoors are stupid."

She blinked as though a feeling had finally registered.

"I didn't mean it to be . . . you're far from stupid, Mr. Qwen. In your world, you're the expert. That's why we came to you."

He looked back at the two men, who looked up hopefully.

"I hope so," he said. "Anyway, gettin' back to my original question. Where did you get the gene from? I mean did you know whose it was?"

"Not exactly." He sensed her hesitation, but he waited her out. "We have arrangements with certain federal correctional facilities for human organs, tissue, et cetera.

"Prisoners? You mean that genetic stuff came out of some convict?"

He thought for a moment. Their pace had slowed. Maggie was pulling farther away and Kevin and Gerson were only ten feet behind.

"Didn't it occur to you that maybe . . . maybe he would inherit evil, too?"

"I don't believe evil can be inherited, Mr. Qwen. There are certain limits, even in our theories."

"Is that right? Well, there's where you and my mother part company. She was right on the money when it came to the kids who would be hell-raisers and criminals."

"To a large extent that was a result of their home environment. I'm not saying the tendencies weren't inborn, but they could have directed their energies, their ruthlessness, if you will, toward more socially acceptable goals. If they had been conditioned correctly, that is."

"All right," Qwen said, "considering the tendencies you put into this dog and the conditioning you gave it, what would you say it's directed toward?"

"You have to understand, Mr. Qwen," she said, her

voice quivering with insecurity for the first time since they had begun the chase, "we're on the frontier of this research. We don't know all the answers yet."

"You mean you might have created some kind of intelligent, criminal animal and not even know that?" She didn't respond. He looked back at the two who had fallen behind a few more feet. "You do know, don't you?" he asked. "That's why you wanted to come along. That's why you think it's so important we recapture him as soon as possible." Still she didn't respond. "Do they know this, too?" he asked, gesturing back with his head.

"No," she said, but it was very low, almost inaudible.

He stopped when the ledge came into sight. Maggie was waiting there dutifully. Qwen broke into a jog and Ann followed right along. Gerson cursed and Kevin picked up his pace. At the ledge they could look down at the lake and the line of houses to the east. It was a picture postcard scene, especially with the rich green maples and tall pine that rimmed large portions of the lake shore. There were half a dozen small sailboats moving so slowly they looked painted on the water. But to Qwen, the peaceful and serene vista looked deceptive. He had the feeling that something terrible could emerge at any moment and turn the water into blood.

The others gathered behind him. He studied the ground by the ledge carefully and followed some signs to the right where he saw the steepness diminished by outshoots of rock and earth, making for a natural pathway down the side of the mountain.

"What's this, a dead end?" Gerson asked.

"Hardly," Qwen said. He looked out over the lake again. They all stood beside him, silently looking in the same direction. After another moment he looked at Ann. He saw immediately that she understood.

"That's the outskirts of the hamlet of South Fallsburg down there," he said.

"So?" Gerson said.

"We'll follow this route down the side of the mountain carefully and go around the lake."

"How can you tell he went that way? Whaddya got, telescopic vision or something?" Gerson asked.

Qwen didn't reply. Instead he went to the edge of the ledge and began his descent carefully.

"For Christ's sake," Gerson said.

"Why don't you shut up?" Ann said and followed Qwen.

"Wait a minute," Gerson said, seizing Kevin's right shoulder before he started after them. "I don't like the idea of headin' directly into population."

"I don't like it either," Kevin said, "but what's our choice? If that's where he went, that's where we must go."

"I don't trust that guy."

"We don't have much choice."

"For now," Gerson muttered and reluctantly followed behind.

The Fallsburg Central Elementary School bus made the turn onto Lake Street. There were only two children on it. Lisa and Bobby Kaufman were the last children on the run. As soon as the bus made the turn, they moved up to the front seats as they always did. Normally, Ed Tooey yelled if any of his children got up out of their seats while the bus was still in motion, but he permitted the Kaufman kids this little divergence from the rule. The bus moved very slowly at this point and he knew how anxious the children were to get home. He smiled and shifted up gear as he finished the turn and went into the straightaway.

Ed Tooey had been driving a school bus for nearly thirty years now, and he never ceased to be fascinated by the faces of children, especially grade school children. There was an innocence and excitement in their faces that made every day bright for him. Other bus drivers, the newer ones mostly, constantly complained about the noise and the roughhousing on their buses. They acted as though the runs were hell for them. He concluded that most of them didn't like children and even if the children sat like zombies, these drivers would still complain.

Tooey took pride in the fact that he developed a good rapport with many of his wards. He made it a point to talk with the children every chance he got, to learn something personal about them. Many times elementary schoolchildren's parents were waiting outside their homes when the school bus pulled up. He always spoke a few words with those who did. Consequently, his runs ran the longest. School administrators had grown used to him over the years, but recently, a new business administrator, with a coldly efficient manner, had been critical of him and the time it took him to complete his route. The business manager had clocked every mile himself and determined with computer accuracy just how long it should take.

"I'm not a piece of machinery," Tooey told him when he was called in for a conference about it. He wasn't exactly insubordinate, but the new business manager was beginning to pressure him into thinking about retirement. He had already threatened to put him on a different run, a high school run that was shorter.

"So how'd you do in school today?" he asked Bobby after the little boy took his new seat.

"Okay."

"He's not havin' any more of those nightmares, is he?" he asked Lisa.

"No."

"That's good. Nightmares ain't nothin' anyway. I

usta have 'em all the time because I ate all sorts of stuff right before I went to sleep. Now I just have hot milk," he said and laughed. "I'm a regular senior citizen."

"I don't like hot milk," Bobby said.

"I'm not crazy about it either, but it sure helps me fall asleep," Tooey said. "Your daddy gettin' you another dog someday?" he asked.

"No," Lisa said quickly.

"My dog's still here," Bobby said.

"Still here? What's he mean, still here?"

"It's a dream he thinks was real," Lisa said.

"Oh."

"It *was* real," Bobby said. "It was."

"Okay, if you say so," Tooey said. He slowed down as the Kaufman house came into view. There was no traffic on the street in either direction, but he turned his warning lights on anyway. By the book, he thought. He always did things by the book. "Looks like you got a visitor," he announced, seeing Carlson's car in the driveway. The two children sat up and strained their necks to look out over the front of the school bus. Tooey brought it to a stop and opened the doors. "Last stop!" he announced. "All off who's going off!"

The children stood up hesitantly. Tooey noticed that the sight of the strange car put a heaviness in their steps.

"Maybe it's a traveling salesman or an uncle. Watch your step, kids."

"So long, Mr. Tooey," Lisa said, remembering to look back. Bobby couldn't take his eyes off the car. When the school bus door closed behind them, they started up their driveway slowly. Ed Tooey did not pull away immediately. He watched them for a few moments and then shook his head. He had heard about the terrible incident with their dog, and he thought it had put such fear into the children that it made everything look ominous, even a strange car parked in the driveway.

He shifted into first and accelerated. It was only when he was half a mile or so down the street that he realized Mrs. Kaufman hadn't come out to greet her children. She didn't even appear in the doorway to wave at him. It was something she always did; she was one of those kinds of parents who showed concern. He called them old-fashioned parents.

Oh well, he thought, so she wasn't there. At least she was there most of the time. He looked at his watch. He was a good ten minutes behind schedule. It wouldn't surprise him, he thought, to find the business manager waiting at the school bus garage, a stopwatch in his hand and a smirk on his face. Well that's just too bad, Tooey thought. I'm cartin' people around, not baggage. He deliberately slowed down so he could relax the rest of the way.

Bobby stopped to take Lisa's hand before going any farther toward their house. It was an instinctive action that Lisa did not question. She seemed to expect it or welcome it. They both looked at the doghouse as though they wanted to confirm the reality of what had happened. Then they went right to their front entrance. They paused on the patio when they saw the front door was partly opened.

"Where's Mommy?" Bobby asked.

"Inside, silly," Lisa said and bravely stepped forward to enter the house first.

# 10

SID KAUFMAN PUT down his clipboard and wiped his face with his handkerchief. He had been working steadily ever since he'd left George Friedman's office. He had decided even to skip lunch, knowing that the moment he paused, he would dwell on the situation back home and lose his concentration. He looked at his watch and nodded to himself. This was a good time to call Clara. She was sure to be home since the kids would be coming home on the school bus any minute.

He went back to Friedman's office. George smiled with expectation as Sid approached. He was talking with his secretary and she looked up at Sid with almost as much anticipation.

"How's it going?"

"Good," Sid said. "I'm afraid I have to ask a favor of you."

"Sure."

"I need to use your phone. It's imperative that I call home now," he added, not realizing how intensely he spoke.

"No problem. Go right on in."

"I'll use my credit card," Sid added as he went by them.

"Whatever you want," George said.

Sid went in and took the seat behind George's desk. After he reached the operator, he debated whether or not he should mention the basement door to Clara. After all, he was adding worries without his being there to comfort and support her. As long as she locked the door now and kept it locked, he thought. He heard the first ring.

He heard the second and the third and shifted the receiver nervously to his other ear as the phone rang again and again and again. After the tenth ring produced no answer, Sid hung up. He looked at his watch again to be sure he hadn't misread the time. He hadn't. She had to be home now. It was not like Clara to let the kids come home to an empty house. She was always complaining about those "latchkey kids" and "absentee parents." She would be home today, especially, he thought, considering all that had happened.

George Friedman's knocking on his own office door almost made Sid jump in the chair.

"Everything all right?" George said, peering in.

"No answer," Sid said as though George knew it all.

"Oh. Is that a problem?" He came further into the office.

Sid looked up at him. Despite his desire to maintain strong selfcontrol, he couldn't help having a quickened heartbeat. He had had a sick feeling come over him ever since leaving the house. He knew it was the result of guilt and worry. There was nothing he wanted more now than to hear Clara's voice.

"My wife should have answered. Our kids are due home from school any moment now. She'd be there."

"Maybe she's outside and can't hear the phone."

"No. You can hear it fifty feet from the house."

George nodded and took the seat in front of his desk. Sid, lost in his own thoughts, didn't realize he was still in the factory owner's chair.

"You have a special reason to be concerned?"

"What's that? Oh, yes. Oh, here, George, take your seat."

"No, that's all right. Sit, sit," he said, waving Sid back down. "You wanna talk about it, or is it private?"

"Private? No. We had some wild things happen recently and it makes you worry," he said. He leaned back in the chair. George looked as if he had nothing else to do but listen, so Sid began to relate the story to him. He had been talking for nearly ten minutes straight before he realized it. Must've been therapy for me, he thought.

"I don't know that much about dogs," George said when Sid paused, "but what you're describing doesn't seem natural."

"That's what I've been gathering."

"What else are you going to do about it?"

"I'm not sure. I was thinking that after I finished here, I would go up to Boston University to try to talk to some expert in animal behavior."

"Oh, I know someone up there. I can make a call for you. My nephew's wife teaches English."

"Great. I'd appreciate it," Sid said. He looked at the phone again.

"Wait a few minutes and call again."

"I will."

"So, while you wait," George said, folding his arms across his chest and sitting back, "maybe you'll tell me some of your initial observations."

Sid smiled. "It wouldn't be fair to make any conclusions just yet, George. There's a lot more to your operation for me to see." Friedman's face registered his disappointment. "But we can make some preliminary comments, if you want."

"Sure."

"With the understanding that I might reverse something later on."

"Of course."

"You're kind of top-heavy in your intake department. Those shifts are too short and they're short because you've got so many men doing that work. I saw the stockpiles. They're actually slowing themselves down because if they didn't, the backup of materials would require another warehouse."

"Really?"

"You need a foreman there, but why two at that price? Your split shift is weak on the downside. I don't think you have to go sixteen hours there. Go twelve and promote someone to assistant foreman to run the other four." Sid looked at his notes for a moment, almost glad that he had agreed to give George his preliminary observations. It was something he didn't like to do, but in this case it was helping pass some very nerve-racking time.

"Assistant foreman, huh?"

"Yes, and even though I didn't watch him enough to make a solid judgment, I think that Crowley fellow looked like the hardest worker in that department. He seemed serious and intent on what he was doing while the others were jawing away and looking at the clock."

"Yes," Friedman said, his face reflecting how impressed he was, "Tom Crowley is a good man. You're a pretty observant fellow, aren't you?"

"That's what they pay me to do, George."

"I bet you'd make a good detective."

"Oh, I dont know. I'm having some difficulty solving a case right now," he said.

"Try again," George said, nodding toward the phone. Sid dialed the operator and went through the process once more. George watched him closely as he listened to the ringing. Sid looked at his watch again. "Maybe your wife had to meet them at school for some reason. Was this some kind of conference day or parent visitation day?"

"No, she'd have mentioned it," Sid said as he put the receiver down. "We have a bulletin board for those things and there was nothing like that on it."

"What do you want to do?" George asked.

"Go back to work, wait a while longer, and call again. What else can I do?"

"That's probably best," George said. "I'm sure it's nothing."

Sid got up but looked down at the phone again. He wished he could crawl through the wires as fast as his voice could travel and be beside Clara and the kids. It was so frustrating. For a moment he thought of Clara and recalled her waving good-bye from the garage. The image left him with such a sense of foreboding that he had to do everything he could to get back to the job at hand.

Lisa hesitated in the entranceway of the house and listened hard for a moment. She was unaccustomed to such complete silence when she and her brother arrived at home after school.

"Mommy?" she called. She felt Bobby's hand on her back.

"My stitches hurt," he said. "I want Mommy."

"Shh." Lisa walked further into the house. When she looked into the kitchen and saw the mess on the floor, she stopped. Bobby was right beside her.

"What happened?" he said.

"I don't know."

"Where's Mommy? I want Mommy."

"Okay, okay. Do you have to be such a whine baby?"

"I'm not a whine baby."

They both turned sharply when they heard something from the area of the bedrooms. Instinctively,

Lisa put her arm around her brother. She placed her school books on the table quietly and then, nudging Bobby, indicated that they should head for that part of the house. He didn't move.

*"Mommy!"* he screamed. *"Where are you?"*

"You don't have to yell, Bobby. You'll frighten her."

"I will not. *Mommy!"*

"Stop it," she said. His shouting was really frightening her. She released her grip on him and started away, herself. He followed slowly. She looked into the living room and saw the smashed lamp. Then she looked down the hallway to the bedrooms. She thought she heard the sound of heavy breathing. It was actually more like . . . like a dog panting. She recalled how King panted sometimes after running around the house with Bobby. After following him into the living room, King breathed so hard he looked as if he would drop on the spot. Usually Lisa or her mother bawled Bobby out for overheating the dog.

"Do you hear that?" Bobby said, coming up beside her. "It sounds like King."

"Stop that. You know King's dead. *Mom!"* This time she couldn't help sounding the note of hysteria in her voice. When Bobby yelled again, she didn't chastize him.

*"Mom!"*

*"Mom!"*

They walked toward the bedrooms.

Lisa stopped at the basement door. Like Carlson, she was curious about the lights being on. She, too, suspected that because her mother was down there, she hadn't heard their bus arrival and entrance. This possibility quickly brought a sense of welcome relief. Without realizing it, she had been holding her breath as she and Bobby started down the hallway.

"Mommy down there?" Bobby asked, pushing past her.

"Probably. Probably in the utility room."

*"Mom,"* Bobby called after peering down the stairs. They both waited for an answer.

It came in the form of a low growl as Phantom stepped out from behind the doorway of Bobby's room. The dog stopped about fifteen feet from them and raised his head. His body seemed to vibrate as a result of his own heavy breathing. He lowered his jaw so his tongue could be fully exposed. It dangled over the bottom teeth. It was dark pink and thick, the sandpapery roughness of which they could see, even from this distance.

The children stared in amazement.

"That's not King," Bobby said. The dog seemed to be laughing. It moved a few inches forward, lowering its head like a hound stalking a chicken. "Whose dog is it?"

"I don't know," Lisa whispered. She was surprised she was able to make any sounds at all. All the strength in her body drained in a flash. She didn't think she'd be able to move, but she understood that she and her little brother were in danger. She had to act quickly.

She brought Bobby up in front of her and placed her hands on both his shoulders, staring ahead at the dog that stared back at them all the while. The instinctive fear that had come alive within her was amplified by the look in the dog's eyes.

She had seen other watchdogs bark their warnings and growl their admonition, but this was a far different thing. They didn't have death written so clearly in their eyes. She was positive that within the next few moments, this dog would attack them. Neither their shouts nor their gestures would dissuade it and, worst of all, a safe flight back out of the house was obviously impossible. They would barely get to the beginning of the corridor before the dog was on them. What would Lisa do if the dog seized Bobby first? She couldn't leave him and she couldn't beat off such a large animal.

"Where's Mommy?" Bobby whispered, his voice hardly audible. He didn't turn back to her to ask the question. He was unable to move his gaze from the dog.

Where was their mother? Lisa wondered. Surely the dog couldn't have gotten into the house without Clara's knowing it, and by now she would have heard them. The dog had already done something to her; Lisa was sure of it. This knowledge crumpled the little composure she had been able to muster. She felt panic rush over her. It was like walking on a frozen lake and falling through the thin ice.

*"Downstairs!"* she screamed and turned Bobby so abruptly toward the basement door and stairs that he nearly fell forward, head over heels down the steps. The moment she took the action, the dog leaped, but Lisa clung to a semblance of logic as she bailed out of the hallway with her brother. She took hold of the basement door and slammed it shut behind them. The sound of the dog's body hitting the closed door sped her flight downward, but Bobby's ungodly scream stopped her midway. It was as though he had torn out his vocal cords with the effort.

They both stared at the bodies below. The gruesome sight of the strange, mutilated dead man crumpled beside their unconscious mother worked like an electrical overload. The circuit breakers in their minds snapped off. All thought came to a stop; even instinctive action shut down. Zombielike, they stared ahead, unable to move, unable to speak. When Lisa had stopped her descent, she had pressed her body against

Bobby's. Now they were conjoined, glued together by their mutual sense of horror. Their hearts beat as one, synchronized in the speed at which they raced the blood around their bodies. Neither could speak. Even the attempt at sound seemed beyond them. They didn't hear the noise behind them as the dog placed its front paws against the door and brought its mouth to the knob.

Neatly stored on the shelves of his mind, packaged like oranges in a crate, were the different new thoughts and new awarenesses Phantom had developed since his escape from the institute. He had handled every original idea carefully, rolling it over and over gently until it became something within his comprehension. To do so, he usually related the new things to old things. Such was the case with the children.

He had been exposed to children in different ways. When he was much younger, he had been placed in a human home environment for a short period of time, his every action restricted, all of his behavior carefully recorded. It was the home of one of the scientists. In many ways that short stay had been the happiest time of his life. He had experienced affection and had seen that humans could be soft and gentle. There were a boy and a girl there too, only the boy was bigger than the girl. They inflicted no pain on him and the tasks that they had him do were far from difficult.

For a long time after he had been taken away from them, he missed them. Whenever a door opened in the lab or a new voice was heard, he perked up in expectation. But a return was not in the design. That portion of the experiment was over; it had served its purpose and those in control of him saw no reason to continue it.

Just for a few moments, when he came out into the hallway and confronted these children, he was thrown back to that time. The images that played on the screen of his memory confused him. All of the recalled stimuli were pleasant and attractive. He half expected the children to come forward and pet him. He listened for the softness in their voices and looked for the pleasure in their faces. But none of this was visible and this wasn't why he had emerged.

Their obvious hesitation and fear ended his reverie. It was natural and logical for him to distrust anything that distrusted him, and it was justification and motive enough for him to go on with his original intentions—to take down the children just as he had taken down the others. When they were able to get behind that basement door before he reached them, he smashed against it, frustrated, and angry at himself for having hesitated. This affection he had recalled, this desire for warm, human contact, was weakness. All that was natural and primitive in him had taught him that survival of the fittest was predicated on an absence of compassion.

Compassion was a human thing, imposed on him only during his short stay within that household. Intelligence had no emotional requisites. He had been developed to seek only clear, logical thought. Because he hadn't moved quickly, he had missed an opportunity. That was an error. Once again he was matched against children in a maze of sorts. Round one was over and the children were ahead. The children would get the reward; he would get the punishment.

They had taught him to be aggressive; they wanted him to want to win. They wanted him to make greater and greater demands on his potential intelligence. This is what he had been taught to do; this is what he would do now.

Right after he had slammed himself against the closed door, he sat back and considered the situation. He knew what was behind the door, what the room below was like and what the exits and entrances were. This was not too dissimilar from a maze in which he had been tested a few times. A small rabbit had been trained to go through a maze that had more than one entrance and exit. He was set loose to catch it.

The maze was very much like others he had been in, except for the extra door. He charged through it after the rabbit, expecting the rabbit to be trapped at the end, with no way out but past him. When he got there, he was surprised that the rabbit was gone. He looked up. There was never a roof on any of the mazes. The scientists stood on a ramp above the maze and watched his actions. They offered no solutions.

He backtracked, sniffing along the rabbit's path, and found the second entrance. He nosed it open and peered out, now understanding how the rabbit had escaped. He was placed in the maze again, only this time he took a different path and arrived at the second door before the rabbit did. When it appeared, he seized it quickly and cut its neck open with a single bite.

It occurred to him that the children could escape through the doorway through which he had first entered the house. He considered going outside and around to it but opted instead to pursue them this way. Even if they did exit through that doorway, he felt confident that he could exit that way as well and catch up to them before they got far from the house. If he moved quickly enough now, he might get to them before they reached that door. In any case, he felt certain they would head in that direction.

Escape from the house didn't enter the minds of either of the children as they stood staring down from the stairway. Instead, they looked for some sign of hope in the yet still body of their mother. When Lisa finally heard the sounds of the dog behind them, she moved slowly down the remaining steps and stepped over the body of the dead policeman. Bobby followed cautiously, afraid even to permit his feet to graze the corpse of the I.D. man.

Lisa knelt beside her mother and shook her body by pushing on her left shoulder.

"Mommy?" she said.

"Mommy, wake up," Bobby said.

Lisa lifted her mother's upper body toward her. Clara Kaufman's eyelids fluttered.

"Mommy," Lisa said again. Both she and Bobby turned and looked up the stairs as the knob on the basement door clicked open.

Clara Kaufman groaned.

*"Mommy!"* Bobby screamed. The upstairs door began to open. Bobby sat down beside Clara and pressed his body to hers. Lisa embraced her even more tightly. Clara focused on the two of them.

"Oh . . . Lisa, Bobby." The pain returned, but she fought it and got herself into a firmer sitting position.

*"The dog!"* Lisa screamed. *"He's coming down!"*

"Oh, God."

Phantom appeared on the top two steps and gazed down at them. He couldn't believe his good fortune. They hadn't gone for the other maze exit after all. It would be easy for him to cut them off from it now.

To the three below, he looked even larger. Because of the angle from which they looked up at him, his size was exaggerated; he took on monstrous proportions.

Clara looked behind her into the utility room.

"We've got to get back in there," she said. She thought about sliding herself along as Lisa pulled her, but Bobby was clinging to her so tightly, she could barely move. He was close to a state of shock because of what had happened with King. She knew he was reliving that terror. His sobbing became more and more hysterical. In a matter of moments, it would be impossible to control him. He wouldn't hear anything she said and he wouldn't feel her hand on his neck.

Even Lisa had begun to cry harder now. The children were entrapping her within the walls of their fear. She looked at the dead policeman and fought back the wave of nausea stimulated by the bloody sight. If only he could be resurrected for a few minutes to protect them, she thought, and then she looked at the gun still in his hand.

A moment after she did so, she looked up at the slowly descending large dog. He stopped as though he realized what she was considering. She was sure that he, too, had looked at that gun. She knew her move would have to be fast and decisive, despite the pain it would bring throughout her body.

She turned and seized the dead man's hand at the wrist and pulled it up to her. The action froze her children for a moment. Their sobbing stopped as they looked on at her effort to free the pistol from the fingers of the corpse. But it seemed glued to the hand.

The dog started a quicker descent and then hesitated when Clara folded her own hand neatly over the dead man's, forcing her right forefinger over the hard, dead one.

Phantom saw the weapon being turned toward him and he crouched down, remembering what the other dog had looked like, how it had jerked about spasmodically after the policeman had shot it in the head.

Clara didn't see his retreat. She thought of all the television shows and movies she had seen where guns had been used, and she vaguely recalled the pulling back of the hammer. She did so quickly and then, with her face turned away from the scene before her, she pressed as hard as she could on the dead man's trigger finger.

Within the closed-in basement, the gun's report was more like an explosion of dynamite. It was deafening. The pistol seemed to jump out of her hand and, with an eerie semblance of life, the dead policeman's arm shot upward and then down. The children screamed. When Clara opened her eyes, the dog was gone from the stairs.

"Quickly," she said when her perusal of the basement showed no signs of the animal, "let's get back into the utility room."

Both of her children gasped for air. Their upper bodies heaved about as though they were both in fits of epilepsy. She could see that they could offer her little assistance. She pressed down on the floor and pushed herself toward the door behind her, but Bobby, clinging to her leg, was like a dead weight.

"Hurry, Bobby, please. Let Mommy go and help get us back in there. Hurry. Lisa . . ." She turned to her daughter. Lisa looked up at the stairs fearfully and then stood up. She went around and tried to get Bobby to release his grip, but the little boy screamed and clung even more tightly.

"I can't . . . he won't."

"All right, baby . . . all right. Just help me go back. We'll pull him along. Take this arm," she said, holding up her right arm, "and pull firmly but gently." Lisa took her mother's wrist and did so. They moved by inches, Bobby too hysterical to give them any real assistance. When they reached the doorway, Lisa looked up at the stairs again. The dog had reappeared. Clara saw him, too. "Don't scream, just pull, pull."

The three of them got into the utility room far enough to start to close the door behind them, just as the dog came charging down the stairs. They slammed it shut only moments before he reached it, all of them screaming at the same time. Clara pressed her body against the door so that her weight would keep the dog from shoving it open. They heard him press his body against it on the other side. Then there was silence.

Clara started to relax until she looked up and saw the handle being turned. It was like a knife through her heart. She stared in disbelief. What kind of a dog was this? Who had trained it to do such things? What more would it be able to do? She looked about quickly and saw the cartons of old things, the dresser they had put down here a year ago, meaning to give it away someday. She knew what had to be done. Some of those things had to be brought to the door to help keep it secure. She was too weak and in too much pain to hold back the large animal for long.

"Honey . . ." She was gasping for breath, herself. What if she blacked out now? Oh God, the children. "You've got to drag some of those cartons over here and we've got to move that dresser against this door. Do you understand?" Lisa nodded. She looked as though she had pulled herself together some. Clara was hopeful. Bobby, almost unconscious now, his body heaving in small, convulsive jerks, still clung to her leg.

Lisa went to the cartons and began pulling on one, sliding it slowly across the cement floor. Clara thought how fortunate it was that they had never carpeted this area. Everything would slide along more easily. Once Lisa got the carton started, she got behind it on her knees and pushed.

"Good, honey. Good. Bobby, help Lisa. Bobby . . ."

Clara felt the door moving inward and pressed her back against it. She moved to the left when Lisa brought the first carton over and pushed it against the door.

"The dresser, Lisa. Try to move the dresser." Clara knew if she lifted her body away from the door to help, the dog would have little to oppose it. One carton was not enough to block the dog from getting the door open enough for him to slip in. In fact, the door opened slightly and she saw the dog's snoot appear.

*"Lisa!"* she screamed, *"Back here, hurry!"* Together they pressed the door shut again. There was some respite as the dog had to turn the handle once more. "The dresser," she whispered. It was more of a gasp. Lisa started for it again.

It barely budged. Lisa began to cry. Clara heard the handle turn open again; she heard the click and felt the dog's power as it pressed its heavy, muscular body against the door. Hope began to sink quickly. Clara felt the blood struggling through her veins. It was as though some great magnet were pulling her down into the floor.

"Back, Lisa, back," she said, and once again the two of them forced the door closed. Clara lowered her head to her chest. She had gone beyond pain. Her adrenaline had taken her beyond normal capabilities, but now, because she felt depressed and defeated, the fatigue and the agony began a slow, definite return. Her body was beginning to turn into dead weight.

Her daughter went back to the dresser. Miraculously, she moved it an inch, then another, and another.

"Good, honey. Good," Clara said. The dresser came closer and closer until Clara had to move away from the door completely to make room for it. Just before she did so, she told Lisa to push as hard as she could so there would be only a short moment without resistance to the dog. The dresser slammed against the door and there was a long moment of silence as they waited to see what effect it would have. The door barely budged. They were safe for the moment.

"Thank God," Clara said. "Good, Lisa, good." She looked down at Bobby. His face was pressed against her thigh; his eyes were closed. The hysteria had driven him into shock and he had fallen asleep. She wiped his face and gently pried his arm loose from her leg.

"I'll put some more stuff against the door," Lisa said. Clara nodded and closed her eyes. She couldn't fight it now. The darkness was coming in, wave after wave. She lowered herself beside her son and tried to embrace him. Seconds later, she was unconscious.

# 11

AT FOUR FORTY-FIVE, Sid Kaufman made his way back to George Friedman's office. Friedman's secretary was getting things together, preparing to leave for the day. When she saw him, there was an expression of guilt on her face. Perhaps she had started this wind-down a lot earlier than need be, Sid thought. At the moment he didn't relish the role of inspector. He smiled and she appeared to relax some.

"Having a productive first day?" she asked.

"Yes, yes I am. Is Mr. Friedman in?"

"No, but he's due back within the hour."

"I was just going to use the phone again."

"Oh, go right in. I'm sure it's all right."

"Thank you," he said. He got behind George's desk, reached the operater quickly, and made the call. Once again, the phone rang and rang. After the third ring, his heart began to sink. By the end of the tenth ring, he was convinced that something terrible had happened. He hung up; then he lifted the receiver and dialed the operator again to place a person-to-person call to Chief Michaels of the Fallsburg Police Department. He was lucky. He caught Harry Michaels minutes before the chief was going to leave the office. Sid explained his inability to reach his wife.

"She wasn't even home around the time the children come back from school," Sid went on, "and she's always there for that."

"All right, Mr. Kaufman. All right. Don't worry. I'll take a ride up to your house myself and check things out, but I'm sure she's probably gone to a relative or a friend. Maybe she's taking the kids to Burger King."

"I don't think so," Sid said. "Listen, are you going to go right up there? I mean, right up there now?"

"I said I would."

"If you get into the house, will you call me? I'll give you the number where I am," he said and recited George Friedman's office phone number. "If you don't get in, call me anyway. Call me collect. I'll wait right by this phone. Please."

"Mr. Kaufman," Harry said, putting on his best fatherly tone of voice, "I know what you've been through. I know what you feel like. I promise, I'm going right up there and I'll call you within fifteen minutes or I'll have my dispatcher call you. Okay?"

"Thank you."

"No problem. Try to relax in the meantime."

Sid hung up and sat back in the chair. He closed his eyes and then opened them quickly to look at the exact time. It was five to five. The police station was only two or three minutes from his house. If he kept to his word, Michaels would call by ten after five, give or take a few minutes. Sid knew it would seem like hours.

As soon as Michaels hung up, he went out to his dispatcher and gave him the phone number.

"I might call you from the car," he said. "You'll call Mr. Kaufman at this number and give him the message I tell you. Got it?"

"Right."

"Where's Sidewater?"

"Hurleyville. There's a cow loose on Brophy Road."

"Great. Why couldn't MacBurn handle that?"

"You told me to send him to Woodbourne today because Philips is out sick."

"I haven't got a patrolman in the South Fallsburg area?"

"Not right now, Chief. You want me to call MacBurn in?"

"No, not yet. All right, I'm heading up to Kaufman's house," he said and went out to his car. His back tires spun on the macadam as he turned around and headed away. He never gave much credence to what some fellow law enforcement officers called the police instinct, but he couldn't help feeling an unusual sense of danger. Maybe it was imposed on him by the note of hysteria in Kaufman's voice, or maybe it was just some delayed reaction to the whole Ken Strasser affair, but whatever it was, it made him tremble. For some reason, an image of Jenny came to mind. He saw her as he'd left her that morning: in the kitchen, gathering the ingredients of the pie she was going to make and bring up to Charley Strasser's house. He smiled at the memory, but his expression changed as soon as the Kaufmans' house came into view and he saw Carlson's car in the driveway.

If Sid Kaufman had called his home only minutes ago, why hadn't someone answered, especially if Carlson was there? he wondered. He pulled in behind the car and studied the front of the house. The front door was slightly open. What could this mean? He opened his door slowly and stepped out. There wasn't a sign of anyone around. The house looked deadly quiet.

He adjusted his gun belt and unclipped the strap holding the pistol securely in his holster. For him that was a considerable action. He had to dig back through his memories to recall the time he had last drawn his gun. In all the time he had been a policeman, he had never once fired at a man, and no one had ever fired at him. He had been in his share of fights; actually, in more than his share.

He started for the house. Sid Kaufman's wife and children had probably just pulled up, he thought, with Carlson right behind them. They'd just forgotten to close the door—probably engrossed with Carlson's methodical questions.

He stopped less than a foot from the house when he heard the phone ringing. Sid Kaufman was most likely trying again. The ringing continued. Why didn't anyone answer it? He looked back at his patrol car, wishing he had brought one of his patrolmen along. Even the dispatcher would have been some comfort. The emptiness of the car, the quiet of the deserted road, and the persistent ringing of the phone filled him with a sense of dread. He was tempted to retreat, but he chastized himself for his uncharacteristic lack of courage.

I'm getting too old for this, he thought again; but he drew his pistol from his holster and went on into the house. Almost as soon as he stepped through the doorway, the phone stopped ringing. The silence that followed was more threatening. He listened for the sounds of people, but there were none. When he continued into the house, he discovered the mess in the kitchen.

"What the hell—" He spun around, his pistol up, anticipating something, but there was nothing there, nothing but the sound of his own heavy breathing. "Carlson!" he called and waited. "Carlson!" He shouted louder.

Then he heard the sound of a little girl screaming. He realized it was muffled and quickly understood that it was coming from the basement. When he reached the opened doorway, he paused and looked behind him because he thought he heard something. The screaming continued, so he started down the stairs.

The moment he saw Carlson's body, he froze. He then brought the hammer back on his revolver and looked about. The girl had stopped her screaming, but he now heard her sobbing behind the closed door. He hesitated to speak, fearing to give away his position without first discovering who or what had done this to Carlson. He moved farther down the stairs and when he reached the bottom, he looked about the basement. He saw nothing.

"Mrs. Kaufman!" he called. There was silence, and then the little girl screamed for her daddy. Harry knelt beside Carlson's body, felt his wrist, and then went for the door. But before he reached it, the dog came out from behind the bar and leapt through the air. To Harry Michaels it looked as if the animal could fly. His jump easily took him across half the basement floor.

Harry had time to raise his left arm protectively and get off one shot. The bullet went wide and the animal seized him at the forearm, snapping the bone almost instantly. Michaels fell over Carlson's body, but he had enough strength and momentum to throw the dog toward the stairway. The dog did not come back at him. It went into a crouch and moved so quickly up the stairway that by the time Harry brought his arm around for another shot, the animal had reached the top.

Harry squeezed off another round. The bullet tore into the doorjamb and sent splinters flying, but the dog whipped itself out of the door before Michaels could shoot again. Just at that moment, the pain in his left arm registered and he fell farther backward. He moaned and took a few deep breaths. There were no sounds coming from behind the door; he imagined the little girl had been driven into a terrified silence.

He struggled to his feet, keeping his eye on the basement doorway. He wanted to put his gun in his holster and hold his left forearm, but he was afraid that the animal would reappear. So he pressed his arm against his body and tried the door to the utility room. It wouldn't budge.

"Hey," he said. "It's the police. It's all right. Mrs. Kaufman?"

"Mommy," he heard the little girl say, "wake up. Mommy."

"Listen, Lisa, it's Harry Michaels. Let me in and I'll help you."

"The dresser is against the door," she said. Her voice was small and pathetic.

He looked back at the stairway and then put his shoulder to the door. It began to give slowly until he built up momentum and shoved it open. As soon as he did so, he saw Clara Kaufman lying on the floor, unconscious, the little boy cuddled up in her right arm. Lisa appeared from behind them, her eyes bloodshot, her face streaked from the tears.

"It's okay," Harry said. "Everything's going to be okay now." He knelt down and felt for Clara's pulse. Satisfied with the strength of it, he turned his attention to the little boy. Bobby's eyes opened slowly and then he sat up quickly, rubbing his face. "Okay, take it easy, buddy. Everybody's going to be all right. Jesus," he said, rising. He stepped out and went right to the phone behind the bar.

After he called for the ambulance and for the dispatcher to bring in all his patrolmen, he dialed the number Sid Kaufman had given him.

"I'm in your house, Mr. Kaufman," he began. "Your children are all right, but your wife's been hurt."

"How badly?" Sid said. "And by what?"

"She'll be all right," Harry said. He had no idea if she would be or not but thought it best to lie at this point. "She'll need some medical treatment, though."

"Can I talk to her?"

"Not just yet."

"She can't talk?"

"Mr. Kaufman, Mr. Kaufman," he repeated. He heard the hysteria in Sid's voice. "I told you I would come right up here and I told you I would call you right away, didn't I? I didn't lie to you, did I?"

"No, no . . ."

"So you've got to believe me now. It won't do you any good not to," he added.

"What happened to her?"

"They had a bad scene here, Mr. Kaufman. They were being terrorized by a dog."

"A dog? A German shepherd?"

"Yes, sir."

"Was she bitten?"

"Just nipped on the wrist. She did a good job of protecting the children. It's all over and I'm getting her to the hospital for a checkup."

"I'm on my way home," Sid said.

"Mr. Kaufman, you'd better drive carefully. It'll do your family no good if you get hurt at this point."

"I understand. Thank you. Chief, Chief," he added before hanging up, "a German shepherd? You're sure it was a German shepherd?"

"I didn't get that long a look, Mr. Kaufman, but I'm sure. I guess your little boy and your wife really saw what they said they saw."

"But why? How?"

"Maybe when you get back, I'll have some answers for you, Mr. Kaufman. Remember, be careful. We'll call the state police and have them on the lookout for you."

"Oh, God," Sid said.

"Amen," Harry said after he hung up.

Phantom heard the policeman arrive; he heard his heavy steps upstairs and knew it was a man. He expected the little girl's scream to bring him down into the basement, and he anticipated that the man would carry a weapon. The way all this came to him surprised him. He was getting better at it. The more he turned to his imagination, the more vivid the images became. It wasn't hard to envision the man on the stairway, and the sound of the man's footsteps helped to create the man's size. Since he was already downstairs, it was difficult, if not impossible, for him to get behind the man, so he decided to hide behind the bar.

He waited, poised. As soon as he saw his opportunity to rush the man, he did so, but he was surprised by the man's strength. After his initial assault, he opted for retreat. He had discovered something unexpected about himself—he did not like head-to-head, face-to-face combat with a man. He needed an advantage, a chance to strike unseen. If that strike did not end the battle, he preferred to withdraw and wait for another opportunity to strike from a hidden location.

With his back to the man, the gunshot filled him with terror. He whined as he rushed around the upstairs corner, and he didn't hesitate in his flight from the house. He went directly to the front entrance and leapt through the screen-door window, tearing the material away from its frame. Once outside, he headed quickly into the forest, half expecting the man to be behind him, firing his gun again and again. He didn't look back until he was deep into the woods, and when he stopped to do so, the sound of his own panting drowned out any sounds that could have come from a pursuer.

Nevertheless, he remained there, studying the trees

and the foliage behind him, looking for some sign of the man or other men. Finally convinced that he was safe, he turned and went on into the forest, moving up the mountain and continuing in a southeasterly direction. When he reached the top, he could see some houses and a major highway before him. The highway was a busy one, but the houses nearbly looked as quiet and peaceful as the ones he had left behind.

He descended the hill, moving with slow but determined steps until he reached the end of the wooded area and entered a long, flat field overgrown with tall rye grass and weeds. No one from the houses before him or the road ahead of him could see him moving over the field. The panic of his flight from the man with the gun had left him. Now he trotted gracefully, almost sleekly, like a fox. His travel through the forest and his escape from the world of men had permitted him to relax his mental powers. He was more of a dog again.

Some bees, working on his right, caught his attention, but he knew enough to stay away from them. He started after a small rabbit but quickly grew bored with the chase. Some field mice looked at him curiously and then burrowed under the earth when he drew too close. He took hold of some blades of grass and chewed them rapidly.

He paused before he reached the highway and sat back on his haunches to clean some stickers out of his fur. He struggled awkwardly with his tail for a while, tearing as much of the annoying weeds from his hair as he could. But, suddenly, he had a whiff of an interesting scent.

Actually, it was far more than interesting; it was enticing. It filled him with a rush of blood. His eyes widened. He held his jaws shut and perked his ears and he felt a stirring in his genitals. Rising to all fours, he sniffed the wind greedily. It was coming from his right. He turned to it magnetically, as if drawn by an invisible leash. He could not fight the urge to go. He wasn't concerned with any dangers, and try as he did to reason with himself, he could do nothing but obey the call of this invisible voice.

It took him to the side of the road, where he paused to study the house and the garage and machinery directly across from him. There were no human beings about, but he sensed that they had been there only a short time ago. To the right of the garage were columns of used refrigerators, a number of electric and gas stoves, and some hot water heaters. A sign braced up against a stick in the ground by the entrance to the driveway advertised the used appliances under the heading, Wilson's Secondhand Shop.

The scent that had brought him here weakened and grew stronger in an undulation that made him dizzy. He didn't seem to notice the cars that whizzed by. Suddenly something caught his eye. He saw the bitch come out of the garage and turn sharply to her right. She headed for the rear of the building. The strengthened scent did not diminish. He tore across the road and leapt over a fallen refrigerator to get to the side of the garage.

The bitch didn't sense him until he was around the corner at the rear of the garage. She was a mixed breed with a good deal of collie in her. Her initial instinct was to growl, but he recognized immediately that the growl was without intent. She was in heat. She wanted the courting to begin.

For the first time in a long time, he was utterly stupefied. Back at the laboratory, they had never permitted him to confront a female dog. That event was a few experiments down on the list. Now, the sexual drive both confused and frightened him.

He went forward. The bitch pretended to snap at him. He feinted and pretended to snap back. She ran into the rear field, but she didn't run hard and when she made a turn to throw him off, she did it so slowly as to invite him to mount her, which he did quickly and firmly. She held his weight comfortably and stood perfectly still, accepting him eagerly.

As soon as he was finished, she shot away from him. Panting, he stood there, watching her run back toward the rear of the garage. When she reached it, she looked back at him as if in challenge, but he wasn't eager for play. He was still fascinated with all that had happened, all that had come over him, and all that he had done. It had gone so quickly, but it had been so satisfying. He had known nothing like it before, and he was eager for it to happen again.

After a few moments, he charged at her. She looked as though she would wait, but just as suddenly, a human voice was heard.

"Candy," the voice cried. "Where are you, you dumb mutt?"

He stopped as the dog went obediently to the front of the garage. When he peered around after it, he saw that a man and a boy had come out of the side entrance to the house. The boy was placing a bowl on the ground for the dog. The dog sniffed it, but then she turned and looked in Phantom's direction. He anticipated that the man and the boy would do the same thing, so he pulled back behind the garage. When he looked out again, the boy was kneeling beside the dog as she ate and the man was walking toward the used machinery.

"She's hungry tonight, Grandpa!" the boy said.

"She's been bumming a lot. She oughta be hungry," the man said. "You'd better take her in, Tony, or she'll be down to Bridgeville again and we'll get a call from the Homestead that she's bothering their customers."

"Okay," the boy said. He went to the side of the house and came back with a leash, which he snapped onto the collar of the dog. After a few minutes, he took the dog back into the house with him and closed the door.

The man remained outside by his used appliances. He went into the garage and came out with a dolly. He loaded a refrigerator onto it and brought it back to the garage. Then he went out and did the same with another and another. He returned one more time for a water heater, but before he returned with that, the side door opened and a woman came out.

"You can't wait for Mac in the morning, canya, Stanley? You gotta do it all yourself."

"Aw, all I'm doin' is selectin' what we're takin'. He'll help me put it on the truck."

"You told Tony you were goin' to take him along."

"So?"

"You know Tami don't like him goin' to New York City, especially that section."

"He'll be with me and Mac. We ain't gonna let him go anywheres."

"I don't know."

"Don't worry about it. She don't hafta know, anyway," he said.

"I don't know."

"You don't know, you don't know. Jesus."

"Well, come in and wash up. It's time to eat."

"Be right there," he said and muttered some more under his breath. The woman went in and, a few minutes later, he followed.

Phantom waited until the door closed and all was quiet. The scent still lingered in the air, holding him close to the house. He was hungry now, but thoughts of going off to search for food were suppressed by his all-encompassing desire to repeat the act of intercourse. He wanted to howl to bring the dog back out to him, but he didn't do it. Instead, he approached the house and searched for ways to enter unseen. He didn't find any. The basement in this house was entered through two metal doors now clamped down over the steps. There was no way for him to get into that.

He retreated to the garage where he could wait and keep an eye on that side door. The sun had fallen low behind the tall trees to the west. Shadows grew deeper, longer. The air grew cooler, although the scent never left. The lights in the house windows became brighter. He could see the people within moving about.

It took some time, but hours later, long after the sun had gone completely, the side door opened again. The boy appeared with the dog on the leash.

"Tie her in the garage," the man behind him commanded. Phantom watched them approach. He slunked in behind the appliances and the truck when the boy reached the garage. The mutt, restless and aware of his presence, struggled against the hold the boy had on her.

"Easy, Candy, easy." The boy set out a dish of water beside the dog. He stroked her a few times and then headed back to the house. Phantom waited until the door was closed again. Then he came out of the shadows and approached the waiting bitch.

Qwen saw that when Maggie reached the lakeside, she became increasingly excited. Her bark was louder, quicker; and she was moving faster. He picked up his own pace to keep up and eventually broke out into a trot as he and the others reached a dirt road that led up from the lake toward a macadam-laid street and the houses. Kevin and Fishman fell farther behind, but Ann remained only two or three yards behind.

The dirt road moved up an incline. It consisted of hard-packed sand and gravel. As Maggie pulled farther away, Qwen envisioned the possibility that Phantom might be just ahead. It was possible they could confront him in a matter of minutes. Up until this moment, he hadn't really given that as much thought as he should have. If the woman was telling him the truth, then it was possible Kevin and Fishman did not realize how dangerous the dog really was. The original belief that they could capture him with little difficulty seemed remote. If there was going to be violence, how would they handle it? How would he?

When Maggie reached the macadam road, she paused and looked back. Turning around, Qwen saw that the two men had dropped considerably behind. Kevin was holding his side and Gerson looked like an exhausted workhorse. Ann, breathing hard but not uncomfortably, caught up with him.

"We're close, huh?"

"Very. I guess it's like perfume—the closer you get to the origin of the scent, the stronger it is. Funny way to identify living things, isn't it—smell?"

"Not really. There are bacteria everywhere; bacteria produce odor."

"For a dog it's like fingerprints," Qwen said, pushing the point. He didn't like the way she could reduce everything he thought remarkable and wonderful to a common denominator, an explainable, scientific fact. When he thought about it, this was what he hated about science—it took the mystery and romance out of life.

Maggie paused only a moment; then she turned left and disappeared.

"Isn't your dog getting too far ahead at this point?"

"She'll know how close to get and where to wait for us," he said. They had both slowed to a quick walk.

"You have such faith in natural things, don't you?" she asked. Her tone wasn't derogatory. It had more the sound of clinical curiosity.

"They're simple. They're honest."

"Are you a religious man? I mean, do you think this

all has some divine design to it?" she asked, gesturing toward their natural surroundings. This time Qwen did detect a note of disdain.

"I don't know for sure, miss, but if there is, you can be sure man is goin' to mess it up." He walked faster and then broke into a trot again. She was right behind him.

"Or improve on it, Mr. Qwen."

He just grunted. They reached the road. Maggie's bark had become shrill. Qwen knew that meant she was at a place where the dog had spent a concentrated amount of time—or she had come upon the dog. He looked back. Kevin and Gerson were into a sprint. They were shouting for Ann and him to wait, but Qwen ignored them. He looked at Ann, and then both of them continued on down the side of the road. They saw Ken Strasser's farmhouse ahead. When they reached it, they stopped to read the sign posted on the doorway, forbidding trespassing or entrance. It was by order of the town police. Maggie had already gone behind the house.

"What do we do?" Ann asked.

"She might have him cornered."

"Then we had better wait for them."

"You wait. I'll start to check it out," he said. He took the safety off his rifle and went to the rear of the house. He stopped when he saw the roped-off area and the diagram of a man's body. Maggie went past it and sniffed the ground before the door of the barn. She looked up at him and wagged her tail as he approached. "Proud of yourself, huh?" His dog came to him and he knelt down to pet her. "But what do you make of all this, girl?" He looked from the roped-in area to the barn door.

"Wait a minute!" Kevin yelled when Qwen stood up and started toward the door.

"What does this mean?" Ann asked. She stood by the diagram.

"It looks like the investigation of a murder," Qwen said.

"Murder?"

"You saw the police sign out there. Something's going on here."

Kevin looked at Gerson. Both of their faces were red with the effort of the pursuit. Kevin was sweating profusely, his hair matted with the dampness. Gerson wiped his forehead with the sleeve of his jacket.

"If he's in there," Kevin said, "I'd better go first. He's used to my voice."

"Suit yourself," Qwen said. "I guess he could open and close a barn door behind him." He stepped back, but he noticed that as Gerson moved forward, his hand reached for his pistol. Kevin went to the door and slowly slid it further open.

"Phantom," he said, "you in here, boy?" He took the chain leash from his backpack and entered the barn. After a moment he announced that it was empty.

"You got one helluva brilliant hound there, mister," Gerson said.

Qwen ignored him and went into the barn. He saw the bed of hay and went right to it.

"He was here," he said. Maggie was at his feet, sniffing the hay and whining. "Wouldn't surprise me if he had something to do with whatever happened out there."

"How do we know the dog was here for sure?" Gerson asked. "This mutt of his could be leading us on a wild-goose chase."

"No, I think Mr. Qwen might be right," Kevin said. "I doubt that his dog has been wrong."

"What do we do now?" Ann asked.

"I don't like this," Gerson said. He stepped forward

to accent his feelings physically. Qwen spit into the hay and walked out of the barn. He stared at the diagram.

"We're going to have to get to a telephone," Kevin said after he came out behind him. "I've got to call Dr. Bronstein."

"There's probably a phone in that house," Gerson said.

"You can't go in there. The police have posted it," Qwen said.

"We're just goin' to make a phone call."

"Trackin' an animal through the woods is one thing, but breakin' into houses . . ."

"Nobody's asking you to do it," Gerson said.

"I've got to get to a phone," Kevin said. "No one expected he'd be out in population and have contact with people."

"Looks like it might be more than contact," Qwen said.

"That's why I got to get to a phone. Can you get in there, Gerson?"

"No problem." He headed for the back door.

"Will Maggie go on?" Ann asked Qwen. "Maybe the dog went back into the forest."

"She can go on, miss. The question is, do I want to?"

"Look," Kevin said. He stopped as Gerson drove his shoulder against the back door of the house and smashed it open. "Let me talk to the director. There might be more money in it for you."

"I got a feeling money's not gonna make that much difference now," Qwen said.

"They'll pay for the damage to the house, don't worry about that," Ann said.

"I ain't worried about that, miss."

He watched Kevin and her follow Gerson in and then he started for the house, himself. He had just reached the back porch steps when he heard the voices and the noise in the nearby woods. He turned to see the policeman and a group of volunteers from the fire department come out of the forest. One of the patrolmen had his gun drawn.

"Hold it," he commanded. "Who the hell are you?"

Qwen dropped his rifle quickly and sat down on the step to wait with Maggie as they all approached. He turned to look into the house and then smiled to himself.

Ain't they gonna be surprised? he thought.

# 12

WITH MAGGIE CURLED up at his feet, Qwen sat on the hard wooden bench in the lobby of the Fallsburg Police Station. The burly chief of police, his forearm now in a cast, and the district attorney had taken Ann, Kevin, and Gerson into the chief's office and left Qwen to wait out here. He had anticipated being called in to join them, but it had been nearly half an hour and no one had sent for him.

Back at Ken Strasser's farmhouse, Qwen had remained outside, too, while the policemen had gone in to confront Gerson Fishman and the two scientists. Not long afterward, two patrol cars were brought up to the house and they were all taken to the station. Qwen was a little surprised that no one had asked him anything.

When he started to talk in the car, Kevin nudged him.

"Just let us handle this," he said.

"I intend to," Qwen said, but when he was left by himself at the station, he began to wonder just how they were handling it. Questioning the dispatcher, he learned the full extent of what the dog had done. He was growing restless and getting ready to demand to know what was happening when two men in business suits, looking like federal agents, arrived and joined the group in the chief's office. The dispatcher had sent out for coffee and sandwiches. Qwen was given something to eat, but his impatience was intensifying. More "agent types" arrived. Some radio and newspaper reporters appeared but were kept outside the station. Maggie grew restless and Qwen demanded the dispatcher to interrupt whatever was going on inside to tell Kevin that Qwen had to see him. A few moments later, Qwen was taken to a small room, reserved for questioning suspects. He waited for a little more than ten minutes before Kevin finally joined him.

"Sorry you were kept waiting so long," he said. He closed the door behind him and Qwen was a little surprised at their privacy and Kevin's calm. Weren't they in trouble?

"Well, what the hell's goin' on? People comin' and goin' . . . I got the full story on what the dog has done."

"I know. It's terrible. Ann's taking it hard. She feels responsible."

"Maybe she is. Maybe you all are."

Kevin looked up at him sharply. Then he reached into his jacket pocket and came out with an envelope.

"This was just delivered for you," he said and handed it to Qwen. He opened it and took out the neatly folded wad of money. "Dr. Bronstein decided you performed your services as requested."

"I don't get it. We didn't catch him yet."

Kevin didn't reply. Then he held his hand out. "Thanks for everything. There's a car and driver out front to take you back to your truck."

"Did they catch him?"

"No, but they will."

"I don't feel as though I earned the money," Qwen said.

"The people who have to pay you feel otherwise. No sense arguing with them."

"No one wants to talk to me to know about trackin' the creature?"

"They feel confident," Kevin said. "You know, bringing in the pro's. Not that you're not one," he added quickly.

"I was all right until the animal did some real damage, is that it?"

"Something like that. I don't know. Look, I've got to get back in there. Dr. Bronstein has arranged everything for you. Good luck and thanks again," Kevin said. "The car's right outside. Oh, and you'd better not get involved with those reporters. A statement's being prepared for them. It's best the—"

"Pro's handle it. I know."

Kevin smiled. "So long," he said and walked out.

Qwen looked down at the money in his hand. "Jesus, Maggie," he said. The dog sniffed at it. "Yeah, something stinks all right," he said.

When he got back out to the station lobby, the dispatcher was waiting for him.

"It's the unmarked dark blue car right out front," he said. Qwen nodded.

The moment he opened the door, the reporters, gathered around their vehicles, turned his way. Some started in his direction, but the dispatcher at his side put his hand up. There were groans and complaints, but no one bothered him. He went directly to the vehicle and opened the back door.

"Hop in, Maggie," he commanded. But his dog cringed and growled. Qwen bent down and looked in.

"You'd think your dog would know me by now," Gerson Fishman said. Qwen didn't move. "Come on, we gotta get back."

"In, Maggie," Qwen commanded with more authority. Maggie got into the back seat and curled up on the floor as far away from Fishman as she could get. Qwen stepped over her and sat down, closing the door behind him. The driver, one of the men in a business suit, didn't even look back. The car started away.

"How can they do without a man of your importance?" Qwen asked, but his sarcasm was lost on the big security man.

"They got me doin' all kinds of things, trapper. It comes with the territory."

Maggie began to growl again, but it was a low, steady, motorlike sound that was barely audible. For Qwen it was enough. He put his rifle beside him on the seat and looked ahead at the oncoming darkness. Fishman lit a cigarette and rolled the window down to throw out the match. He sat back and stared ahead like a man being taken to his execution.

"Nobody really knows what's goin' on, do they?" Qwen said.

"The people who hafta know, know," Gerson replied. "Whaddya care? You got paid, didn't ya?"

"Yeah, but I'm not sure for what."

"Money's money."

"Not all the time," Qwen said.

Fishman laughed. "Give me whatever you don't think is right," he said. Qwen looked at the driver, who still hadn't turned around or said anything.

They continued on out of the hamlet and rode steadily toward the highway that would get them back to the institute the quickest way. The traffic was light, and for long periods of time they were alone on the road.

"Hey," Fishman called to the driver. "Don't this vehicle have a radio?"

The driver said nothing. He leaned over and turned on the radio, tuning in quickly to a loud rock station. Fishman didn't mind and the driver seemed oblivious to everything. The music bothered Maggie. She lowered her head between her paws as though to block it out.

"What's everyone, deaf in here?" Qwen asked.

"What's that?" Fishman laughed.

Qwen knew the road. He had been on it many times before. He was familiar with the billboards and the signs. They came to a long stretch between communities. Houses could only be seen in the distance. The driver looked into his rearview mirror. There were no cars behind them or oncoming. He reached up and adjusted the mirror while slowing down at the same time. Qwen understood it to be some kind of signal.

He knew there was a side road just ahead, so he anticipated the turnoff. Just before it happened, Fishman reached in under his jacket. Qwen, just as quietly and as unobtrusively, put his finger around the trigger of his rifle and let the barrel fall across his lap. The moment the car came to a stop, Qwen saw Fishman's hand emerge with the pistol in it.

There was no mental debate, no indecision about what he would do. A life in nature had taught him the validity of instinct. For many animals in the wild, a moment's hesitation was the difference between saving themselves and sudden death. They didn't have the luxury of philosophizing; that was a privilege only the truly civilized enjoyed, and Qwen understood that he wasn't in a civilized environment at this time, not by any stretch of the imagination.

He lifted the barrel of his rifle just as Gerson brought the pistol around. Qwen squeezed the trigger. His bullet struck Fishman in the forehead and ripped through the brain before settling against the skullbone. At the same time, the driver spun around with what looked to be a thirty-eight special in his right hand. Qwen brought the stock of his rifle up in a swift, swinging motion and caught the hand and the pistol squarely, sending the gun flying into the door window. Maggie was up, growling. She leapt into the front seat as Qwen reached over the slumping body of the dead security man and grasped the driver under the chin. He pulled the man's head back as hard as he could and brought his rifle barrel across the man's adam's apple, seized both sides of the gun, and pulled it up. The driver gagged. Satisfied that the man was incapacitated, Qwen reduced the pressure and brought the rifle barrel back, placing the end against the driver's head.

"Open that door slowly," he commanded, "and step out. Keep your hands where I can see 'em."

The man coughed and gasped to get back his breath, but he reached for the handle. Maggie remained close to him on the seat, her teeth flashing. The driver stepped out of the car and Qwen climbed over the seat to get to the wheel.

"Tell whoever it is you work for that now they have two wild animals on the loose. Only, this one can talk," he added and closed the door. Then he turned the car around and went back to the main highway to chauffeur the corpse of Gerson Fishman back to the institute. He wanted to leave this car and get his truck.

He went only halfway up the side road that led to the secret complex and got out of the car. Something told him that it would be better to go the rest of the distance on foot, keeping to the shadows. Maggie sensed the need to be surreptitious. She kept close to his feet and moved as silently as Qwen.

When he got close to the complex, he crouched in the brush and studied the scene. There were two security guards at the gate and another one of those men dressed in a business suit. They spoke in low murmurs but it was obvious to Qwen that they were interested in what was going to come up the road.

Looking all the way to the right, he noted that his truck wasn't where he had left it. It occurred to him that if his demise had been as well planned out as he now imagined, the truck, of course, would have been disposed of, too. It was better for them if all traces of his involvement with the institute were erased.

He went back to the car and considered his options. Once the driver got in contact with his superiors, they were sure to send people to Qwen's home. He had to go somewhere where he would be safe for a while, so he could think and make some decisions. He certainly couldn't use the vehicle much longer; it was too easily identified. He decided to leave it where it was and head into the forest. There was enough moonlight for him to make his way.

He would go east to old Sam Cohen's shack. The old coot had been a friend of his father's and lived just the way his own father had lived fifty years ago. There was no running water, no electricity, and no indoor bathroom facilties. To Qwen it was as though the old man camped out year-round. He was sure Sam was a little senile.

Looking back one more time before disappearing among the trees, he thought about Gerson Fishman, dead in the backseat of the car. He didn't have any regrets about it; it had been either kill—or be killed. He just wondered how he would explain his side once they'd had a chance to rearrange the facts.

And then he realized wherein his hope lay—once people discovered what kind of creature these people had created, they would understand what kind of people they were and would give credence to his explanation. How ironic, he thought as he broke out into a trot, that his fate might very well be tied in with the dog's fate.

And like the dog, he thought of ways to throw off the same pursuers and put distance between himself and the institute that loomed behind him like a nightmare remembered from a sleep of madness.

* * *

The state police called Harry Michaels at home to let him know that Sid Kaufman was less than an hour from the hospital. He had asked them to call because he felt that he should be there to greet the man. Of course, Jenny bawled him out for it.

"You've got a fractured forearm, you've been through more hell in one day than you've been for an entire career, and you want to get up and go out again. It's almost midnight, Harry."

"I know, but that man's goin' to have a lot of questions."

"Do they have to be answered tonight?"

"I feel a little responsible," he said. He rose from the couch where he had fallen asleep in his clothes while watching the late news. Jenny had made him hot milk and had remained at his side, sitting in the old soft-cushioned chair, his chair, the chair she had threatened a hundred times to donate to the dump. Tonight she enjoyed sitting in it; she enjoyed the feel of its worn material and the weakness in its springs. It symbolized her husband, a part of him that was worn but precious; tarnished with age and use but as valuable as a youthful memory. For the first time in a long time, she felt the fragility of their lives. From the moment she had learned of all the terrible events, she hadn't stopped shivering inside. She did a good job of hiding it, covering it with her shell of sarcastic wit. Even so, she sensed that Harry saw through her. He was just playing along for both their sakes.

"Good lord, Harry, how the hell are you responsible for this?"

"I should have paid more attention to the stories Sid Kaufman told me."

"What stories? His son's dreams about a dog, and his wife imagining their dog came back to life?"

"It wasn't a dream and it wasn't someone's imagination."

"You sent patrols up there, you went there yourself."

"I sensed something was wrong. I felt it, dammit," he said.

"You know Harry, you should have been a rabbi or even a priest. You have the personality and the mentality for it."

"I won't be long."

"I'll be asleep. I shoulda gone to sleep an hour ago."

"I'm just going up to the hospital and back," he said, answering her unspoken question.

"I'm not interested. And besides, I don't believe you."

"Jenny, if you saw those children—"

"I don't want to hear any more about it," she said quickly. He smiled and kissed her on the cheek. "I'm not waitin' up for you, Harry Michaels."

"Good."

"How can you drive with that arm like that?" she asked as he went to the door.

"It's no problem."

"My mother warned me about you. She told me not to trust a man with bushy eyebrows."

"Your father had bushy eyebrows."

"That's how she knew."

He left his laughter behind him, but on the way to the hospital, he made a firm decision about himself. He decided that he would give it a couple of weeks and then inform the town board that he intended to retire as soon as they had determined a replacement for him. He told himself that he was doing it for Jenny, but in his heart he knew that he was tired. His time had come.

Sid Kaufman arrived at the hospital only fifteen minutes after Harry did. He knew the man had been traveling fast. At this late hour, there were few non-hospital personnel around. Lights had been turned down low and a quiet, subdued mood prevailed. He and one of the men on the hospital's security staff had a conversation carried out in low tones.

But Sid Kaufman's entrance shattered the mellow atmosphere. He rushed in, exhausted from the drive, his face filled with anger and anxiety. Before he even reached the receptionist at the front desk, he demanded to know his wife's whereabouts. Harry moved forward to greet him.

"Mr. Kaufman. I'll take you to her."

"Chief. How is she?"

"She's all right, she's all right."

"What the hell happened to you?"

"It's part of it all. I'll explain as we go up. She's on the fifth floor."

"ICU?"

"Yeah."

They stopped at the elevator and Sid straightened his posture.

"I'm here. No more bullshit. What happened?"

They got into the elevator and Michaels pushed the button.

"The dog got into the house and attacked her. He came at her more like a bull than a dog, striking her in the ribs with his head. He cracked her rib and . . . the rib punctured a lung. They call it pneumothorax. I'm not trying to impress you with big words. I just wanted to remember everything right."

The elevator stopped at the fifth floor.

"What are they doing now?"

"It's going well. They inserted a chest tube to depressurize the area around the lung. The lung will self-inflate and she'll heal."

"Christ, where are my children?"

"Your in-laws took them home with them. They're okay, but they had another terrible scare. A policeman was killed in your house."

"What? The dog did all this? What kind of a dog was it, for Christ's sake?"

"A military dog," Harry said. "The government fucked up."

"Military dog? What's a military dog doing around my house?"

"Apparently it escaped from a training center, a secret one. They've been doing new things with the training and this dog went berserk."

"That's the story?"

"That's what they told me. They were out looking for it and had tracked the animal to Ken Strasser's house not long after all this happened. I'll tell you more in the morning. They promised to have someone at the station when you're ready."

Sid nodded and started for the door to ICU. Then he turned back.

"Your arm? You got that in my house?"

"Yeah."

"I guess I owe you my family."

"No, sir. I'm just doing what they pay me to do."

"No one gets paid to do this," Sid said and went inside.

Harry stood there a moment and then nodded. "You might have something there, Mr. Kaufman," he muttered. "You might have something there."

When Michaels got to his car, the fatigue hit him, but he couldn't keep his mind from working all the way home. The government people, especially that woman, struck him as odd. Everything had become so specialized these days, even the training of a dog. With all the new technological weaponry this country had, why be so interested in developing better attack dogs? he wondered. It was probably just another way to waste the taxpayers' money, he thought, only this time there were going to be a good many red-faced officials, even with the subdued way they were presenting the facts to the press.

At least these military people were in charge, now; they had the responsibility of finding the animal and protecting the population. By now a contingent of soldiers from Fort Drum was on the way. At first light they would comb those woods so thoroughly they would find Indian arrowheads. It was all right with him. They should clean up their own mess, Harry thought.

Hopefully, they would do it quickly and this would all be over. It was already over for poor Ken Strasser and Tom Carlson. He shook his head and tried to remember how it all had started. And then he recalled Sid Kaufman's dog and that bizarre event.

It was beyond him what that had to do with all this, and he was tired of thinking. He couldn't wait to get home and crawl into bed beside Jenny. He knew she'd be wide awake when he arrived, but she wouldn't let on that she had waited up. Just before he turned over and closed his own eyes, he'd say, "Good night, Jenny," and she would poke him. He smiled, thinking about it.

Phantom lifted his head from his paws and listened intensely to all the sounds that entered the garage. It was as though he had been kicked, but it was his sixth sense, his undiminished animal instinct that stirred him from his sleep. He recognized the feeling. It was the same one he had experienced back in that house, sleeping on the little boy's bed. It told him that he was still being pursued and that the pursuers were drawing closer.

Only moments ago, at the crack of dawn, the woods around the Kaufman residence had been deliberately filled with bedlam. The search had been designed in the fashion of a battle. The forest had been divided into sectors, and in each sector men were driving toward each other in pincer movement. In less than an hour, two helicopters would be brought in, and army personnel in jeeps were being sent to patrol the surrounding highways.

Phantom looked at the bitch. Since she was not the object of any hunt or the potential victim of a predator, she slept peacefully. Nothing alarmed her. She continued to enjoy a sleep of contentment and fulfillment. But he stood up and sniffed the air to sift the breezes caught in the garage doorway. The scents discouraged him and filled him with fear. They warned him of packs of men, but packs of a larger number than he could imagine.

He whined; he couldn't help it. The vaguely lit world was fraught with danger. The bitch opened her eyes and, seeing him up and about, rose quickly in anticipation. But he was concentrating on avenues of escape. He walked right past her as though she weren't even there; he stepped out onto the driveway. The sun itself was not visible because of the heavy forest to the east, but the dawn light filtering through the trees made the leaves look phosphorescent. The darkness, which had been a friend to him, was in retreat everywhere.

He turned and started to the right, but after traveling only a dozen feet or so, he stopped. They were coming from that direction, as well. They were as clear to him as if they were standing right before him. Spinning quickly, he went into a run and headed toward the rear of the house. He drove himself through the heavy brush and splashed through some swampy ground. There was forest this way, too, but no sooner had he reached the rim of the trees than he heard the not too distant bark of hound dogs. He was going directly toward them.

Frustrated, he stopped and remained in the same

spot for nearly a minute. Not since leaving the institute had he felt so restricted. It was as though they had thrown invisible chains over him. How could he flee? In what direction should he go?

He looked back at the garage. The bitch had started her own barking, calling to her masters, demanding food. He trotted to the right and then moved back slowly until he reached the rear of the garage. The side door of the house opened and the boy emerged with a dish of food. While the boy walked to the garage, Phantom slunk against the opposite side of the building. There he waited, listening to the boy talk to the bitch.

"Okay, Candy," the boy said, "you can run loose a while, but I gotta tie you up again before we leave. Grandma says so."

The bitch didn't run off. She stayed there, eating her food. A few moments later, the boy was called back to the house. After he went inside, Phantom appeared in the garage entrance. The bitch had cleaned her dish, but she growled possessively, anyway. He ignored her and went toward the rear of the garage instead, hiding himself behind sacks of fertilizer and a small tractor.

The bitch looked at him curiously, but she didn't follow him to the rear of the garage. Instead, she took advantage of her freedom and headed off down the road to the right. Almost immediately afterward, a car pulled into the driveway. The man who got out was big, over six feet four and easily two hundred and fifty pounds. Before he reached the side entrance, the door opened.

"On time for a change," Stanley said. "That's good."

"Well, I promised Dora I'd be back 'for seven. She's got somethin' goin' for her sister. Hiya, Tony."

"I'm goin' too," Tony said.

"No shit."

"Don't make a big thing of it. His grandmother's pissed off. Okay, boy, get your jacket. Mac and I are goin't' finish loadin, the truck."

"Right, Grandpa."

The two men came down to the garage. Phantom lowered himself as close to the floor as he could, but it didn't matter. The two men were intent on the loading of the used appliances and didn't look into the garage once.

Just after they finished, a helicopter was heard coming from the east. They looked to the tops of the trees and saw it sweeping over the forest. Its low altitude made it curious, but their curiosity was whetted even more when a military jeep went by.

"What the hell is it, an invasion?"

"Beats the hell out of me," Mac said. They watched the helicopter go over the house and head south. Tony came charging out of the house to see it.

"What's that, Grandpa?"

"I don't know, son. You say good-bye to your grandmother?"

"Yep. Oh, I gotta tie up Candy. Where's Candy?"

"We don't have time to go looking for that mutt. Your grandmother'll do it. Get in."

"How many stops do we have, Stanley?" Mac asked.

"Four this trip."

"All in the Bronx?"

"Yep. Just finish tying down that canvas and I'll be right out," Stanley said, and he went to the house. Mac tightened the rope of the canvas so the rear of the truck was somewhat closed in. All the used appliances were secure as well. Satisfied, he got into the truck cab and he and the boy waited. A few moments later, Stanley emerged. He took a quick look at the rear of the truck and then got into the driver's seat.

Almost as soon as he did so, Phantom emerged from

the rear of the garage. Crouching down and keeping to the side, he moved with the muscular sleekness of a bobcat. The truck engine started, and the vehicle began to move forward slowly. Phantom paused at the garage entrance. Despite the sound of the truck's engine, he could hear the voices of men approaching from the forest to the left. They had successfully followed his path. In a few moments they would be on him. He saw and he understood.

Just as the truck reached the bottom of the driveway and began its turn onto the highway, Phantom shot out of the garage and ran after the vehicle. He leaped onto the rear and landed between an old refrigerator and a porcelain stove. The two men and the boy inside the truck cab did not hear him or see him. They were talking loudly and laughing.

He crouched down and worked his way in between the used appliances, keeping himself well under the canvas as he did so. A moment later, he was out of sight. The truck picked up speed and continued on down the country highway that would take it to Route 17 and east to New York City. They passed a military jeep coming from the opposite direction, but the two soldiers in it did not look at the truck. They thought their mission was somewhat stupid, anyway, and they were involved in their own conversation.

As the truck disappeared down the highway, a group of ten soldiers emerged from the woods. Soldiers also emerged from the forest behind the house. The groups joined up on the road and the soldiers traded jokes and cigarettes. Someone shouted as Candy came trotting back up the road and there was a lot of laughter. Mrs. Wilson came out her front door and stood on the porch.

"What the hell's goin' on here?" she demanded. All of the soldiers quieted down quickly and one of the sergeants stepped forward.

"Sorry, ma'am. We're on a search."

"What?" She looked at them as though they had stepped out of the evening news.

"We're looking for a dog, a big German shepherd. Have you seen any?"

"You're all out looking for a dog?"

"It's not just any dog, ma'am. This one is kinda dangerous. If you've seen one around here . . ."

"Do you know what time of the morning it is? I haven't even finished breakfast."

"Sorry. That your dog?" he asked as Candy stopped on the front lawn and gaped inquisitively at the soldiers.

"It is, and it ain't a German shepherd."

"Oh, we know that, ma'am."

"Come here, Candy," she called and clapped her hands. The dog ran up to the porch. She looked out at the soldiers again, shook her head, and then went inside with Candy.

A moment later, orders were given and the soldiers broke out into new directions. The second helicopter appeared from the northwest and crossed over the field. And then, all was quiet again.

A few miles down the road, the truck bearing used appliances turned onto the entrance to the quickway route to New York. This far from the city limits, there was barely any traffic; but even when the truck rode into some traffic, it was difficult for any of the drivers behind it to make out the large German shepherd neatly settled in the rear. He knew what it was to travel in a vehicle, but what pleased him most was that as the miles ticked off, the sense of danger he had experienced back at the Wilson house lessened and lessened until it became nothing but a memory.

# 13

QWEN SLEPT LONGER than he had expected to, but what eventually woke him was the sound of music. He opened his eyes, thought for a moment, and then reached for his rifle and sat up quickly, so quickly that he frightened Sam Cohen; the seventy-four year old man lost his grip on the small frying pan, letting it fall into the sink. Qwen had sacked out on the naked mattress placed on the floor of the kitchen in the two-room shack.

He knew there wasn't any point in explaining any of the situation to Sam, so he merely told him he needed a place to stay for a while and the old man brought out the mattress. Despite his forgetfulness, he was still quite capable of taking care of himself. He had two sons living less than fifty miles away. They took turns visiting him once a week, but they had given up on all attempts to get their father to leave his primitive living conditions.

The music surprised Qwen because he knew there wasn't any electricity. He spun around and saw the battery-operated music box on the front windowsill.

"When the hell did you get that?"

"Donald brought it up yesterday. Says it'll keep me from talking to myself so much," Sam said and ran the fingers of his right hand through some of the loose, thin gray hair that still grew in patches over his freckled skull. Qwen remembered when he'd had rust blond hair. He used to keep it long and brushed back over his neck. Whenever he went into town, strangers thought he was a hippie or an older rock musician. "It's got a clock on it and it just comes on by itself and goes off by itself. I forgot all about it. Sorry."

"That's all right. I slept too long as it is."

"Figured I'd make some eggs. Ain't often I get an overnight guest."

"Can't imagine why not," Qwen said, and they both laughed. There was an affinity between them, making Qwen seem more like Sam's son than Sam's sons did. Qwen understood this; he understood why there could be a warmer relationship between Sam and him than between Sam and his sons. His sons, although they didn't vocalize it often, were embarrassed by a father who rejected most of what was called modern society. He wasn't illiterate, but he had little formal education. He'd spent most of his life as a farmer and a hunter, working with his hands. After his chicken and dairy farm had become too much for him, he sold his property but kept the shack used for hunting and fishing trips. It was where he had spent many happy days, so it was most logical to him to hold onto it.

"You're just an older version of Huckleberry Finn," Qwen told him.

Qwen got up and went to the hand pump. The cold water shocked him into complete alertness.

"That's the best cure for a hangover I ever felt," he said.

" 'Cept you didn't have one, so it's a waste of a cure." They laughed again and Sam put up the eggs.

Qwen opened the door and stepped outside. Sam had let Maggie out earlier to do her business, and she was sprawled comfortably at the entranceway, soaking up the early morning sun. There wasn't any fog this morning; the air was sharp and crisp. Qwen took a deep breath. Memories of the night before seeped into his consciousness with the impact of polluted thoughts. They poisoned his joy. If he hadn't been alert enough and Gerson Fishman had gotten off that shot. . . .

It made him angry to think about it and also to think that he had become something of a fugitive. If anybody should be a fugitive . . .

His thoughts were interrupted by the voice of the radio newscaster. News headlines were being announced, and the dog story was number one. Qwen rushed back inside and turned it up.

"A military dog has gone berserk in the Sullivan County area," the newscaster said. "Two men are dead, a woman was badly injured, and she and her children were terrorized for hours by the animal. Fallsburg town police chief, Harry Michaels, reports that the dog was part of a new training exercise carried out by the army in a nearby secret compound. The dog escaped and made its way to the South Fallsburg area where it committed the violent acts. Chief Michaels went on:

" 'The dog is still loose, but a contingent of soldiers from Fort Drum are searching the area thoroughly. They have two helicopters and a number of vehicles. They expect to either capture or destroy the dog in a matter of hours. They have asked to handle the problem themselves and frankly, I'm happy about that.'

"Government officials are embarrassed by the event, and talks which will result in significant compensation for the families of the dead and injured are already underway. Military officials have declined to make any comments until the situation is under control. In the meantime, any residents of the area who see a large German shepherd in their vicinity are asked to call the Fallsburg town police, whose dispatcher will forward the information to the army command post.

"On another front, the proposed hearing for the Loch Sheldrake sewer treatment plant renovation has . . ."

Qwen turned off the radio. Why weren't they reporting the death of Gerson Fishman? Why wasn't there a story about him? And what was this fairy tale about a military dog gone berserk?

"I'm scramblin' 'em," Sam said.

"Huh?"

"The eggs."

"Oh, yeah. I've got to get to a telephone," Qwen thought aloud. Sam looked at him.

"You'll hafta get back to town," he said.

"I don't wanna go back to town. Not just yet."

"Well . . . I'll tell ya what you could do. Go down to the river and take my rowboat to Keebler's Landing. They got a phone."

"Yeah. Yeah, that's a good idea, Sam. Thanks."

The old man smiled. "Still some smoke in the old chimney, eh?"

Qwen laughed. The coffee began to perk and the aroma of it and the eggs awakened his appetite. The food filled him with encouragement. He had seen and spoken with that police chief for only a few minutes, but it had been long enough for him to make an initial impression, an impression, admittedly, heavily dependent on instinct. The man's too small-town, too honest to be part of all this, he thought. He was being used, just as Qwen was being used. He was the man to whom Qwen wanted to talk as soon as possible.

"So tell me," Sam began as he poured the coffee and put down the platter of eggs, "what have you been doin' with yourself lately?"

Qwen laughed, thinking about what it would be like

to tell the story. "I've been on a hunt," he said, "only I think I was after the wrong animal most of the time."

"No shit. That happened to me once. I was trackin' a fox with my dog, Mike, when . . ."

"Where is Mike?" Qwen asked, realizing the dog wasn't around.

"Somethin' caught his attention a few days ago. He went off trackin' it and he ain't been back since. Probably after a bitch in heat. Which just goes to show you what a piece of tail could do to a good friendship," Sam said.

Qwen laughed, but he couldn't help wondering how close the German shepherd had come during his zigzagging away from the institute and if Mike had crossed his path. There was no sense in bringing it up. It would only lend an element of darkness to a world the old man still saw as bright and alive.

"Sam," Qwen said, "the more I see of the world, the more I think you're smart stayin' out here in the lap of Nature."

"Well," the old man said chewing his eggs slowly and thinking about it, "I got no complaints about the landlord."

Phantom awakened when the truck was halfway across the George Washington Bridge. The sound of traffic hadn't bothered him. In fact, the monotonous sound of the truck's engine and the tires whistling over the highway had lulled him into sleep. What stirred him back to consciousness was the scent of the sea water. It intrigued him. He stood up and shook himself quickly. Then he peered out between the used appliances and saw the line of cars and trucks. The sight amazed him. Some of the drivers saw him, too, and stared back with almost as much amazement. He backed up as the truck exited to the Cross-Bronx Expressway and picked up speed. Twice when the truck slowed down behind traffic, he was tempted to jump off, but he hesitated because he was disoriented.

From the Cross-Bronx Expressway, the truck turned onto Webster Avenue and headed south. He peered out again and saw the people and the traffic and the hubbub of the city world. The sight was both fascinating and frightening. He alternated between growling and whining. As he stepped farther forward, people along the sidewalks and the streets began to see him. Most accepted him as some kind of guard dog taken along to protect the merchandise, even though it was used appliances.

He turned his head from side to side to catch the origin of the sounds of horns, squealing brakes, a whistle, people shouting, and the terrific sound of a wrecking ball as a crane operator sent it crashing into the side of a partially demolished building. The activity and noise were abusive to his nervous system. He had experienced nothing like it in the laboratory. He longed to be back in the forest, traveling through the shade of trees, moving through a world that was so silent at times that he could hear himself breathing.

The truck turned off the avenue and continued down a side street. The reduced activity was welcome, but the closeness of the buildings and the overall sense of being entrapped within stone and steel angered him. He went to the edge of the truck bed and when the truck slowed down to squeeze between a double-parked car and another vehicle, he jumped into the street.

For a moment after the truck began moving again and started away from him, he had the impression that he had made an error. The truck was, after all, his only contact with the world in which he felt secure and dominant. Here he was so unsure and confused that he was nearly in a panic. He took a few steps toward the departing vehicle and then stopped. It had picked up speed and gone on to the end of the block, where it turned left and then disappeared.

He looked about. The line of apartment houses on his right ran uninterrupted to the end of the block, but to his left they were broken up by a vast lot of demolished buildings. At this point, the pile of rubble was more attractive to him than the houses. He went to it and sniffed about, looking for some signs of other wildlife. His inspection brought forth some rats that scurried in and out of the chunks of concrete and stone. He didn't chase them.

Across the street two men came out of a doorway but paid no attention to him. He watched them walk off and then he went out to the street again. He started to cross it, but an oncoming vehicle, being driven too fast by the teenagers inside, drove him back. They shouted at him from the car windows. He stood on the side and watched the car squeal around the turn at the end of the street.

For the first time, he noticed a man lying on the sidewalk twenty feet or so ahead of him. The man was curled up on a piece of cardboard. There was an empty bottle of gin in a paper bag beside him. When he went up to the man and sniffed his face, the man's eyes fluttered, but he only groaned and turned over; he was no threat and of no interest.

There was nothing to do but go on exploring. He reached the end of the street and turned down the direction the truck had gone. When people on this street saw him, they either stepped aside or crossed to the other side. He noted how no one wanted to confront him directly. This was encouraging to him and he sped up. Now his interest was in finding something to eat. He picked up the scent of food being cooked nearby and stopped when he reached a stoop. Without hesitation, he ran up the steps to the pale brown door of the aged brownstone. He had no problem with it; it opened when he merely pressed his head against it.

The odors in the hallway of the building weren't all appetizing, but his hunger had grown now, and he was willing to ignore everything but that. He trailed the scent of the food to a door at the far end of the hall. He stopped, sat back on his haunches, and tried the doorknob. It didn't turn. Frustrated, he growled and then pawed the door. Moments later, an elderly black man, dressed in a pair of white pants and a plaid flannel shirt, opened the door. He stepped back in amazement.

"Holy shit, where'd you come from?" he said.

Phantom didn't hesitate. He shot through the opening and entered the run-down apartment. He went right through the living room, jumped over the worn couch, and trotted into the kitchen. The old man had put out a plate of bacon and eggs for himself.

"Hey, what the hell—" He came up behind the dog as quickly as he could, but Phantom didn't hesitate. He leapt onto the table and attacked the plate of food. "Get the hell outta here. Hey!" The old man lifted a kitchen chair and swung it at the dog. Phantom took the blow as though it had been delivered by a five-year-old. He didn't let it interrupt his wolfing down of the food. The man struck him again and again.

When the food was gone, he turned his attention to the man. The old man saw this and suddenly realized the size of the animal he was attacking. He had seen dogs before in the neighborhood, but most of them looked mangy and underdeveloped. This animal was healthy and strong, and unlike the other dogs, this one didn't cower and slink away when chastised or threatened.

He was first puzzled and then terrified by the calm way in which the dog looked at him. He told himself that if he didn't know better, he'd think the animal was trying to decide whether or not he was worth the effort.

Actually, that was exactly what Phantom was thinking. He sensed no danger from this man. The man carried no terrible weapon and exhibited very little physical strength. Arrogantly, Phantom turned away from him and scrutinized the kitchen. The old man saw this as an opportunity to effect an escape. He stepped back and ran out of his own apartment, screaming for help, first in the hallway and then from the stoop of the building.

No one opened a door in the building. Cries of help weren't unusual in this neighborhood, even in broad daylight. Out on the stoop, he attracted the interest of some passersby, but it was a group of three teenagers who crossed the street to listen to his story. The youngest was fifteen, but they all wore a streetwise look that made them appear older. The fifteen-year-old was white, and the two older boys were black.

"What the fuck's the matter with you?" the bigger of the two black boys said.

"There's a fuckin' monster dog in my apartment, dammit!"

"No shit."

"I can't get it out."

"What's it worth?"

The old man looked back through the building's hallway and then at the teenagers.

"All I got is two bucks," he said. He reached into his pants pocket to show it.

"Two bucks? To get a monster?" All the boys laughed.

"You got any cigarettes?" the fifteen-year-old asked.

"Yeah. There's a pack in the kitchen on the counter. You can have it," the old man said. The boys sensed that he was lying, but their curiosity about what was in his apartment got the better of them.

"Take the two bucks, Tutu," the big black boy commanded. Tutu scooped it out of the old man's fingers and the three boys went into the building. They stopped at the opened apartment doorway and listened. Phantom, unable to open the refrigerator, had opened a cabinet door and was pawing out all the contents.

"Maybe we'd better forget this," the white boy said.

"Take it easy. The old man might have something in here worth something."

They entered and paused in the living room. Phantom heard them and stopped his foraging. He took a few steps to the left and watched the kitchen doorway. The bigger black boy inched forward and put his head around the corner of the doorway. Phantom lowered his body and moved forward, more like a cat than a German shepherd. The boy didn't see him to the left and stepped fully into the doorway. The moment he did so, Phantom sprang forward and up. He clamped his jaws firmly on the boy's throat and tore into it, his razor-sharp teeth slicing the arteries and the neck muscles like a hot knife through butter. The boy tried to scream but gagged on his own blood, instead.

His two friends, seeing the attack, ran from the apartment. In a moment, Phantom was after them. They shot out the front door and rushed past the old man. When they got to the sidewalk, they split up, the smaller, white boy going to the left and the other black boy, Tutu, going to the right.

"Hey," the old man said, but a moment later the dog went by him.

Phantom paused at the bottom of the steps and watched the faster black boy running down the sidewalk. He turned and saw the white boy cross the street and head for the corner. When he looked back, he saw that the old man had closed the front door.

Because none of the choices really attracted Phantom, he ignored them all. He didn't go back up the stairs; there was nothing more of interest back in the apartment, and pursuing either of the boys was pointless now. They were fleeing from him and they had nothing he wanted. He continued on down the block, instead.

Some people along the street, looking out of windows, standing by their own apartments, had heard the commotion and watched the teenagers. No one wanted to come to their aid or challenge the dog. Whatever was happening looked to be over, anyway. Before the old man came out screaming again to announce the ghastly scene in his apartment, Phantom had turned the corner and run up the next block.

Without realizing in what direction he was heading, he found himself back on the major avenue, where the traffic and noise were immense, from his perspective. He could think only of escaping from it, so he charged forward, unused to these many cars and people. Some automobiles had to swerve; others put on their brakes; there was a quick fender-bender behind him. People were shouting; horns were blaring. He ran faster and harder, avoiding the people who waved and gestured in his direction.

Panicked, he headed directly down the avenue, running between oncoming vehicles. Cars continued to swerve, brakes squealed, and more people gathered. Finally, a police car appeared near the traffic light directly ahead of him. The policemen stopped their vehicle and stepped out, looking with amazement at the traffic mess being caused by a large, stray dog. The dog kept coming at them.

It wasn't in the experience of either of the policemen

to deal with such a situation, but the driver had the instinct to shout for his partner to get the shotgun. He didn't start to do so until Phantom had gotten within ten feet of them and it was obvious to him that the dog was not going to veer off. He was attacking.

Phantom almost welcomed the sight of the police car and the men in uniform. This was something he could deal with; this was something he understood. He had confronted a man in a similar uniform before, and he knew that the man was a danger to him. He lunged at the men, thinking that they were somehow keeping him in this terrible place, blocking him from escape.

The driver started to unholster his pistol, but he hadn't cleared the barrel from the holster by the time Phantom was at him. He seized him at the wrist and spun him around. The policeman slammed against the car and crumpled to his knees. Phantom merely reached out with his iron jaws and clamped down on the side of the cop's neck, tearing away the artery. With the blood spurting freely, the policeman fell forward.

His partner came around the front of the car, his gun drawn. He had nowhere near the time he needed to get the shotgun from the trunk of the car. Phantom did not challenge him, for he was a man with a gun. Instead, the dog, despite his size, lowered his body and slipped under the rear of the vehicle. The policeman was shocked at how agile the dog was. He couldn't get off a single shot, and his attention had to be directed to his mangled partner, whose bleeding had become life-threatening.

Traffic had stopped all around them. People were gathering in groups. There was general bedlam, but even so, Phantom shot out across the street. The people in his way had seen the commotion. They parted quickly, no one daring to remain in his path or trying to stop him. He rushed through the crowds and headed blindly down a side street, running as hard and as fast as he could, driven by the fear of what awaited him and by the impact of what he had just been through. He expected more men in uniforms around every corner, but none appeared. He ran on and on, crossing streets, winding around cars, charging past people until he came to a section of rubble and demolished houses. There were empty buildings and long stretches of garbage-strewn lots. He didn't pause; he went directly into it. There was something about the area that suggested the wild. He saw places to hide and he was encouraged by the emptiness and desolation. In it he saw hope and safety.

He looked back only once. Satisfied that none of the men in uniform had caught up with him, he slipped into one of the half-demolished structures and disappeared into the darkness of its hollow interior. In moments, all was as quiet as before and he found a cool spot. He lowered himself to the floor and listened, but he could hear nothing over the sound of his own quickened breathing and panting. For the moment he cared about nothing but rest.

Qwen stepped out of Sam Cohen's rowboat and tied it to the dock at Keebler's Landing. Since he had last been here, the owners had built on to their small motel, adding rooms that were mainly used by trout fishermen who drove up from the city. They could walk up or down the river to stake out their lucky spots. He had seen a few on his way down and now saw that the motel was almost full. He walked up to the office where he knew there was a pay phone. They had a small sporting goods store in there, as well.

It was a beautiful spot, shaded by tall pines. If one approached it from the highway, he traveled for a good mile and a half down a hard dirt and gravel road. It was an ideal escape for the devoted fisherman. There was really nothing else to do here.

Qwen didn't know the owners personally—a couple and the husband's brother—but the woman, a salt-and-pepper-haired chunky lady in her mid-fifties, gave him a warm hello and smile when he entered the office. He explained that he was there only to use the phone.

"Help yourself," she said. He thanked her but saw that the phone was on the wall, just to the right of the counter. He wished he could have some privacy for the call, but it was either this or head back into town. He asked the operator to connect him with the Fallsburg police department and then looked back over his shoulder. He couldn't tell whether the woman was listening or not. As soon as the dispatcher answered, he asked for the chief.

"Tell him it's Qwen, the trapper who was with the dog group," he said, thinking that was the best way to describe himself. He wondered if there was an APB out on him for shooting Fishman. The dispatcher hadn't acted excited when Qwen mentioned his name, and when Harry Michaels came on, he sounded quite nonchalant.

"What can I do for you, Mr. Qwen? If you're calling to find out about the dog, I got nothin' to tell you. They haven't located him yet."

"And they won't," Qwen said. He figured he might as well be direct, as quickly as possible.

"I don't know about that. There are an awful lot of men out there with some pretty good equipment. Shouldn't be much longer."

"It's more than a dog, Chief. You remember me? No one's lookin' for me?"

"For you? Yeah, sure, I remember you. Who should be lookin' for you?"

"That so-called security man who was with us last

night tried to kill me. He and the driver, I should say. To make a long story short, I killed him."

"Huh?"

"What I really want to tell you, though, is they gave you a bunch of bullshit about that dog. That dog is no military dog in special training. It's an experimental animal, created in a laboratory."

"What is this, a joke?"

"I wish it was, Chief. You and me got to get together right away."

There was a long pause, during which the operator came on to demand more money. Qwen was out of change.

"Charge the remainder of this call to this number, operator," Michaels said. "This is a police matter." She said she would. "Qwen, I never really got to talk to you last night. Who the hell are you? What do you have to do with all this?"

"They hired me to find their dog. They told me a cock n' bull story too, at first. Then I began to realize things about the dog and they were forced to tell me the truth. That's why they tried to get rid of me."

There was a long pause before Michaels spoke again.

"What was that about killing someone?"

"I told you, they tried to kill me on the way back to the institute."

"Institute?"

"They probably called it a training center. Look, don't you think it might be better if we met?"

"Who'd you say you killed?"

"The guy's name was Fishman, remember?"

"The big guy?"

"You got it."

"Where are you now?"

"I'm at Keebler's Landing. It's about two—"

"I know it," Michaels said. "My oldest boy fancies

himself a trout fisherman. You stay there. It'll take me a little over half an hour."

"I know. Only, Chief, I wouldn't advise your telling anyone from the institute that you're going to meet me."

"All right," Harry said. "You stay put."

After Qwen hung up, he turned to the counter and saw that the woman was gone. He imagined she had either overheard his whole conversation and had gone back to tell her husband and brother-in-law about it, or she hadn't listened in at all. He smiled to himself and went back out and down to the dock, where Maggie waited obediently in the boat. There wasn't much for Qwen to do either but wait to see whether or not Michaels would arrive. He still believed in his instincts, and his instincts told him that the police chief was a down-to-earth fellow who was as overwhelmed by all this as he was.

He sprawled out in the boat, put his hands behind his head, and looked up at the bright morning sky. There was no sense in being tense and nervous about it. Maggie seemed to sense his mood. She got up, shook herself, and then lay down again, planting her head over his stomach. The two of them often slept this way on the rug in the living room of his home.

"There comes a time when you just have to wait it out, Maggie, my girl. That time's come now." The dog opened and closed her eyes, as if in agreement. Qwen closed his. It was close to forty minutes later when he opened them again.

Chief Michaels was standing alone on the dock. He had his hands on his hips, the sleeve of his bandaged arm rolled back, and his hat tilted to the rear.

"I called about that Fishman guy, the one you supposedly killed," he said.

"So?"

"They said he was transferred. They way they talked, I gathered it was because he fucked up."

"He fucked up all right." Qwen sat up. Michaels stared at him.

"Why wouldn't they tell me you killed him? Try to get you for murder?"

"They can't have any investigations. They don't do things that way, anyway. I'm learning that fast. Did you let on where you were headed? Because if you did . . ."

"No, but I didn't leave the office before I got a call back. A doctor Bronstein wanted to know what I wanted with Fishman."

"What'ja tell him?"

"I told him I thought he might be able to help with the search since we still haven't found the dog."

"He didn't buy it," Qwen said. "He knows I got to you. I wish you would've believed me."

"Now look, I admit that the whole thing's been botherin' me and I—" Qwen put his hand up to indicate that Michaels should wait. Another vehicle was coming from the dirt and gravel road. Two men sat in the front seat and one sat in the back. None of them looked like fishermen.

"You told someone at the station where you were goin'?"

"Just my dispatcher."

"And you didn't tell him it was to be kept quiet."

"Well, I didn't think that—"

"You'd better get in the boat," Qwen said. He reached for the oars.

"Huh?" Michaels looked back. The car kept coming slowly.

"Get the fuck in the boat," Qwen commanded. He started away from the dock. Michaels looked behind again. The car had stopped and the men were getting out. Without hesitation, he stepped off the dock and into the boat. Qwen's big thrust with the oars sent him into a sitting position. He took care not to bang his arm on the side.

The three men came down to the dock as Qwen drove the boat into the downstream current. One of the men reached under his jacket for what looked like a pistol, but the other two stopped him before he brought it out. They looked for another boat and found one, but it was without oars. One of the men was sent to the office to get them. Before he returned, Qwen had brought his boat around the first bend in the river.

"They're after us?" Michaels asked.

"Me, mostly, but now you, too. I suppose they could make it look like I killed you."

The river turned again about two hundred yards down. Qwen considered it and then made a quick decision. He turned the boat in toward the shore. As soon as he hit it, he got out.

"Use your good arm and push the son-of-a-bitch," he said.

Michaels saw what Qwen wanted to do. They got the boat out of the water and dragged it back behind some bushes. Then they crouched down and waited. Less than a minute later the three men appeared. Two of them were telling the one who was rowing to row faster.

Qwen waited until they had disappeared around the far bend and then he led Michaels into the woods. They made their way back to Keebler's Landing quickly.

"They must have turned around by now," Qwen said. "Let's get goin'."

They got into Michaels's patrol car and Harry started away. "I don't know what the hell's goin' on," he finally said.

"You know those guys ain't fishermen. That's for sure."

"Tell me how this all started and what you know about the dog," Harry Michaels said. As Qwen talked, Harry thought about the way Ken Strasser had died, about Carlson's body on the basement floor, and his own confrontation with the dog.

"Do you think it could have influenced other animals, too?" he asked, thinking about the Kaufmans' dog.

"Who knows? They don't even know what it's capable of doing."

"I don't know. I'd like to believe you, but—"

They were interrupted by a radio call.

"I figured you'd want to know this, Chief. There's a wild story comin' out of New York City. It's about a dog."

"What about a dog?"

"A big German shepherd . . . invaded some old man's apartment, killed a teenager, caused a traffic tie-up, and nearly killed a cop."

"Where'd it happen?"

"South Bronx."

"Did they get the dog?"

"Not yet. It disappeared somewhere in the slums."

"Could there be more than one of them?" Michaels asked Qwen.

Qwen thought for a moment. "No," he said, "it's our dog."

"But how did he get to New York City? Take a bus? Come on!"

"I don't know how he did it, but it doesn't surprise me that he did."

Michaels went back to his car radio.

"What about our dog? Any progress?"

"Not a thing, Chief."

"Because he's not here," Qwen said.

Michaels looked at him again. Then he looked into his rearview mirror. There was no one behind them, but he sped up, anyway. "What the hell do we do?"

"We go to the Bronx," Qwen said. "Maggie and I will find him. I gotta find him. I want the world to know."

"Hunt a dog in the city? You know what that area's like?"

"It can't be any wilder than where I've been," Qwen said. "All I know is, I gotta get him."

# 14

HE HEARD THE sound of human voices. They seemed to be coming from everywhere. He heard many different sounds; many were alien; some were familiar, but most of the scents he smelled were strange. He had no concept of anything he could think of as home, but he fondly recalled the time he had spent in the forest.

There was nothing to hunt here. The air wasn't as clear and the solitude wasn't real. The animals, mostly rodents, were unlike the field mice. These rats and mice had the scent of death about them. They were more like parasites feasting on decay. He sensed them eyeing him from dark corners. They wanted his flesh. He was sure that if he were to die here, they would consume him to the bones. He could face other dogs, vicious dogs; he could taunt a snake and he could even challenge a bear if he had a mind to, but there was something about these vermin that made him cringe.

This reaction came from a part of him that he didn't quite understand. It brought with it memories that seemed more like dreams. He didn't know how to deal with them. They weakened him. He had the urge to bark, to growl, to snap his teeth at the rats that were gathering, but he backed away, instead. He didn't like fleeing, but he didn't want to remain in so small an area with so many of them scurrying about on all sides and even behind him. He turned and went deeper into the shell of the wrecked, degenerated building.

With its windows out and gaping holes in some sections of its walls, the building's interior was a curious mixture of darkness and light. Broken ceiling panels dangled from above; torn Sheetrock revealed the intestines of the structure. The rays of light that streamed in illuminated particles of dust, making them dance in the air with the brilliance of tiny gems. He saw broken bottles, empty cans, and articles of old clothing strewn about, but nothing really attracted his interest.

When he came to a stairway that still had integrity, he gazed upward into the vertical corridor. Behind him the rats squealed and danced nervously over the loose floorboards. The human voices grew louder and he understood that people were approaching the building from at least two different angles. He decided to go up, but when he turned the corner of the first landing, he came upon a man sprawled out on the floor, his back against the wall, his eyes closed. His right hand still clutched a syringe, but there was the definite scent of death around him.

As Phantom drew closer to the body, three rats poked their heads out from under the man's torn overcoat. When they saw him, they scurried into the holes between the floor and the walls. He didn't hesitate; he heard the sound of footsteps below and he continued up the stairs. He climbed five flights before pausing and listening to the sounds below. The voices were muffled and indistinct. He waited to see if they would remain so or if they would grow louder as the men began to climb the stairway to come after him. He assumed that they could track him as well as he could track them.

But they didn't come. Their voices grew lower and lower until they were gone altogether. Even so, he climbed another three flights before stopping. This time he entered the floor, taking care to avoid the weak boards and large holes. He kept to the side of a wall and reached a room on the northeastern end of the decayed and deserted structure. He made his way to an opened window and got his paws on the sill so he could look out at this strange and unfriendly world into which he had somehow been dropped.

The sight dazzled him. He saw all the movement and activity below, but its diminished size made him feel much bigger. He grew dizzy from the constant traffic on the major highway in the distance. To his left he could make out what looked to be a pack of those men in the uniforms. They had gone past the building he was in; they looked like insects crawling in and out of the rubble and sifting the area for something of value.

He went down to the floor again and thought. It was difficult, if not impossible, for him to understand this world, but his biological clock told him that some time had passed and daylight was on its final half. He had to remain safely in hiding and wait. Night would come as it always had, even to this world. Darkness had always been his friend. He was secure in it; it made him stronger, especially if he had to do battle against men.

He looked around the room. It was empty, except for a large carton in the far right corner. For now, that was a most attractive place. He went to it and, as comfortably as possible, curled himself up within the carton. He wasn't tired, but he didn't want to chance any more travel through the building and he didn't have his usual curiosity in things. If anything, this place depressed. Even the most hateful room in the laboratory was preferable to this.

He thought about the laboratory. Being there seemed so long ago to him. He went back over the journey that had taken him from there to this point. Most of the challenges had been invigorating. Now his mood was characterized by foreboding. The shadows in the room darkened and took on the shapes of monsters. Fears instilled in him as a puppy came to the fore.

He recalled being afraid of being crushed by objects much larger than he was. He remembered whimpering and shivering in a cage. He thought about being lifted and transported in the night. He remembered the first time he had heard a truck engine and felt the vibrations. He thought some terrible creature was going to come through the metal walls and tear him apart. None of this happened, but still these were some of the images that often made for sleepless nights. The fact that he thought of them now dispirited him. He lowered his head to his paws and looked out at the naked room. His breathing was soft; he made no sounds, but he felt the heavy thumping of his heart. He didn't even care about being thirsty. All he could do was lie there and wait in anticipation. For now he hated the brightness of the daylight and the sounds that came up from the hard, cold cement and metal world below.

He tried closing his eyes, but the moment he did so, he envisioned a pack of those rats coming up the stairs after him. There were so many of them that their bodies rubbed against the sides of the stairway walls. Some walked over those in front and some drove others into the gaping holes, sending them to their deaths below. He opened his eyes quickly and growled, but all he heard was the echo of his own voice. Still, he was distrustful of the silence within the building. Perhaps these rats were as quiet as the mice in the field. Perhaps they were already just outside this door.

He stared at it and waited. He wanted to relax and end the tension, but he couldn't. He had to keep his eyes open; he had to listen, and as he did so, something in the back of his mind came alive—a tiny electrical reaction in the deep caverns of his brain sent a signal into his consciousness. It came in the form of a large, black bird swooping down from the mountains, soaring above the tall buildings and then diving in between them as it headed toward him.

It was coming with two hot coals for eyes. It would come through the window and drive its razor-sharp beak into his head. The picture was so vivid he couldn't help but whine like a puppy.

"I was thinking to myself how that dog killed old Ken Strasser," Michaels said, "and how it got into Sid Kaufman's house and took down Carlson. I wasn't particularly crazy about him, but he was a good cop, a smart policeman. Then I thought how Clara Kaufman and her children were terrorized to such an extent that they pushed furniture up against that basement door."

"Opening a door isn't much of an accomplishment for him," Qwen said. "That woman, Ann, she told me some of the clever things he did in the laboratory."

"Yeah, well anyway, I listened to their explanation and I thought to myself, something don't sound right, but what else do I have to go on? Then you called. If I didn't have this gut feeling that they were full of shit, I would have written you off as some loon."

Qwen nodded and turned around to see how Maggie was doing in the rear of the police car. She looked up quizzically, her tongue extended. They were more than halfway to the city limits, Michaels cruising at eighty to eighty-five all the way. He had contacted a friend of his on the city police force and been quickly placed into contact with the captain whose precinct covered that section of the Bronx in which the dog had done its damage. He told him he was coming down with a trapper who was trained to tracking such animals. The captain said he welcomed any professional assistance.

"He heard what happened up here, didn't he?"

"Oh yeah, but he didn't see how the events were related. The army dog trainers didn't contact him about any dogs trained in or very close to the city."

"You didn't try to explain any of what I told you then?"

"I thought about it and decided he'd probably think I was crazy."

"Tell me about this section of the Bronx. I don't get into the city very often. I've got to have real earth under my feet most of the time, if you know what I mean."

"Sure I do. I'm a country boy, too. This is the South Bronx. Maybe you remember President Carter was going to do something dramatic about it years ago. It looks a lot like Berlin immediately after the Second World War."

"What did he say about the search so far?"

"They've combed ten square blocks but found no sign of him."

Qwen sat back and thought. He had to admit that by this time, one of the major reasons for his wanting to do this was to set eyes on the animal. When Chief Michaels described his confrontation with the dog, Qwen felt the hunter's envy. Michaels's description was far from adequate. He had been too excited; the attack had been too quick. In his eyes the animal appeared to be six feet tall and weighed over two hundred pounds. It was a ridiculous description, the description of someone who had been in a panic.

Michaels didn't make excuses for himself.

"I know I'm a cop; I've been a cop for years, and I should have been more professional about it all, but there was something more about this animal. It wasn't just a big, angry dog. I've had my times with dogs before, even mad dogs. Christ, I felt like a kid in the movies lookin' up at a werewolf. Don't laugh, you bastard."

"I'm not laughing," Qwen said. "It's just that you described what I imagined as I tracked him, what I accused them of doing—creating a freak."

Michaels nodded.

"If I had only gotten off a better shot . . . two more people dead. Damn!"

"If you're lookin' for someone to blame," Qwen said, "you just have to go up to that secret compound."

"Um. And that's just what we're going to do when this is all over."

They crossed the George Washington Bridge and went to the Cross-Bronx Expressway. The late afternoon sun hung above the city, inflaming the thin clouds that passed over it. When they took the Webster Avenue exit and entered the inner city, Qwen understood what Michaels meant by "like Berlin immediately after the war." He gaped in disbelief, amazed that human beings could live in such conditions. Even old Sam Cohen's shack looked like a palace, compared to some of this.

After they parked at the precinct, Qwen stepped out of the car and opened the door for Maggie. The dog looked unhappy about it. The warmer than usual spring made the city air feel more like hot summer air. Qwen felt oppressed by it and by the lack of a breeze. Maggie's tail drooped as she waited for them to move over the sidewalk and up the steps. Michaels came around the car and looked about.

"How do you like it?"

"Harder than hell to find good fish worms here," Qwen said.

Michaels laughed. "Let's meet the captain and find out what's going on. Maybe they've got the bastard, already."

Qwen, with Maggie at his feet, followed Michaels into the police station. Two patrolmen coming out nodded to them. When they got inside, the desk sergeant looked up quickly. He saw the insignia on Harry Michaels's hat and badge.

"Town of Fallsburg police department? Where the hell's that?"

"Upstate New York, Sullivan County. Is Captain O'Keefe in?"

"Yeah."

"Did you find the dog yet?" Qwen asked quickly. The sergeant just looked at him.

"He means the German shepherd that went wild down here," Michaels said.

"I know what he means. No, not yet. Whaddya know about it?"

"That's why we're here to see the captain," Michaels said. "He's expecting us. Tell him Harry Michaels, will ya."

"Charlie!" the desk sergeant yelled. A hatless patrolman, carrying a clipboard, came out of an office in the corridor to the right. "Tell the captain Harry Michaels from upstate New York is here, will ya?"

The policeman nodded and went on down the hall. A moment later he returned to wave them in.

"What kind of dog is that?" the desk sergeant asked when he saw Maggie trailing along behind them.

"A country police dog," Michaels said. Qwen laughed. They found Captain O'Keefe alone in his office, talking on the phone. He gestured for them to come in and take seats.

"I've got every available man out there, sir," he was saying. "Right now we think it's someone's animal and it's back in the apartment. That's our best bet.

Yes, sir. I know. I'll do my best, Commissioner. Thank you." He hung up, wiped his brow with the palm of his right hand, and then sat forward.

Qwen couldn't help contrasting the two policemen. Although Harry Michaels was along in years, he still looked virile and rugged. Of course, his size made a difference, but Qwen believed that even if Harry Michaels were fifty pounds lighter and five inches shorter, he would have a worn, tough look about him. There was nothing slick or polished in his demeanor.

On the other hand, this New York City police captain looked more like an agent in the FBI. He looked professional but also bureaucratic. Qwen wondered just how much real experience in the field he had. He was a slim man. In fact, he looked like someone who had recently been on a diet. The suit he wore seemed a size too big. To Qwen he looked more like an actor portraying a big city police captain.

"As you can imagine, this thing's heating up. The media are having a field day. A few hours ago it was bedlam out in that lobby. There are network cameramen out there on the streets, just hoping for some action. I hope none of them get mugged." He looked at Maggie, who sat obediently at Qwen's feet. "We're bringing in some dogs, too. Something special about yours?"

"Yes," Qwen said. "She's been trackin' your dog."

"Oh?" He stood up and walked around to the front of his desk. "Might as well introduce ourselves proper. I'm Captain O'Keefe."

"Harry Michaels," Harry said. "This here's Mike Qwen."

"So you're a trapper? You do that for a living?"

"Among other things."

"What'ja mean, she's been trackin' your dog?"

"The dog you're after down here came from our area," Qwen said.

"Came from? Whaddya mean, someone down here bought him up there and brought him down here? That's great. If we have the name, we . . ."

"No, Captain, that's not what Qwen means."

"It's not? What do you mean then? You said he came from your area, didn't you?"

"I meant the dog came from our area, himself."

Captain O'Keefe looked at Michaels and then at Qwen. He leaned back against his desk. "Didn't you say you came from upstate New York, around Sullivan County?"

"Right," Michaels said.

"That's about ninety-odd miles, isn't it?" Qwen nodded. "You mean that dog walked down here?"

Qwen looked at Michaels.

"We don't know how he got down here, Captain, but we're fairly sure that's our dog."

"Wait a minute. When you say 'our dog,' you're talking about the military dog that killed some people?"

"Exactly."

"Only it wasn't a military dog," Qwen said.

"How do you know all this?" Captain O'Keefe asked.

"I was hired to track him. Me and Maggie, that is."

"And you've tracked him to the city?"

"In a way. Look, Captain, I don't want to get into the whole thing right now, but believe me when I tell you this is not an ordinary animal. It's smarter, wiser. It knows it's being hunted. Take my word for it for the moment and let us help you. Show us where the dog did its damage and where it was last seen. We'll do our best from there."

O'Keefe looked at Qwen and then at Michaels. He thought for a moment and shrugged.

"Okay," he said. "But when this is over, someone's

going to have a lot of explaining to do. I almost lost a good officer out there."

"That's why we've come here, Captain," Qwen said. "To make damn sure that explaining gets done."

Qwen sat with Maggie in the back of the patrol car. His dog seemed just as disgusted as he was by the things they saw as they rode along. Young children played in lots strewn with garbage. There were wrecked and deserted automobiles everywhere, most stripped of their valuable parts by unseen junk parasites. Qwen wondered how anyone could feel any sort of dignity living in such an environment.

Although Michaels wasn't as shocked by the decrepit neighborhoods, he anticipated Qwen's reactions and shook his head in silent agreement. He sat up front with Patrolman Horowitz, the twenty-eight-year-old policeman Captain O'Keefe had assigned to them. His first duty was to take them to the apartment building in which the dog had killed the teenager.

At first the young patrolman was upset with his assignment. He thought it was just his bad luck that he was available to play chauffeur to a small town policeman and a hick who looked like someone as out of place here as an Amish farmer on Forty-second Street. Who the hell came into New York with a hound dog and was surprised to learn that the subway came out of the ground?

But as he drove them to the apartment building, he heard things that made him wonder. Perhaps these two knew what they were doing, even here. After all, dogs were being used to sniff out drugs and fires and bombs. And when he thought about it, he had nothing to brag about; the dog had eluded a big city police force up until now.

"I was just thinking," Qwen said as they turned

down one street and started up another, "that to the dog, this might be something like being in a maze. It certainly feels that way to me."

"So maybe moving through the streets wouldn't be so terrifying to him," Michaels said.

"Yeah, and in that case, every obstacle would become a test, and with the way he likes a challenge . . ."

"You guys talk about this dog as though he's a person," Horowitz said. Michaels looked at him and then back at Qwen. Horowitz caught the smile between them and questioned what was going on here. Who the hell were these guys? "This is it," he said, turning onto the block.

Some people were still gathered in front of the building, listening to the elderly black man retell the events from beginning to end. He had been out there all day, relating the tale to anyone wanting to hear it. Actually, after what had happened to him, he clung to company and put off going back into his apartment for as long as he could. But as soon as the police car pulled up, everyone turned away from him. They watched Qwen and Maggie, Michaels, and Patrolman Horowitz get out.

"What made him stop at an apartment on this block?" Michaels asked. Horowitz's eyes widened. Could Qwen answer that?

"Just the scent of food, I'd say. There's nothing that resembles anything back home, nothing that would bring him to it in a search for something familiar. The apartment belongs to that old man on the stoop?" Qwen asked.

"Huh?" Horowitz said. "Oh, yeah. His name's Russel."

Qwen nodded and went to him. The crowd parted as he and Maggie approached with Michaels and Horowitz right behind.

"Howdy."

The old man looked up at Qwen and at Maggie. "Who the hell are you? The dogcatcher?"

"Sort of." Qwen laughed and took out a chaw of tobacco. He bit into it and looked up the street. "Mind if I ask you some questions about what happened?"

"Get in line."

"Know what you mean . . . quite a thing, quite a thing. Tell me, how the hell did he get into your apartment? Was the door open?"

"Door open? In this neighborhood?" Everyone laughed. "Hell no, mister. I even had my chain lock on, but I heard this scratchin' and I opened the door. Stupid, plain stupid."

"He just went chargin' in?"

"Like he owned the place. He went right to the kitchen. Knew I had my breakfast out on the table. Jumped right up on the table. I couldn't get him out."

"What'dja do?"

"I hit him with the kitchen chair, but it might as well been a fly swatter. He was a big bastard. Maybe it was a wolf."

"No."

"Escaped from some circus." He played to his audience. Some heads nodded.

"No, no way. Besides, a wolf's half the size."

"Oh yeah?"

"Yes, sir," Qwen said. He looked up the stoop. "I see the front door is closed. Is it always that way?"

"Hell, yeah. We got a spring on it makes it shut. It don't lock, though. The lock's broke. Still, some son-of-a-bitch let that dog in, huh?"

"I don't think so," Qwen said. He looked at Michaels, who closed and opened his eyes. "Did you see him kill the boy?"

"No, sir. I was out here. He just chased the other two out and went right by me."

"Okay, thanks." Qwen turned to Horowitz. "Take

us to where he attacked the policeman. Any doubts about it bein' our dog?" he asked Michaels.

"I'm losin' 'em."

They got back into the car and started away. The crowd watched them until they disappeared around the turn.

"From what we got," Horowitz said, "he entered Webster Avenue from here. He met the patrol car just at the traffic light."

"Pull over," Qwen said. After he did so, Qwen looked out at where the policeman's blood still stained the street.

"From here he headed east. Everyone lost sight of him at the end of the block."

"Okay." Qwen got out of the car. Maggie followed but remained very close to his feet. When the light turned red and the traffic stopped, Qwen walked out to the spot. Maggie sniffed about and then Qwen and his dog started east.

"Hey!" Michaels called.

"Just follow along in the car," Qwen said. "Maggie's excited. She recognizes the scent and she knows what I want."

"What's he saying?" Horowitz asked.

"Please just do what he says," Michaels replied. The policeman shrugged and made the turn at the intersection. He drove very slowly as Qwen moved up the sidewalk. Maggie picked up her pace, seemingly oblivious to the noise and activity around her. When they came to the end of the block and saw what seemed to be an endless strip of crumbled buildings and piles of rubble, Qwen stopped.

"Holy shit," he said. The patrol car came up beside him and Michaels leaned out.

"What'sa matter? The dog's still goin'."

"It looks like the end of the world."

"Maybe it is."

Maggie's bark grew louder and shriller. She went through a pile of cement blocks and worked herself around some rolls of wire.

"We were up and down this place," Horowitz said. "We went in all those buildings—or what's left of them."

"You went through them from top to bottom?"

"We didn't go up no decaying stairways. In most cases, there's nothin' to go up to. Anyway, a dog wouldn't do that."

"Maybe a dog wouldn't, but he would," Qwen said.

"Huh?"

"Better hand me out the tranquilizer gun," Qwen said.

"Tranquilizer?" Horowitz smirked. "We aim to kill that bastard."

"Not before he talks," Qwen said.

"Talks. What the hell is he talking about?"

Michaels didn't answer. He handed the rifle out to Qwen and got out of the vehicle.

"We'll walk from here on," Michaels said, but when he turned around Qwen was already trotting down the street. "I mean run." He started after him.

"What the fuck?" Horowitz shook his head and picked up his radio mike to call in and report his location. After that, he got out of his car and followed the two men into what he had come to call the land of the dead. He saw the dog was moving quickly and barking madly. Qwen was into a run and Michaels was doing his best to keep up, but he was falling behind. Horowitz started to run himself, his heart beating with excitement.

Did that hound dog from the boondocks really know what it was doing?

Who the hell were these guys?

# 15

EVEN BEFORE HE heard the dog barking, he knew they were coming. Before, when he had picked up the sounds of the city policemen below and sensed their presence in the building, he had prepared himself for the inevitable battle; but he had done so with a sense of optimism. It was true that they had come in a pack, and a pack was the worst thing to fear. Animals that gathered together to hunt down and share the prey were unusual in his experience, even his race experience. If anything, it was his genetic lineage that traced itself back to such creatures. It was his ancestors who had been gregarious, who had seen the advantage in moving together in numbers. But for him, now, there was something mystical and horrifying in such an occurrence.

When he had moved through the forest and heard sounds around him, he had looked into the darker areas and imagined such herds of marauding creatures. To come upon them was to come upon Death itself, for any animal alone had no chance of escaping them or defeating them. Nothing was truer than the knowledge that the strong survived and the weak perished; and he knew without ever having personally experienced it that even an animal half his size was stronger when it was in a pack.

But he had been so successful in eluding and defeating men, even those in the uniforms, that he viewed them now almost the way he would have viewed a colony of rabbits. They were animals; even when they were in large numbers, they were no match for him. Now he was suffering from the belief that man was that way, too. When he had heard them below, he hadn't felt that all-encompassing, deadly fear that could move with electrifying intensity throughout his entire body and could leave him disheartened and weak.

Suddenly it was different, though, because he sensed something familiar in these oncoming pursuers. They had been behind him before. This knowledge came from an instinctive awareness, honed through centuries of species development. It was a marvel of nature, the result of thousands of years of adaptation, the evolution of those wild elements within him that were now given at birth. It was why baby birds flew, why newborn horses stood almost instantly after birth, and why squirrels knew to hoard. Scientists had come to describe it as the sixth sense; they struggled to dissect it, to understand it. Maybe it was electrical; maybe it came like radio and television waves, or maybe it was extrasensory perception. Whatever it was, it was there.

He raised his snoot in the air and sniffed, as though to confirm it. What could have followed him so far and located him so quickly? Whatever it was, he hadn't yet defeated it. All he had done was postpone the face-off. He growled in anticipation and stood up. The sound of the dog barking outside grew louder and closer. He stepped out to the middle of the room and tuned in his hearing to any activity below.

Qwen paused as he approached the gaping hole in the side of the building. Maggie had stopped before it, not crossing through to enter the partially wrecked structure. The moments of silence between her barks had grown shorter and shorter until she delivered almost one continuous yap, high-pitched and excited. It excited Qwen; he knew what that meant. She would do it only a few feet from a fox or a coon. A well-trained hound dog didn't go farther without command at this point. Maggie had done her job well—she had brought her master to the kill.

"Hold on!" Michaels yelled. He was a good twenty-five yards behind. The short, quick run had brought home his weight problem, his age, and his fatigue. He had to slow down to a quick walk. Even that seemed too strenuous. How embarrassing it would be for him to keel over in the South Bronx, he thought. Jenny didn't know he was down here doing this. If he didn't die from it, she'd kill him. He cursed under his breath as the younger city patrolman caught up with him and passed him.

"What the hell does this mean?" Horowitz asked when he reached Qwen.

"He's definitely in there," Qwen said, his gaze set firmly on the opening in the wall.

"I'd better go back and radio the station, first. Everybody's at least a half dozen or so blocks to the south and west of this. We checked this place out."

"If he wanted to do it, he could hide right below your feet and watch you walk by," Qwen said. Horowitz swallowed hard and turned to Michaels as he approached. "What kind of dog is this? A circus dog?"

"He's part human," Qwen said without cracking a smile. "We've got to approach this the same way we'd approach it if a man we was huntin' was in there."

"Part human?" The patrolman looked at Michaels, but the upstate police chief didn't change expression. Horowitz began to feel as though he had been dropped onto the set of *The Twilight Zone*. He looked back longingly at his patrol car, hoping for the sudden appearance of another black and white. Then he looked at the excited hound dog. "I'd better go back and radio the captain," he said.

"Go ahead," Qwen said. "You're not going to do me any good in there, anyway."

Horowitz didn't reply. He turned around and quickly shot off toward the patrol car. Qwen took a few steps toward the opening and Maggie put her front legs up on the crumbled stone. Her barking, now directed into the building, echoed, reverberating throughout the structure and upward. Then she stepped through the opening, with Qwen only a few feet behind. Harry Michaels drew his revolver and followed.

The dog continued its barking, but she paused intermittently to sniff the crumbled floor. Qwen and Michaels looked around the room expectantly, neither saying a word until Maggie went farther into the building.

"Go slow," Harry Michaels said. "She came at me from outta nowhere."

"Keep yourself a few feet behind. Leave a good space between us," Qwen said and started after Maggie.

They stepped over broken Sheetrock walls and loose boards, slowing down before every pile of rubble behind which a dog could hide, but when Qwen saw Maggie at the bottom of the stairway, he sped up. She went up a few steps and stopped, not barking as much now as she was sniffing. Climbing the stairs seemed curious to her. Qwen thought it was almost as though his dog doubted her own findings. It made him suspect, and he paused to turn about very slowly. Michaels did the same, lowering his upper body into a kind of crouch, as if he expected the dog to come leaping out at him at any moment. He brought back the hammer on his pistol. Qwen heard it and suddenly realized it might not be so smart to have a nervous man with a loaded gun, primed and ready, walking behind him. He never liked it when he went hunting with someone, and he certainly didn't like it now.

"Look," Qwen said, "it's what I thought. He went above them, crawling over places they never imagined a dog would go. They missed him because they didn't think of him as anything more. I want you to stay here at the bottom of the stairs in case he gets by me."

"You wanna go up there yourself?"

"It's the best way to approach this."

"Maybe we oughta wait for reinforcements. It shouldn't be long."

"Naw, they'll all be trigger-happy. You know how they feel. It's not something they deal with every day."

"Who does? Christ, I don't know," Michaels said, looking up to the first landing. "Those steps might give way under your feet after a while."

"Then it's best only one of us attempt it. From the way this place looks, chunks of it chopped out here and there, this is probably the only way down. If he gets by me, you'll have to shoot him."

"You don't hafta worry about that. Be careful," he added as Qwen started up. "You're not walking through some forest in the Catskills, now."

Qwen nodded. That was so, but in a strange way, he felt at home. A hunt was a hunt, and although there weren't trees and grass and rocks about, there was still something wild about this place. True, they were in a part of the city and there were thousands and thousands of people around them, but to Qwen this was just another kind of jungle.

The dog's paw prints were now visible in the dust on the steps. He knelt down to study them. For him they were like fingerprints, and they served as final confirmation.

"He's here," Qwen said. "For sure." He stood up and followed Maggie to the first landing. The rats, feasting on the corpse of the junkie, scattered as quickly as they had when Phantom had appeared. "Shit!" Qwen shouted.

Harry rushed up the stairs. "Looks like an O.D.," he said. He indicated the syringe. "This place must be a shooting gallery."

"In more than one way, maybe," Qwen said. He studied the steps before him. They didn't look as secure as the first set.

"Go slow," Michaels warned. Qwen continued. Harry watched him until he reached the corner of the landing above. Maggie had paused by it as if she wanted assurance before going farther up. Qwen raised the rifle and started around. The step second from the top gave way and his foot went through. Michaels started up after him.

"I'm all right," he said. "I'm all right." He got his balance again and whipped around the corner. There was nothing above him but another set of steps, this one missing the second, fourth, and seventh. "All clear," he called behind him and continued on.

He read the other dog's bark; it was clear to him what this other animal was doing. For the first time since he had heard the barking of dogs sent to pursue him, he felt a sense of betrayal. It was funny that it hadn't occurred to him before, but his mental powers and his awareness about the world around him had grown considerably during the last twenty-four hours. It was as though he had lost track of who and what he really was. Accordingly, his view of things began to change.

Every time he closed his eyes and opened them, he focused in on parts of his surroundings he had neither seen nor considered before. Subtly, the borders of his vision expanded, but even more importantly, the contents within multiplied. For all of his life, until very recently, nothing had interested him unless it had carried with it the promise of food and comfort. Of course, he had a puppy's curiosity in small movements and in other animals, but like any other animal, he tended to see everything in an isolated sense. Most of the relationships between things were lost to him.

Now it was different—he not only saw things for what they were in themselves, but he also saw their significances. The barking dog was not just a barking dog following a rote command to pursue; it was intrinsically linked to the man who was its master. In his eyes now, this dog was no longer a dog. It had become part of the man.

It seemed to him that all the world was closing in—animals, men, and even the very surroundings. Now he understood why this place had depressed him. It was a place of death. Buildings died, as well as living things, and sometimes they took living things with them. Maybe that was why the man was on the stairway; maybe that was why this was the kingdom of rats and other vermin.

He was sorry now that he had entered it, and as he looked about the room and realized the height he was at, he concluded that he had made a very big mistake, a mistake similar to taking the wrong turn in one of the test mazes back at the laboratory. In a real sense he had trapped himself. He had made it easy for the man's dog and for the man. Such mistakes were tragic, and he knew that there was no room for tragic mistakes in the world of kill-or-be-killed.

He sensed that the man and the dog were only a flight or two below him now. All he had left to choose was where to do battle. This room was too small and too confining. It was better to go to the stairway, where he would have the advantages of height and surprise. He trotted out of the room, staying closely to the wall again, and made his way over the partially demolished hall floor.

Maggie went wild. Qwen was amazed at the intensity of her reaction. She started up the steps of the landing and then came back down. Each time she did this, she inched up a little farther. It was as though she were pressing against an invisible wall, pushing it back slowly. Qwen studied the top of the landing, looking for some sign of the animal. He felt certain that it loomed just around the next corner.

Although all the steps in this section of the stairway looked intact, he saw that the header holding the stairs to the landing floor had slipped a few inches. It was possible that his added weight would send the entire set of steps falling downward and him along with it. He placed his left foot gently on the first step and leaned against what was left of the corridor wall. There was nothing to grab onto if the floor should give way beneath him, he thought.

"Go ahead, Maggie, go ahead," he said in his most encouraging tone of voice. His dog looked back at him and then climbed another step. Her bark was sharp but full, and in the narrow stairway corridors it was amplified tenfold.

Qwen took another step. He thought the stairway trembled beneath his feet, so he paused, hoping to be able to jump back down to the more secure flooring behind him if the section began to crumble. In the back of his mind was the thought that the whole thing could come down.

Maggie was four steps ahead of him. He could see that this was as far as she would go. There was no point in sending her up any farther anyway. He checked the tranquilizer gun. They had loaded it with serum darts strong enough to bring down a dog twice the size of the normal German shepherd. He hoped to be some distance from the dog before he shot at it. He needed some room to retreat while the tranquilizer took effect. He expected the wound would surprise the animal and disorient it quickly. Once Qwen had captured the dog, he would tell the whole story; the authorities would have the animal to test and examine as a way of validating Qwen's claims. They would no longer be able to hide Fishman's death, and the attempt to have Qwen killed would be exposed as well. The potential realization of all these goals motivated him to take another step and then another.

And then something happened that he had never anticipated. Maggie stopped barking and lowered her body to the steps, crouching as though she expected to be run over. She inched down. Qwen looked up at the corner just as the great dog put its head out from behind the wall. For a long moment, during which Maggie produced a thin, subdued whine, Qwen and the German shepherd faced each other.

He had the rifle about chest-high, but he didn't lift it into position for firing. He and the dog studied one another with an almost similar curiosity. Qwen saw something familiar in the dog's eyes. It was easy to detect a higher intelligence behind its gaze, but along with that was the look of something wild. For Qwen it was as though he were looking at a different form of himself—something that loved and belonged in nature, but something with an awareness and perception far beyond anything born and bred in the wild.

This sight took Qwen by surprise and it was a long moment before he realized how close he was to the animal and how dangerous a situation he was in. When he did so, he raised the rifle and took a step back. The dog did not charge forward, though. Instead, he retreated behind the wall before Qwen could get off a shot.

"Are you all right?" Michaels called up the stairway. "Qwen?'

"Yeah, yeah."

"Two patrol cars just pulled up."

"Keep them down there."

"Any sign of him?"

"Not yet," Qwen called back. He couldn't tell Michaels what had just occurred, because he couldn't explain it to himself. "Easy, girl, easy, Maggie," he said. He moved up the stairs to the landing and looked down the corridor. Much of the floor was gone. Beams running beneath it were clearly visible. There was just one large, gaping hole at the end of the corridor where the wall had been. Qwen hesitated before going forward. He hoped the dog would reappear and he could get a clear shot, but it didn't.

Qwen stepped farther into the hallway, balancing himself on the more secure portions, and inched his way toward the doorway of the first room on the right. At this point Maggie remained a foot or so behind him. He paused and listened. He heard the voices of the policemen below and he heard Harry Michaels's voice. He looked down through a hole in the floor. It seemed as though the opening went all the way down to ground-level. Then he moved a few feet more. He was less than two yards from the doorway of the room, and he was sure he heard sounds coming from it.

Qwen lowered himself into a crouch and brought the rifle stock against his shoulder. He heard the policemen below start to make their way up the stairs behind him. There were a number of them now and they made considerable noise.

Phantom heard it too, and to him it meant that the pack was closing in; it would be only moments now before he would do deadly battle. He knew where Qwen was and he knew where he had placed himself in relation to avenues of escape. He looked at the carton in the corner. A part of him wanted to retreat to it, but there was something else in him that longed for the fight.

These conflicting drives made him pace up to and back from the doorway. Finally, driven by a rush of anger and frustration, he turned and charged out. Qwen fired the moment the dog's head appeared, and the dart struck him in the neck. The gunshot and the blow sent him reeling to the right. He stumbled down the corridor toward the opened wall.

Qwen stood up and moved slowly toward him. He saw that the dog looked confused. He wavered to the right and then to the left, leaning against a part of the wall to steady himself. The policemen were shouting now and moving faster up the stairs. Qwen heard Harry Michaels shout his name, but he couldn't respond; he couldn't do anything but watch the dog as it turned and faced him, battling against the effects of the serum.

Phantom started toward him, stumbled, and fell to the right. Then he struggled to get back to his feet and fell farther to the right. Qwen saw what that meant. The floor was obviously weak there, it was cracked, and there were small holes along the boards. He moved as quickly as he could toward the animal, but when the dog raised himself again by pushing downward, his forelegs went through the decayed floorboards and his body slammed down on the weakened slats.

The rear portion of the great dog disappeared first. He struggled to maintain a hold on the firmer portions of the floor, but he sank lower. Qwen charged forward, disregarding his own safety. He took a position on the solid side of the corridor and reached out to grasp the dog's collar. He caught it just as the rest of the floor gave way under the animal; Qwen tried to hold on, but the weight of the dog was tremendous. He could hold it for only a few moments.

The dog looked up at him then turned its head as though to snap at his wrist. Qwen released his hold and the great German shepherd fell into the dark, hollow guts of the deteriorated building, disappearing within as if he had been swallowed into the mouth of Hell. Qwen heard a crash, but no sound came from the dog. Qwen imagined it had lost consciousness before it hit.

# 16

WHEN THEY FINALLY located Phantom below, Qwen determined that the dog's neck had been broken. Blood streaked from its mouth, and there was a deep gash in its right shoulder. Dead within the ruins of the building, the German shepherd somehow didn't seem as big as it had in life. For Qwen, and especially for Harry Michaels, it was as though the dog's body had already begun to decompose.

"It's not as big as Ernie said it was," said one of the policemen standing by.

"When it's comin' at ya, it's twice the size," Michaels said. He held up his arm. "Believe me." All the policemen looked at him and then back at the dog. Qwen stood up. "Too bad," Michaels told him.

"Too bad?" Horowitz said. "Whaddya mean?"

"We needed it alive," Qwen said.

"For what?"

"For proof."

"Proof of what?"

"It doesn't matter now," Qwen said. He started out, Maggie at his heels. Michaels started after him.

"Hey, where are you going?" Patrolman Horowitz called.

"Take us back to my car," Michaels said. He kept walking.

"Wait a minute. Hey. Listen, the captain wants you two back at the station. You're going to meet the commissioner."

"Shit," Qwen said.

"We don't have time for that," Michaels said. "I got a town to get back to. We got our own problems up there."

"But—"

"Just drive us back to our car," Michaels repeated.

"What the hell are you guys so unhappy about? Jesus, you two act as though you killed Lassie."

"We needed that dog alive," Michaels said. They all got into the patrol car and Horowitz started away from the demolished building. Qwen looked back through the rear window.

"I had him by the collar," he said, "but I couldn't hold him, and before I could get another grip on him, he turned to bite me, even though he knew he was goin' to fall."

"Maybe he didn't want to go back to where he was," Michaels said. Horowitz looked at him and shook his head again.

"Maybe. I got the feeling he knew it was over."

"You know somethin'," Horowitz said, "listening to you guys talk about that dog gives me the creeps."

"Join the party," Michaels said.

When they got back to the station, Horowitz pleaded for them to go inside, but they refused again.

"Just tell the captain thanks for the use of his city," Michaels said.

Horowitz watched them get into the Fallsburg patrol car and drive off. He pushed his hat back and scratched his temple.

"Who the hell were those guys?" he muttered and went in to tell the captain that they wouldn't stay to meet the commissioner.

On the way home, Qwen described to Michaels his

battle with the dog. Now, with the two of them alone, Qwen had more time to reflect on what had occurred. He decided he would try to explain to Michaels what it was like when he had his first face-off with the German shepherd. He wanted to see if Michaels understood what Qwen meant when he talked about a mesmerizing effect.

"Of course, I didn't have time to look into his eyes like that," Michaels said, "but I imagine it would be some helluva experience if I was a few feet from him and he just stared. Now me, I'd probably piss in my pants. Especially after our introduction," he added, holding his arm up.

"You know," Qwen said, almost as if he didn't hear a word Michaels had uttered, "old Maggie here can look at me and I can look at her and we can talk to each other, express feelings, if you know what I mean. But there's never a doubt as to who's the dog and who's the man. It was different on those stairs."

"I wish we woulda gotten him alive," Michaels said.

They were quiet for a while, both lost in their own thoughts. Maggie had curled up on the back seat, where she was now asleep. The sun had dropped below the mountains in the west; darkness crawled over the landscape, dropping first like a thin veil of shadows and then thickening into a heavy blanket that made houses and trees and portions of highway disappear with an eerie magic.

"Shit," Michaels said when a New York State Thruway road sign announced a roadside restaurant, "I can't even remember when I ate last. What about you?"

"Yeah."

"Let's have a quick bite. You'll probably wanna get somethin' for the dog, too."

"She likes cheeseburgers," Qwen said.

After they'd gotten their food and taken a table,

Michaels went to make a phone call. He thought it was best to check in and tell the dispatcher to call Jenny to let her know where he was and when he'd be home. Qwen looked up as Michaels returned to the table. He knew immediately from the look on the police chief's face that something was wrong.

"What is it?"

"Sometime during the late afternoon they claimed they got the dog."

"What?"

"They killed a German shepherd, a big one. Pictures and all."

"It wasn't ours," Qwen said. Michaels nodded, but Qwen saw that there was doubt in his face. "You saw what this dog did. It wasn't ours," he repeated. Michaels nodded and finished his coffee.

"No chance of them havin' more than one?"

"Not from what I learned. This was part of an experiment. The dog was special. What they claimed up here is bullshit just to throw off any connection with what went on in New York. It calms everyone down and it's all forgotten." Michaels nodded again, but Qwen felt uneasiness. "Look," he said, "they sacrificed some dog, that's all. I know what," he said, an idea coming to him, "let's not go right back to your police station."

"Whaddya mean? Where the hell else should we go?"

"To the institute. Let's confront them directly. You call in when we get within radio range and let your people know where we're going—just in case."

"I don't know."

"I got to get my truck back, anyway," Qwen said. "Listen," he added, "you're into it this far, you might as well finish it with me. People in your town were hurt and killed. You got a right to know whatever there is to know."

Michaels thought for a moment. "My wife's going to kill me," he said.

"There are worse ways to go," Qwen said.

Michaels laughed. "You don't know Jenny."

After Maggie had feasted on her cheeseburger, they continued up the thruway. Qwen described the institute compound and told Michaels as much as he could remember of what Kevin Longfellow and his assistant Ann had explained about the experiments and the conclusions they had made about the dog. Michaels listened, but the darkness and the day's events had left him tired. It was a deep fatigue, one that went through more than just his muscles and bones. It was as though a very heavy weight had shifted within him; he had all he could do to keep it from toppling. It would take a younger, stronger man to set it all right again. He was eager for that to happen. He was eager to walk away.

He couldn't help thinking that he was a holdover from an older world, a very different world. The villains in this new world were hard to recognize. If Qwen was right about it all, they were articulate, intelligent people in highly respected positions, doing work subsidized by a blind financial machine that responded to computer punch-outs. The differences between what was right and what was wrong had become muddled. Somehow, the priorities had changed, and Harry Michaels thought there was no way he'd be able to adjust. Surely, it was time to go, to retreat to some back porch and, among old friends, relive the past. Perhaps that was one of the benefits of age—a man could take such pleasure in a simple memory.

It was close to eight-thirty by the time they turned off the main road to take the side road that led to the institute. To Michaels, the uninhabited route with its surrounding dark forest looked ominous. Qwen added to that atmosphere when he pointed out where he had left the car after he had done battle with Gerson Fishman and the driver.

The moonless, partly cloudy night sky offered little illumination, but the institute complex loomed before them in an inky silhouette. No lights were on in the building. The only light came from the security booth at the gate. Michaels turned on his revolving roof light as they approached.

"Might as well make this look official," he said. He leaned on the horn at the entrance. "Where's all that security you described?"

"They were here before."

"Looks like everyone's asleep." He pressed his horn again. A figure appeared in the window of the security booth. After a moment the man emerged. When he stepped into the illumination of the patrol car's headlights, Michaels and Qwen saw that the man looked elderly. "What's he, part of another experiment?" Harry rolled down his window as the man came through the gate.

"What's the problem?" he asked.

"Where is everyone?"

"Who you lookin' for?"

"We want to speak to Kevin Longfellow," Qwen said.

"I don't know who that is, but they're all gone."

"Whaddya mean, they're all gone?" Michaels asked. "Isn't there anyone in that place?"

"Not anymore."

"What do you make of this?"

"I don't know," Qwen said. "There's my pickup truck, though. They put it back where I left it."

"That yours?" the old man asked. "They said someone might be comin' for it. I was supposed to have it towed off if you didn't come in a day or so."

"They're all gone?" Qwen asked again.

"Yep."

"When are they comin' back?" Michaels asked.

"Don't know as they are."

"What about the animals that were in there?" Qwen asked.

"Animals? I didn't see any animals."

"This is bullshit."

"We want to go in there," Michaels said.

The old man shrugged. "They turned off the electricity in the building. You're better off comin' back in the daytime."

"I got a flashlight."

"I guess it's all right. They told me only to watch out for vandalism and you ain't about to vandalize."

"Thanks," Michaels said and drove on into the compound. The old man followed them. He wore a ring of keys, one of which opened the front door.

Harry directed the beam of his flashlight around the small lobby of what had once been a rest home for the elderly. The furniture was covered and looked as though it had been that way for years.

"Is this what it looked like when you were first here?"

"I never came inside. There wasn't any reason to."

"So you never saw what was going on?"

"No."

They walked farther in. The security guard remained outside. They came to a small landing and followed it up into the corridor that went to the right. As they walked down it, they opened doors and Michaels shone the light within each room. Maggie sniffed at each doorway, but she did not enter any. In every case they found small rooms with beds of naked mattresses, small dressers, and night tables. When they reached the end of the corridor, they took the stairway up to the next floor. Some of the rooms were similar to those below, but they found two large rooms, rooms that Michaels surmised had once been used as recreational areas. Now they were completely empty. Maggie sniffed about the floor, but she didn't grow excited over any scents.

"Smells like a room full of mothballs. You sure this guy was telling you the truth?"

"What they obviously have done is stripped the place clean."

"It's spic-and-span, all right. Where are these mazes? The other animals? Maybe most of it was bullshit."

"Bullshit? How can you say that after what we've been through?" Michaels started out of the building. "How can you even think it? You're not buyin' this, are ya? Why would they have that fence put up? To keep in the ghosts of old people?"

"Naw, it's not that," Michaels said. They started down the stairs. "Somethin' else occurred to me, though."

"What?"

"Maybe they were afraid to tell you the truth . . . that they had simply developed a better killer-dog. For the military, like they said."

"No way, my friend. I tracked that animal—or whatever it really was. I faced it, just as I told you. You faced it!"

"I don't know what the hell I faced. I faced a vicious, big German shepherd, I know that."

"But what about Fishman?"

"What about him? I push to find out about him and they block it under the excuse of confidential information. What's the difference anyway?" Michaels said. They walked out of the building and the elderly security guard approached them. "Hey, what kind of stuff did they take out of here?"

"Can't tell ya. If anything was taken out, it was done before I got here."

"This is bullshit," Qwen said again.

"Well, what do we do now, put out an APB for a missing secret laboratory? Come on, let's see if your truck starts."

Qwen looked back at the building and then went to his truck. Maggie leapt right into the front seat. Qwen put the key into the ignition and started the engine.

Michaels closed the door and leaned against it. "Sounds better than my car, even though it looks like shit."

"I like it that way," Qwen said. "My mother used to say it's what's on the inside that counts."

"She was right. Why is it mothers are always right?"

Qwen laughed. They watched the security guard go back to his booth. "What are you goin' to do now?"

"Check in at the station and then go home. I'm tired. Tomorrow's another day. I'll make some phone calls and see what I can find out."

"It'll probably be like you said—doors shut everywhere."

"All we can do is try," Michaels said. Qwen stared ahead. Harry reached in to pat him on the shoulder. "Go back to the forest, my friend. Life's simpler. One of these days I might come out there and join you, so keep the fire burning."

Qwen waited until Harry walked to his car; then he backed up his truck and started out of the compound. The elderly security guard peered out the window of the booth. Michaels followed Qwen out to the main road and then turned right when Qwen turned left. He beeped his horn and was gone, his lights, reflected in Qwen's rearview mirror, diminishing until the darkness swallowed them completely.

# EPILOGUE

THE MID-AUGUST sun hung accusingly in the sky. It looked like the inflamed fingertip of an angry God. For the past two weeks, there had been a terrible drought in the Catskills. The reservoirs serving the New York City area were just above forty percent of their capacity. The fields across from Wilson's Secondhand Shop had turned a pale brown. Color came only from the resilient weeds that flourished on whatever disastrous conditions affected the rest of nature. Even the birds were lethargic. They fluttered their wings nervously and waited in a subdued manner. When they sang, their songs had half the volume. Only the bees were vigorous. They seemed to be in a panic as they searched the dried flowers for pollen.

In the forest, animals retreated to the coolest and darkest part to seek relief. It was as if the world had tightened into a protective fist. The air was so still that the smallest sounds carried for what appeared to be infinite distances.

A young boy's voice rose to a pitch of excitement; the high volume was shattering. It put a sudden surge of energy into the birds and they rose out of the trees like multicolored rocks flung at the reddish sun.

"Grandpa!" Tony shouted. He was standing by the large old refrigerator left on its back. It was doorless.

It had been the boy's idea to put a blanket in it and let it serve as a place for Candy. "Grandpa, come quickly."

The screen door slapped the doorjamb as its springs pulled it back behind Tony's emerging grandfather and grandmother. They hurried across the driveway to the lot of old appliances. Mrs. Wilson wiped her hands on her apron as she walked quickly.

"What is it? What is it, Tony?" she called.

The boy was gleaming. "Look," he said.

The three of them stood around the old refrigerator and looked down into the cabinet. Candy had given birth to six pups. Four of them were suckling, but two of them were climbing over her body, working their way toward the rim of the cabinet.

"Well I'll be a son-of-a-bitch. Ain't this a pretty litter," Stanley Wilson said. "Look at how vigorous those two are."

"They look like they know where they're goin', Grandpa."

"Smart little buggers," he said as the puppies reached the sides and put their paws up on the ledge.

"Don't they look so much older than just born?" Mrs. Wilson asked.

"Yeah," he said and scratched his unshaven chin. The puppies pulled themselves up and out of the refrigerator with amazing grace. Both landed solidly on the ground. Almost as soon as they did so, two more stopped suckling and began the same journey. The ones that had gotten out were moving quickly away from the refrigerator. They sniffed and approached everything and anything in their way.

"What kind do you think they are, Grandpa?" Tony asked. He reached down and picked up one that was trying to get out of the refrigerator.

The old man studied it for a moment. "They look like they got a lotta German shepherd in 'em," he said.

"Goin' to be pretty dogs. We won't have any trouble givin' 'em away. Might even be able to sell 'em."

"Oh, Stanley, who's gonna pay money for a mutt?"

"They're mutts all right, but they're pretty smart ones," he said. "Look at those two go at it. They're almost as eager to learn as could be."

"Let me see that one," Mrs. Wilson said. Her husband handed it to her and she held it up so she could look into its face. The puppy stared back at her with almost as much interest. "My God," she said, "it looks like it has human eyes."

In the forest, the birds had returned to the branches of the trees, positioning themselves under the shade of the leaves. They stared out at the world and waited as though they expected to see the earth catch on fire.